The Detective and the Burglar

by

Kirsten Paul

Calendar Men of King Court,
Book 2

The Detective and the Burglar

Cover Art by *Debbie Taylor*

The Wild Rose Press, Inc.
PO Box 708
Adams Basin, NY 14410-0708
Visit us at www.thewildrosepress.com

Publishing History
First Champagne Rose Edition, 2020
Trade Paperback Print ISBN 978-1-5092-3140-9
Digital ISBN 978-1-5092-3141-6

Calendar Men of King Court, Book 2
Published in the United States of America

She plowed down the embankment through snow up to her knees. Her pants were wet, and ice crawled into the tops of boots, but she didn't care.

"Hey!" He raced after her, grabbed the back of her coat, and pulled her to a stop. "What are you doing? You can't go down. It's dangerous."

Emily pulled her coat free. "It's my car and my belongings and I'm going after them." She set out again, but her heel snagged something. She tugged at it. "I am quite capable of—" She pulled her heel free but stumbled and fell flat on the snow.

"Ma'am." He picked her up like a cloth doll and set her on her feet. "Please, let me go down. You're going to get hurt."

Emily brushed her face clean, hoping her mascara didn't run down her cheeks. She didn't want to look like a racoon. He was a man of the law but one of the best she'd ever seen. "I'm not a ma'am. My grandmother is a ma'am. Now, I may be small, but I don't break." She forged ahead.

He raced after her. "Can I at least hold your arm to help you down? Those heels are high. They must be awkward."

"Thank you but I can do a lot of things in heels. Dance, run, and have sex wearing them and nothing else." She covered her mouth with both hands. Did that come out of her?

Amusement sparked his eyes. "Is that a bribe?"

"Of course it's not a bribe! I didn't mean anything. I'm…flustered. I have to get my stuff." She had to watch what she said. She couldn't be arrested for bribing a police officer with sex—even if he was the hottest one she'd ever laid eyes on.

Praise for Kirsten Paul

"Chemistry, humor, intrigue, heat, and hockey—what else could you want in a romance??!!"

~The Indie Express

~*~

"*THE HOCKEY PLAYER AND THE ANGEL* is a fast-paced romance that is full of love and humor…a story that is sure to sweep you away to another time. Paul has created a world that is full of romance and magic with well-developed characters that are realistic and relatable. *THE HOCKEY PLAYER AND THE ANGEL* would make a lovely weekend read."

~Truly Trendy

~*~

"Take a hockey player out to make money, pair him with type A chef about to lose her family's legacy, throw in a power outage and watch the sparks fly. This book will make you smile, shed some tears, and eventually make you go "awwww". Paul has a smart writing style with great characters and good story flow. I obviously liked the book…a lot!"

~Susan G.

~*~

"I was laughing so loud at times. This book was read within a few hours. It was fast-moving with great description of the characters and the setting of the scenes excellent. I thoroughly enjoyed this book and would recommend highly."

~Christine

Dedication

To the real Marilyn, Lubna, and Tatyana

Chapter One

I'm sorry, will return it ASAP.

Armand stared at the hand-written message on the red, heart-shaped sticky note.

"Does this note really say, '*I'm sorry, will return it ASAP'?*" he asked King Court's antique dealer, Mrs. Halloran, who doubled as his high school teacher before retiring.

"That's what the pretty little note says," Mrs. Halloran replied.

Armand turned it over. Nothing on the back. In all his six years on the police force, a thief had never left a note apologizing for stealing something and promising to return it.

The block letters were non-descript. Nothing unusual about them. "If the thief signed it, my job would be much easier. Did he take anything else?" Antique furniture, coins, decorative plates, crystal vases, artwork, and knickknacks of all shapes and sizes covered every inch of wall space, including the front window. Thrown in at random were Cupid sculptures with heart-shaped cut-outs the extent of Mrs. Halloran's window dressing style. Armand didn't know much about antiques, but he was positive there were more valuable items in the store than a wooden horse the size of a tablet.

"Nothing. I checked. Everything is here. Except for

the horse."

Armand stuck the note inside a paper envelope. "When did you realize it was missing?"

"I opened the store this morning as usual and began dusting when I noticed a space between the wooden train car and miniature totem pole in the curio. The note's in the exact spot where the horse sat."

"Your alarm didn't go off?"

Mrs. Halloran laughed, her perfectly arranged hair never moving. "This is King Court, Armand. Never in my forty years here, selling antiques, was the store robbed."

Yes, good and solid King Court where nothing happened. The most exciting things he'd investigated since graduating from the police academy were missing farm animals, under-aged teenagers, boozing it up Friday nights or tipping cows, and the occasional misplaced tractor. How would he earn credibility and sound experience to join the Ontario Provincial Police or any big city police force when King Court was so boring? He didn't want to spend the rest of his career investigating petty crimes.

"Was the Post-it Note one of yours?"

"It was. I keep a pad near the cashier. Heart ones for Valentine's Day. They used my pen, too. Black gel. I used red gel to grade your history papers."

"I recall." Including her notes about dangling modifiers. "I'll need to take them too. Any surveillance cameras?" He didn't know why he asked. He knew the answer.

Mrs. Halloran's eyes rounded with disbelief as much as amusement. "Really?"

"We have more people coming through the town.

You need to think about installing security cameras to protect yourself and your business."

She flicked her hand as though he spoke gibberish. "You're far too uptight, Armand. I know you've told all us store owners to install security systems, but I've been here all my life, like you. A few more people coming through King Court won't make me rethink security."

"I'm just doing my job, Mrs. Halloran."

"Yes, yes. You're serving and protecting, and you're doing a fine and upstanding job. You're the very model of the noble warrior and will get my vote if you run for office." She grimaced. "On second thought, you're far too honest to be a politician. Those buffoons would eat you and your smart suits alive."

Was that a complement or an insult—for him and his closet of well-tailored suits? "Luckily, I have no intention of running for office." He slipped the envelope in his coat pocket. "So, you don't know when this wooden horse was stolen?"

"Of course, I do. During the night. The horse was here when I closed the shop at 6:00. I know where everything is, and I knew the instant I saw the space with the Post-it Note between those two other wooden pieces."

"Was anything else tampered or moved?"

"Nothing. Even the note pad and pen were in the exact spot as I always leave them."

Armand checked the lock on the front door. Not one scratch on the metal to indicate it was picked.

"You can save yourself the trouble of checking the back door, too. The thief came in through my office window." She led him to a back room, cluttered with antiques and boxes, some opened, others not. Her desk was invisible under mounds of leather or cloth-bound books. "I draw the drapes together, so no light comes in and damages any wood or artwork. There's a sliver between them. The thief came in through the window."

Armand picked his way to the window, maneuvering like a giant through the obstacle course of boxes. He slit the drapes apart still wearing latex gloves to examine the lock. If it was scratched, he couldn't tell. "I have to get my fingerprint and evidence collection kit from my car. I'll need to do a thorough check." If he was in Ottawa or Toronto, he would call in forensics officers to assist in the investigation and collection of evidence. Hell, if he was in Ottawa or Toronto, he would investigate big time thefts or drugs or homicides. He wouldn't waste his time looking for the person who stole a wooden horse the size of an over-sized collectible.

He went out the back door and trudged through the well-packed snow, his shoes leaving deep impressions. Someone had brushed the snow beneath the window, leaving it free of boot or shoe prints. He followed the smoothed-over trail around the store to the side lane and road. It stopped there. Snow was cleared and there were neither footprints nor tire marks on the road. Other than a few customers at the Koffee & Tez Shoppe across the street and a few cars parked in front, the stores lining both sides of King Court's downtown were empty. His black Taurus was the only vehicle on this side of the street.

He went inside. The top of Mrs. Halloran's hair peeked out from behind an old-fashioned push-button cash register "Can you tell me about the horse?"

"I can do better. I can show you a picture. I always take photographs of everything I buy." She returned to her office and opened creaky wooden filing cabinets. Armand moved to the glass curio from where the horse was stolen. Wooden objects. Miniature totem poles, canoes, teepees, train cars, farm animals, cradles, bows, arrows, and figurines of farmers, fishers, weavers, and trappers filled the shelves.

Mrs. Halloran returned with a file folder and handed him a photo. The horse was hand carved out of wood he couldn't identify. The etching on the saddle resembled a First Nations' headdress. "What can you tell me about the horse?"

She scanned the fact sheet. "I bought it on a reserve in Northern Ontario almost ten years ago. It was made by a First Nations' artist around the turn of the twentieth century. It may be part of a larger project."

"A larger project?"

"Sometimes an artist makes other pieces to go with each other, like horses or a cart for this particular piece. He puts symbols about his life on them. It's like a totem pole but on a personal level instead of a tribal level. A memoir of the artist's life."

"Do you know the artist?"

"Oliver Fines. He was a furniture maker. His furniture brings in a lot of money, but he only made a few small objects like the horse."

"How much is it worth?"

"On its own, I could sell it for a couple hundred dollars if I got lucky. If it's part of a set, then depending on how many pieces, it could be worth more."

Armand was investigating the theft of a wooden horse valued at a couple hundred dollars. Could policing in King Court get any worse? "Can I take the print and spec sheet?"

"Will you bring them back?"

"Of course."

She put them in the folder and gave it to him.

"Don't touch the curio, anything in it, the office window, or the note pad and pen. I'm getting my kit and camera to dust for prints, take photos, and collect the things the thief used." He headed to the front door. "You should consider an alarm system. You're on your own for most of the time when Mr. Halloran is away on trips."

Mrs. Halloran laughed. "You're as funny as those dangling modifiers in your essays, Armand."

****

Emily stared down at Isla, sitting on the edge of the bed. "You did what?"

Isla slipped on her furry boots and jumped up. "I couldn't exactly buy it and return it. It doesn't work with antique dealers. I also didn't have any money. As usual."

Emily grabbed her black coat from the other bed and threw it on. "So, you decided to break in and take it?"

"It worked, didn't it?" Isla threw a toiletry bag into her knapsack. "It's such a sleepy small town. The antique dealer didn't have an alarm system or cameras. Not even the stores around her did."

Emily took Isla's arm. She wished her younger sister was sitting. Even in her high heeled boots, Emily looked up to scold her. "We gave up our little game of stealing years ago. Why would you jeopardize everything you've achieved for a figurine of a horse?"

"It's not any horse." She shook her arm free and zipped up the knapsack. "It's made from the same wood as your little figurine. It could lead to your family."

"It could lead to jail time for you, Isla—and for me for not turning you in." She buttoned up her coat. "Your future could be ruined. *My* future could be ruined."

Isla moved to the other side of the bed and grabbed her parka. "Nobody saw me. And I left a note. On really cute heart-shaped Post-its."

Emily grabbed her suitcase but stopped. "You did what?"

"I apologized and said I would return it."

"Well, that makes all the difference in the world. What store owner would charge you with breaking and entering and stealing when you were polite and promised to return it? You couldn't have brought me into the store? We would have asked the owner to see the horse. Then I would have nicely asked if I could plop my figurine on it to see if they went together. If they did, I would have bought the horse to add to the mystery of my past and the owner would make a sale."

"How boring. I wanted to see if I still had it." She smiled, her eyes lighting up with mischief and delight. "I do."

Emily threw her leather gloves at her. "Don't be so smug. This is dangerous business."

Isla picked the gloves off the floor. "Will you at least look at the horse?"

Emily snatched her gloves back. "No. I don't want anything to do with it."

"It's for you."

"I don't have to find my family. I have you and Mom and Dad. You're my family."

"I see the way you look at your figurine. You want to know your real mom and dad. You want to know where you came from. You especially want to know why you were left with the figurine when you were adopted by Mom and Dad."

Emily did want to know. Her adopted mother and father were the most important people in her life along with Isla, who came as a big surprise two years after Emily became part of the family. Isla looked like her parents. Tall, slim, with blonde hair, blue eyes and skin that burned easily. Emily was the opposite. She was at the top end of short with black hair hanging heavily below her shoulders, equally dark eyes with random specks of silver, and a complexion she thought should be olive but was light. She was the exotic to Isla's ethereal. She couldn't even flirt with a resemblance to her adoptive family. There wasn't any.

Isla plopped her purse on the bed. "You could at least check if your figurine sits on it. It is the same wood. Basswood as you repeatedly tell me. If it is, you have a little more scene to work with. There's a design on the saddle. Some decorative headdress. I'm sure both your art degrees could identify its origin. It could lead to your family's home and possibly to your family."

Emily stared down at Isla's oversized purse. "My family gave me up for adoption when I was one year old, Isla. Why would they want to see me again twenty-five years later?"

Isla put her hands on the side of Emily's face. "You don't know why they gave you up, Emmy. Maybe your parents were kids and had to. They tried to keep you. You were one when they gave you up. You have every right to find out where you came from."

She did. She just didn't want to find out why they gave her up. She'd rather believe in her own romantic notions of necessity or poverty or even illness—anything except a reality indicating she wasn't wanted.

"Okay." Her voice was under a whisper. "Let's see it."

Isla tore open her purse and pulled out the horse. Emily's heart missed a beat. It was made of basswood like her figurine.

Emily removed her little girl figurine with finely etched overalls, sneakers, and a baseball cap from her purse, where she always kept it. Her hands trembling, she mounted it on the horse. The figurine wavered back and forth and toppled over.

Emily's heart toppled over, too. She seized on the hope it would fit and have an answer to her family, but her hopes were false. The world was telling her something. She wasn't to know her real family.

"Oh, well," Isla said. "At least I tried." She took the horse and wrapped it in her scarf. "I'll spend another night here and return it tonight."

"No, you won't." Emily took the scarf and removed the horse. "I'll return it." She handed the scarf to Isla and headed to the bathroom. "You need to get back to Toronto and write your final exam." Using a towel, she cleaned it to a buff to make sure there were no fingerprints. She wrapped it in tissue paper and her silk scarf for added protection. "I'm here for a week if not more. I'll return it tonight."

"There may be security people or cameras set up now."

"When did a security camera or guard stop me?"

She put the horse in her briefcase—next to her lock pick tool set and furniture appraising kit of brushes, tweezers, and cleaners. "You forget. Mom and Dad taught me. I taught you." She closed her briefcase with a loud click. "And you are never to tell them."

"You know I wouldn't—even though, I'm sure they know. But it was such a rush going in the way you taught me and quietly coming back out."

"It's time to give it up. We're in the real world now and we have to make good. Otherwise, all we've done and achieved in the last ten years since our last escapade will mean nothing. Our future will be nothing."

"You sound like a Country and Western ballad."

"Good, because I don't want to turn into a Country and Western ballad. It's Halloran's Antiques, right?"

"It's the only antique shop in the small town."

"I'm not due for a couple hours at the Acadia Inn. I'll go by and check it out."

"You excited about the job? You look like an up and coming executive in your prim coat and suit. The high-heeled boots are the only things screaming fashion. They're too sexy for the coat, by the way."

Emily ignored Isla's last remark. "Of course, I am. And thank you, if what you said was a complement. From the few pictures I saw, it has incredible nineteenth and twentieth century Canadiana furniture and pieces. I saw some interesting artwork, too. It's my first solo job for the company. If I do this well, I'll become a full-fledged furniture appraiser and hopefully, art appraiser."

Isla slung the purse over her chest and the knapsack on her back. "I don't know what you see in all this appraising business."

Emily draped her purse over her shoulder and picked up the briefcase in one hand and the suitcase in the other. "And I really don't know what you see in all those numbers."

Isla laughed. "When I become a stockbroker, you'll thank me for setting you up a financial portfolio."

"Good. Until then, thank you for spending the weekend with me but no more breaking and entering. No more thieving. Nothing. Your financial career will be out the window and my art appraising career, too, if any firm ever found out that once upon a time in our crazy teen years, you and your equally crazy older sister used to break into stores, steal things, and then see who could return them without setting off alarms."

Chapter Two

Emily dropped Isla at the Ottawa Station. Half an hour later she was in King Court's downtown area. The town's main strip wasn't anything like Toronto's that ran from Lake Ontario all the way north to mid downtown and even farther to upper downtown. King Court's central shopping and business area was two blocks of one-of-a-kind stores, owned by individuals or families and not big box companies or franchises.

Halloran's Antiques sat snugly between Fabrics & Wools and Books Galore and across from Koffee & Tez Shoppe, Savory and Sweetie, and Wonders of Costumes. A Valentine theme ran through them, tying them together like one big happy family. Lots of red, bold hearts, and Cupids. A parking lot was missing, which was unheard of in Toronto. Instead, car owners parked on the street. In the morning on one side and in the evening on the other side.

At Koffee & Tez Emily asked the barista if she could leave her car on the other side of the road without paying or fear of a tow truck carrying it away. The barista, a woman of about her age with red-streaked hair and multiple earrings, piercing the edge of an ear laughed. "You're not from King Court, are you?"

"Toronto."

"No joke. You can park and it's free. Really."

Emily took out her wallet. "Then a jumbo-size of

your Valentine's roast, please."

As she waited for the coffee, she took in the photographs hanging on the brick walls. Portraits of everyday people with distinguishing features or props told her in a glance about them or their jobs. The photograph behind the counter was of an elderly woman, her hair tied back in an old-fashioned chignon, her face lined with deep wrinkles. But her electric smile, pulled the viewer into her eyes and made her an ageless beauty.

Emily took the coffee. "Great photographs."

"Thank you."

"You took them?"

"Since you like them, I admit I took them."

Emily was surprised. "What's not to like? They're astounding portraits. They scream out the person's personality and your voice." She moved closer to read the artist's signature, but it was too fine. "Some of them look familiar. Were they in a gallery or show?"

"Only school. Ontario College of Art and Design."

"OCAD? I've been there for special workshops and classes."

"You're an artist, too?"

"Art historian—and future art appraiser. I'm appraising the furniture at the Acadia Inn for Kanata Auction House." She put her coffee down and extended her hand. "I'm Emily Atterberry."

"Jessica Saunders. You're in King Court for a while?"

"Just a week, but I expect to come back until everything is sold."

"Could I shadow you one day and see appraising in action? Since," she indicated the photographs, "art won't make me money and," she held up the carafe, "coffee pays the rent."

Emily picked up her coffee. "Sure. I'll even give you a rundown of the training program."

A group of about eight women came in, bundled in coats and hats.

"My Monday morning book club group. Lady Bookworms."

Emily nodded in approval. "Great name."

Jessica leaned forward. "They dived into erotica last week in honor of Valentine's Day," she whispered. "Can't wait to be the fly on the wall and hear what they say."

Emily held up her cup. "Enjoy."

"I will."

She put her coffee down and gave her a card. "Call me and we can set up a time."

"Will do. Good morning, Lady Bookworms."

"Good morning, Jessica," the women replied, moving to a table at the back of the café. "The Valentine's brew for everyone," one of them said and laughed. "We have much naughtiness to discuss."

"Wish I could be a fly on the wall, too," Emily whispered. She fixed her coffee and sat at the high counter in front of the window, facing Halloran's Antiques. The street was dead for mid-morning, also unheard of in Toronto. Only one dark car was parked behind her silver rental. The Lady Bookworms walked.

She sipped at the coffee, enjoying the espresso taste. She could see the appeal of Halloran's Antiques to Isla. It screamed come and break in. I'm easy. Antique front door and from what Emily could make out a vintage lock and handle that added classical-movie style charm but no defense. Everything it sold was on random display in the huge window. Emily couldn't see much inside except for the top of a man's head. Separating the stores from each other was an alley, which Isla said led to the back. A wooden door with a similar lock and handle as the front door led into an office and the store front. The store overflowed with what Isla called junk. Emily corrected her. It was treasure. Anything from the past was a treasure. Clutter added fun and adventure.

Isla had climbed in through the window, leading into an office, overflowing with more junk. She would have gone through the back door but didn't have her picks, hooks, or wrenches. Tonight, after settling at the Acadia Inn and her colleagues from Kanata Auction House were fast asleep, Emily would take a drive, leave her car down the street, walk to Halloran's Antiques, go in through the back door, and return the horse to its curio between a wooden totem pole and a train car. It would be a simple job. There were no security cameras at any of the stores on the street, and they all closed at 6:00 except for the coffee shop which closed at 10:00.

Even she recognized a simple break and enter. Halloran's Antiques screamed I'm easy picking, but so did the other stores.

Emily took a sip of her coffee. A thin person wearing a military parka approached the black sedan parked behind her rented silver Camry. She couldn't tell if the person was a male or a female. The hood and a scarf were over the person's face as well as sunglasses. The person peered in but sauntered to her car.

Her phone rang. It was Isla. "You scouted the

place?"

"Doing it now. You're right. It's a quick in and out job."

The person plied him or herself against the driver's seat of the Camry. He or she pushed something against the window.

What the heck was the person doing? Was he—

"Holy shit!" Emily jumped up and dropped her cell on the floor. Jessica gasped and the Lady Bookworms' chairs shrieked as they turned.

"What is it?" Isla shouted.

Emily grabbed her phone. She knocked her head on the counter and gasped. "Someone is stealing my car!" She snatched her purse but knocked over her cup. The coffee streamed into her purse and onto her pants. "Shit, shit, shit!" Heat stung her. She set the cup straight, but coffee floated in her purse. If she dumped the coffee, everything would fall out. She zipped it closed and pulled her coat from the back of the chair. But the buttons caught in the bars.

Jessica rushed to her with a tea towel. "Are you okay?"

"That person is stealing my car." She pointed and tugged at her coat. The chair crashed to the floor.

"Let me." Jessica set it upright.

Emily pulled at her coat again and freed it. A buckle snapped from a sleeve and a button popped. *Shit* she wanted to scream. Her brand-new executive-style coat. Ruined, and on one of the most important days of her career.

She glanced outside. The person sat in her Camry. "I have to stop him."

She stuck her cell in her pant's pocket, held her

purse in one hand, her coat in the other, and raced outside. A blast of freezing wind pushed her against the door. She pressed but was pinned to the spot. "Stop!"

The person ducked. Was he or she working the wires? This was not good. She had to get to the thief but couldn't move.

The wind relented. Emily raced across the street, throwing her coat over her shoulders. A car swerved to avoid her. "Sorry!" She pulled one sleeve on as she navigated snow and ice patches in her high-heeled boots.

The car started.

"No!" Emily banged on the driver's window. "Get out."

The person sped off, knocking Emily to the ground.

"Stop!" She bolted up as the back tires threw snow and ice onto her.

A big man in a dark woolen overcoat and suit raced out of Halloran's Antiques. A small elderly woman followed.

"My car," Emily shouted, disgusted at the foul taste of snow in her mouth. "Someone stole my car. Call the police."

The man strode to her side and took out his cell. "I am the police."

"Go after him!" The police officer was as tall and broad as her father. But even through her agitation she saw that under his smart, business-looking coat and suit was solid muscle. Definitely not the amiable shape of a man who enjoyed watching police shows and munching chips.

"What's your license plate?" he asked.

"My license plate?" Emily shrugged. "I don't know. It was a rental. I need my car." Her lock picking utensils and the stolen wooden horse were in her briefcase and the car. If the thief or the police broke the lock of her briefcase, he'd find them. Emily would lose her job and credibility and everything she did to get to where she was. Hell, she would land in jail. She would have no career and no future. "We have to go after it."

"Stay here." The man strode to the black sedan. Emily pulled on her other coat sleeve and raced to the passenger side.

The man peered over the car. "What are you doing?"

"Getting my car back." She jumped in and closed the door.

He gazed at her through the window. "*I'm* getting your car back. *You're* waiting here."

She glared at him. She didn't care the green eyes staring back were what artists called green topaz or his nice GQ and professional haircut was referred to as espresso brown black. She didn't care if she acted foolish in front of a hunky specimen of a police office or was covered in ice and snow or smelled of eau de coffee. Nothing mattered except getting her Camry and briefcase. "I need my car now. I have important documents in there. I have my laptop and my—working tools. Without them, I'm lost. Now get in or we'll lose the thief."

The man didn't move.

Emily's face burned. "Do I have to drive?"

"Go get the woman's car," the elderly woman shouted, startling the police officer. Even the Lady Bookworms, who stood outside the coffee shop with

Jessica screamed and waved him on, too.

"This is against the rules," the officer told the women.

"Rules, smules. Go," the Lady Bookworms shouted back.

"Live on the wild side," the woman in front of Halloran's Antiques said.

Shaking his head, the officer sat behind the wheel and drove off.

But he didn't put on the sirens.

Emily peered at him, her mouth dropping open. "Aren't you putting on your flashing lights and sirens?"

"Do you see cars on the road?"

Emily didn't see any. But the wooden horse. Her lock-picking tools. Her future. They rested on no one finding them. "Could you go a little faster? You'll lose the car."

The man sped up to fifty kilometers.

"You're kidding me, right?" She pointed to the speedometer. "I could run faster in my heels."

He took a deep breath. "Why don't you get your leasing agreement out and give me the license plate of the car. I can get the number out on the airways and other police will look for it."

Was he really so cool, calm, and collected or did his training kick in? "You mean this sleepy small town has more than one police officer?"

The officer pulled a tight smile. "The town may be small, but we have a capable police force."

He really *was* cool, calm, and collected. Any other time she would think the professional demeanor in that solid six-pack-looking male package would set her on fire with lust but right now it set her on fire with rage.

She wanted to press her heels on his nice leather shoes and make the car go at lightning speed.

"Call all of them," she shouted. "All one, two, or three. I need everyone looking for my car." She didn't care if she was rude. She had to get her car and now!

The officer picked up his radio and called in the theft.

Emily opened her purse. Coffee swam inside. He sniffed it. "My coffee fell into my purse when I saw the person take my car." She took out her wallet. Coffee dripped from it. She didn't have anything to dry it. Even her tissues were drenched.

"The Valentine's brew?" he asked.

It wasn't funny. Nothing was funny right now! Taking in a deep breath to calm herself, she opened the wallet and removed the car rental agreement form. It was dry. She rang off the information, and he relayed it.

Emily spotted the silver Camry ahead. "There it is." She jumped up, hitting her head on the top. "Oh no." It sat on the edge of a hill, most of it facing down into a valley of trees and snow. It tittered, tottered, slid over, and, she gasped, disappeared.

Chapter Three

The officer swung his car to the side of the road. Emily raced out and to the edge of the precipice. The car rolled down the embankment, cracking branches and flattening dried bushes. It hit a grove of trees and stopped. Its back wheels jumped up and down, whipping slush everywhere.

He appeared beside her. "Stay back. The thief may be hurt and trapped inside."

Stay back? Not on her life! Her future depended on this police officer not finding her lock-picking kit and the stolen horse.

She slung her purse over her chest and plowed down the embankment through snow up to her knees. Her pants were wet, and ice crawled into the tops of her boots, but she didn't care.

"Hey!" He raced after her, grabbed the back of her coat, and pulled her to a stop. "What are you doing? You can't go down. It's dangerous."

Emily pulled her coat free. "It's my car and my belongings and I'm going after them." She set out again, but her heel snagged something. She tugged at it. "I am quite capable of—" She pulled her heel free but stumbled and fell flat on the snow.

"Ma'am." He picked her up like a cloth doll and set her on her feet. "Please, let me go down. You're going to get hurt."

Emily brushed her face clean, hoping her mascara didn't run down her cheeks. She didn't want to look like a racoon. He was a man of the law but one of the best she'd ever seen. "I'm not a ma'am. My grandmother is a ma'am. Now, I may be small, but I don't break." She forged ahead.

He raced after her. "Can I at least hold your arm to help you down? Those heels are high. They must be awkward."

"Thank you but I can do a lot of things in heels. Dance, run, and have sex wearing them and nothing else." She covered her mouth with both hands. Did that come out of her?

Amusement sparked his eyes. "Is that a bribe?"

"Of course it's not a bribe! I didn't mean anything. I'm…flustered. I have to get my stuff." She had to watch what she said. She couldn't be arrested for bribing a police officer with sex—even if he was the hottest one she'd ever laid eyes on.

One of her heels snagged on something again. She pulled, but it wouldn't budge.

"May I help?"

"Go ahead." She snapped. Her face turned hot. "Sorry, please, yes, if you can. Thank you." Now she babbled like a repentant nun. *Control, Emily, control!*

He bent down, brushed snow from around her boot, wrapped his big hand around her ankle, and tugged as she pulled. But it wouldn't give. "It's really stuck. The whole heel is in mud." More tugging. "Or ice." Both hands went around her ankle. "Or both."

She spied a low branch and grabbed it. "Try now." As he pulled, she held on and yanked her foot. It came free, kneeing him in the face.

"Ow!" His hand went to his nose as he fell on the snow.

"I'm so sorry!"

Blood smeared his fingertips. "You're strong for your size."

Add bodily harm to the charges piling up against her. "I didn't mean it." She pulled tissues out of her purse, but they were soaked with coffee. "I'm sorry, but I don't have anything. And I really have to go." She moved forward but slipped and toppled onto him. Her purse smacked his face.

He groaned in surprise as much as pain. "Are you okay?" His voice croaked.

"Yes—" She yanked her head up as her purse opened. Coffee flowed onto his face and into his mouth.

"The Valentine's brew." He didn't savor the taste. Her wallet followed, hitting his nose, and drawing more blood. "You are one dangerous woman."

"I'm not doing it on purpose." She rose. Material slashed. She gulped. Did her heel rip his pants?

He stiffened. "Were those my pants or yours?"

"Yours." Her voice was small. She tried again, this time scraping his knee or shin or both.

He flinched, and a spark of pain flashed in his topaz green eyes. "And now my shin."

Emily cringed. "It's not my day."

He grimaced. "Please let me take matters into my own hands. Don't move."

Afraid of doing more harm to him, she waited. She was quite comfortable on his polished coat and nice hard chest and knew she shouldn't be.

The officer wiped the coffee from his face with his coat sleeve and handed her the wallet. He went on his elbows, but the snow gave way under him. His eyes rounded and so did hers. She gripped him and yelled as they slid down the hill and landed in a puddle of slush and dried leaves.

Emily lifted her head. He was drenched in mud and snow, his nose bleeding, his face smeared with coffee, his pants torn, and his leg scraped. And all compliments of her.

"Are you all right?" He spoke like he was in church, but it was tense.

Emily stared into those vibrant green eyes. She wanted to lose herself in them. They were one of a kind. Just her luck to meet a great-looking man and create havoc. Worse, pain. "Yes, thank you." Her tone was a contrite schoolgirl. She raised herself. "And you?"

He cleared his throat. "Could be better. Could be worse, too."

Her hands slipped in slush and she fell back on him. Her stomach landed on his firearm and handcuffs. She gasped in horror.

"It's my gun." His eyes rounded. "Nothing else."

"Of course, it's nothing else." She had better ideas for foreplay. And they didn't include snow, mud, or the Valentine's brew. "My apologies again." She slid off but plied her hands on his chest, smearing the front of his coat with mud. She grinned apologetically as she stood and extended her hand. It was filthy. She wiped it on her coat, and gave it to him again. "May I?"

The officer shook his head. "I can manage on my own, thank you."

"Wise choice," she mumbled.

He stood, shook the mud caked on his coat and

pants, and pulled a tissue from his pocket. She put him through an obstacle course, ruined his nice suit and coat, and gave him a bloody nose and shin. She was in a frantic state, but he was a damn turn on—dirty and clean! Why couldn't she meet him under different circumstances?

He patted the blood from around his nose and cleaned his eyes of coffee. "You maneuver well in heels."

She managed a weak smile. "You would too if your life was in the car." His calf bled. "You're bleeding. Down there."

He picked up clean snow and applied it to his calf.

Emily wanted to leisurely take him in, but she had to get to the car. She trudged up the hill, shivering from the snow, ice, and mud seeping through her clothes. The driver's door was ajar. She peered inside. Her briefcase was open, and her utensils were scattered on the back floor. The wooden horse sat upright among them.

A person jumped out of the passenger door, startling her. The person hit his or her head on the door. The hood of the coat slid down, the scarf flung open, and the sunglasses flew off.

Emily flinched. The thief was a girl. Her hair was dyed vibrant red and straightened and styled into a long bob and thick, theater-style makeup coated her face. She could be in her twenties, but she wasn't out of her teens. Emily recognized the collar of the white golf shirt. She wore one in high school, too.

"Are you hurt?" Emily asked.

Tears jumped into the girl's deep green eyes, turning her into a frightened child, but she shook her head.

Emily glanced back. The officer dabbed at blood on his leg.

"Please stand away from the car," he called out to Emily. "The thief may still be in there. He may be armed."

The girl ducked behind the door. The officer climbed toward them. But he snagged his shoe or pants on branches and bent to loosen it.

Emily's pulse raced. She had to do something. The girl was too young to be in trouble with the law. She was also frightened. She may have been forced to steal the car. Just like she had been coerced to steal at one time, too. If a policewoman hadn't let her go when she was barely sixteen, after one of her more challenging theft jobs, she would not be standing here in her executive style coat, high heeled boots, and with two art degrees to her name. She would have gone through the court system and have a juvenile record. Instead, the policewoman believed in her and set her straight. She didn't want this young person to start her life the wrong way.

"There he is, Officer." Emily pointed to a grove of trees in the opposite direction of the car. "Right there."

The officer unsnagged his shoe and bolted away from the car. "I don't see him."

The trees brushed against each other. "Behind you, now." The officer raced toward the trees.

The girl jumped. Her tears stilled, but she didn't move.

"Go," Emily mouthed.

The girl balked.

"Go."

The girl came to life. She picked up her sunglasses and rushed off, losing herself in evergreens.

Emily pulled open the back door and dived into the car. She wrapped the horse in the scarf and was about to throw it in her purse when she remembered it was drenched in coffee. She couldn't ruin it.

She threw her lock picking kit in her purse, not caring if it became soaked, and stuffed the horse in her pocket. But her pocket was too small. She had to put it somewhere or the officer would see it.

She stuffed it in her jacket under her arm and squeezed so it wouldn't fall.

The officer headed toward her. "He disappeared. He's obviously not hurt, either. Is anything missing?"

"No, my briefcase is still there and unopened." She swallowed the lie. "I need to check the trunk." She trudged to the back and opened it. Her suitcase was also there. The car was deep in snow and mud and it was a steep climb to the road.

"Unless you and your heels have superpowers and can drag the car back up," the officer said, "we're going to have to get a tow truck here."

Now that she had the wooden horse and lock picking tools, Emily was relieved and laughed. She was surprised when his cool and collected demeanor allowed him to break into a smile. She held up her briefcase. "I have what I need. My job, my life depends on everything inside." And especially what was under her arm.

"We have to dust it for prints."

"It was exactly where I put it. It wasn't touched at all."

She hooked the briefcase over her shoulder along

with her purse. She took the suitcase, but the man put his hand over hers. "Please. I don't want to do battle with your heels again." He pulled her suitcase out and gave her his arm.

Emily decided to play humble. Pressing her arm around the horse, she hooked her other arm through his and they moved up the incline. "I'm sorry about the cuts and the sliding and my rudeness. I didn't mean to be. My mother would be appalled."

The officer surprised her by laughing. "My mother would applaud." She gasped. "I don't like to get dirty." His eyes widened. "Mud and snow dirty."

"I understand." But she couldn't resist a smile.

"May I be frank?"

Emily shrugged "Why not? We've shared a dirty intimacy of sorts."

"I've never had so much fun in all my six years as a police officer—even if it was in mud and snow. You are my most entertaining victim to date."

Emily laughed. "I didn't mean to be." If he found the wooden horse, it would mean the life of a certified criminal instead of a certified art appraiser. She wouldn't be an entertaining victim but a handcuffed suspect.

They reached the top without any more incidents. A white police car parked behind the officer's car. The uniformed officer, a big man with a mid-life circle of belly, walked toward them.

"You got here quickly, Bassam," the police officer said, putting the suitcase down.

Bassam's lips twitched with amusement. "You two okay?"

"We're fine."

"If you say so." He spotted the car in the ditch. "Are we up to ten cars in four weeks now?"

"Looks like it. The thief got away."

"I'll start looking." He moved down the hill.

The officer pulled out his cell phone. It had mud on it, but he cleaned it off. "Can you give me a description of the thief?"

"I didn't see the thief's face."

"What about a physical description? You saw what he wore."

"He had on a military parka, which was probably a couple sizes too big, a hood over his head, and a scarf around his face. He also wore sunglasses."

"So, it was a he?"

Emily didn't say anything for a long moment. "Possibly. I don't know. I didn't see her face."

His eyebrows raised. "Her?"

Emily knew she slipped but kept her expression neutral. "Her. Him. I don't know. His or her face was covered up."

"Was this person tall or short?"

Emily didn't like "short". "A little taller than me but very thin. The coat was big, so it could be an illusion. I really couldn't tell you."

"Did you notice anything else? The pants, boots, or did he or she say anything?"

"I'm afraid not. Ten stolen cars in the last four weeks?"

"It started with one during the first two weeks and escalated with regularity. Usually they're at night, some even from people's driveways but this is the first time it happened in broad daylight. This thief is either super confident or utterly rash. You were the closest anyone was to him—or her. You must have noticed something."

Emily didn't let his little dig bother her. He was pressing. He knew she was lying or hiding something. He had his professional demeanor on again and wasn't about to call her bluff. But that could change. If she were interrogated.

She squirmed. "I'm afraid I didn't see anything except the coat." She didn't like telling lies. "He didn't look at me even when I banged on the window."

"Armand, can you bring me the camera?" Bassam shouted from below.

Armand, Emily thought. A sexy name for a sexy officer of the law. She wanted to say it out loud and roll it around on her tongue until she reached the right pitch and heat.

What was she thinking? She would be arrested for soliciting an officer by simply toying with his name. How unfortunate. Valentine's Day was at the end of the week.

Armand moved to the trunk of his car and removed a camera bag. "I'll be back for a statement." He disappeared over the incline.

Emily sat on her suitcase. She had to stop thinking about him. About *Armand*. She popped open her briefcase, pulled the wooden horse from under her arm pit, and put it inside. She clicked it shut and locked it.

That was one close call.

She checked her watch. She didn't have time to give a statement. She had to get to the Acadia Inn. She pulled out her cell phone and googled the directions. Two kilometers down the street. She could get there in time for the meeting. She'd explain what happened, get cleaned up quickly, and start on the evaluations.

She stood up, threw her purse over her chest, saddle bag fashion, hiked her briefcase over her shoulder, and wheeled the suitcase away even though her heels got stuck in snow. Sorry, *Armand*. At the end of the street, she turned toward the Acadia Inn. The street was cleared of snow, which made the walking and pulling easier.

That hopefully was her last brush with the law.

Pity. Armand was the most gorgeous law enforcement officer she and her high heels had the pleasure not to have foreplay with.

Chapter Four

Armand wanted to shake the mud and snow from his coat and pants. But he didn't want the spitfire to think him a dog. She already thought he was an inept, small town police detective.

It didn't help matters she was one of the sultriest women he had ever met—if one of the pushiest, too. It took all his professional composure not to wrap his arms around her compact body as she rode on his chest like a toboggan. Or to lose his fingers through her hair as it slid across his face like a cool waterfall just before her cold coffee washed it and her wallet slapped him. The fire in her dark eyes was as much a turn on as a warning not to mess with her—at least in her mood. But there were specks of silver in those discriminating eyes, daring him to try his luck.

His shoes crunched through ice and into mud as he moved toward the passenger side of the car.

If he saw her sitting at the bar or a table of the Coyote's Hole, he would introduce himself in a flash. She was sleek and smart as much as she was fire and wind and he had never come across those extremes in any other woman. But it was his luck to meet her while on the job. He now had to be professional and treat her as the victim of a crime.

He moved to the back door and stopped short in a puddle of mud. "Shit."

Bassam took photos of the car from the other side. "Did you say something?"

"Yeah. Shit." He pulled his shoes out and dragged them across a flat stone. "There are shoe prints in the snow and mud, leading from the passenger door." The incline was thick with evergreen trees. "All the way from the passenger door to the trees and probably up the hill to the road." And in front of where he stood, along with the shoe prints were the fine imprints of his spitfire's high heels. Did the spitfire lie? Did she see the car thief but make him rush off in the opposite direction? Only one way to find out. Corner her— literally speaking, of course, and ask.

"Can you take pictures from this side, Bassam. I'll get impressions of the shoe print." He climbed up the hill. "But first, I have to," he wanted to say interrogate, "get a statement from," *spitfire* almost slipped out of his mouth, "the victim."

At the top, he looked one way and the other. Where the hell was the spitfire? He strode to his car in case she sat inside to keep warm, but she wasn't there. Did she decide to walk back to town—drenched in mud and snow, carrying a briefcase, dragging a suitcase, and in those damn high heels, which ripped his pants and scraped his shin?

Could she?

He remembered the fire in her eyes and talk. He wouldn't put it past her.

Hell, he needed a statement—a statement he sure would include a physical description of the thief. He was sure she saw him—or her. Worse, he didn't have the spitfire's contact information. He didn't have her name.

Bassam came up beside him. "Where'd the pretty lady go?"

"I have no idea."

"Really?"

"Really."

Bassam took in Armand's coat and tapped his nose. "What did you do? Mud wrestle with the little lady? Looks like she got a good hit in." He indicated the rip in his pants. "Or two or three."

Armand touched his nose, but it was dry of blood. "No comment." He was about to pull his impression kit from the trunk when he spied heel and suitcase wheel marks in the snow. He gave the case to Bassam. "Start without me. I'll be down in a minute."

Bassam took the kit and moved down the hill.

Armand followed the heel marks to the end of the road, but they disappeared. A wintry blast of wind made his torn pants flap from the calf down, chilling him.

The spitfire could go three ways. Straight ahead toward Hewett Equestrian and the end of King Court. Left toward the Acadia Inn and the opposite end of King Court or right and to the center of town. His best guess was to the center of town, where she had her coffee—before it spilled into her purse and flowed onto his face. He took the brunt of the snow, ice, mud, and coffee but she got wet, too. Did nothing bother her, including the wind and chill?

He jogged toward his car, removing his drenched coat, and peered over the incline. "I'll be back in a minute, Bassam." Shoe impressions and dusting for prints could wait. He had to find his star witness.

He drove to the intersection, turned right, and

headed toward the center of town. He thought he'd see her trudging along, her head held high, but she was nowhere. He went through the center of King Court, looking into the stores but nothing.

Where could she have gone? Without a statement or her name, he'd be teased endlessly at the station.

He made another sweep of the downtown center, turned, and headed to the stolen car. Bassam left him to take impressions of the shoe prints and to sweep the car for fingerprints and other evidence. But there weren't any either of the thief or his spitfire, who wore gloves. He took photos of the inside of the car, called for a tow truck to pull it out, and arranged to have it brought to a garage for further investigation. He headed to the police station, a one-story building the size of a big bungalow. He parked in between two marked police vehicles and went into the squad room, carrying the camera and kits. Bassam and Sergei stood up at their desks and clapped. Patricia, his supervisor, came out of her office, clapping also.

Great. Bassam told them everything. It wouldn't be long before all of King Court knew of his escapade down a snowy hill and into a muddy ravine with a beautiful woman riding on top of him. A beautiful woman *and* the star witness, whom he lost.

Patricia came around the counter to get a good look. Her eyebrows lifted. "You've never had a hair out of place, a wrinkle in your shirt, or a shaving cut on your face. We could put you on the cover of a men's fashion magazine. But at this very instant, you look like you went for a swim in a muddy ravine with a moose."

"Tobogganing, actually. And believe me, she wasn't a moose."

"Tobogganing? Were you the toboggan?"

Armand didn't say anything. Laughter broke out.

Sergei sat on the edge of his desk, folding his thick arms across his equally muscle-enhanced chest. "I gather the rip in your pants, the gash on your shin, and the bruising around the nose was compliments of your ride?"

"Actually, the gash and rip were compliments of the lady's heels. The bruise from the lady's knee. My coat was the toboggan."

"And the lady?"

"No damages." He bowed still holding the camera and kit. "I went beyond the call of duty and saved her from any and all discomfort."

More laughter erupted. Patricia slapped him on the back. "I'm looking forward to your report—Sir Armand."

Armand plopped the camera and kit on the farthest desk in front of the holding cell. He remembered the envelope with the Post-it Note from Halloran's Antiques in his jacket pocket and handed it to Patricia. "I dusted Halloran's Antiques. I have to dust this note now."

Patricia put on her glasses and widened the envelope to read the note. "What a nice thief. Too bad he didn't sign it." A piece of ice fell from Armand's jacket onto her boot. She kicked it off and handed back the envelope. "Maybe you should clean up before you," she indicated the camera and kit, "start processing everything and update me—on all your escapades of this morning."

Armand removed some muddy leaves from his jacket pocket and dumped them in the nearest garbage bin. "My exact sentiments." He dropped the envelope on his desk and moved down a corridor to a locker room equipped with a shower. He put his firearm and handcuffs in his locker, stuffed his clothes into a big plastic bag, and took a quick shower. His nose was slightly bruised. It wouldn't be the first time and he didn't think it would be the last either. He put rubbing alcohol on his gash, followed by a big bandage, and changed into one of his old police uniforms, clipping his firearm and handcuffs around his waist. He hadn't worn the uniform in two years. He was going back in time instead of forward. But at least he was clean again.

In the forensics room, he dusted the Post-it Note for prints. But, as he suspected, there were none. He returned to his desk, wrote his report on the theft of the wooden horse, and examined the shoe print taken from around the stolen car. It didn't take him long to identify it as a Dr. Martens boot. The thief wore a size seven. A size seven in ladies' Dr. Martens boots.

His spitfire lied. She saw the thief. She said "she" and then explained it away. So why did she deny it? Why the lie?

His cell rang. "Hey, Nicole. You all right?"

"Yes, but I need a favor. Darryl is supposed to spend the night here at the inn, but he's stuck in Montreal, waiting for a flight out. I was going to stay but I don't want Carli to spend the night on her own. She's been out of sorts lately. Spending a lot of time on her own. I don't know what's bothering her."

"She's a teenager, sis."

"I think it might have to do with a boy."

"Boys, already?"

"She's sixteen, Armand. She noticed boys at ten."

"You want me to speak to her? Her wonderful Uncle Armand can wrangle anything out."

"You can give it your best shot if she'll let you near her. But right now, I was wondering if you could come by the inn after your shift and wait until Darryl gets here."

"Not a problem. We had another car theft."

"I heard. Same MO as the others?"

Nicole still spoke like a police officer even though she and her husband, also an ex-police officer, had been out of the force for two years. They started a private security and alarm company and it was doing better than they imagined.

"Same MO but only a shoe print to go on. Then, believe it or not, I have to dust for prints and take photos at Halloran's Antiques. There was a robbery. I should be there around five or five-thirty."

"A robbery at Halloran's Antiques?" Her voice was incredulous.

"My exact reaction. Small theft but the thief broke in. Is Lowan and his crew still there?"

"They are. They're filming in the lobby but should be gone by eight or nine. Katrina and her parents went to Ottawa, some unexpected business with the sale of the property, but a few appraisers from Kanata Auction House are arriving tonight. They're bunking in the family quarters. Theresa and Jerome will take care of them. All you have to do is keep an eye on the monitors and enjoy a beer or two with Lowan. I have two guys taking care of the film crew's equipment."

"Sounds easy enough. Everything okay with baby Ashlee?"

"We're fine, but I think she wants to be a dancer."

"Are you sleeping?"

"Well, it's interesting. I get home and Ashlee could be doing the rumba, but I sleep right through it. I even sleep through Carli's music. Talk later."

Armand went back to his report on the car theft. He gazed at the screen, pulled himself back in his chair, and fiddled with a pen. He didn't want to report the victim disappeared before getting her statement *and* name. It wouldn't make him look good.

But Mariana at King Court Car Rentals would know, along with his spitfire's address, phone number, driver's license, and so on. His pride was saved.

He found Mariana's number. The phone rang twice, and the store's voice mail clicked in. Armand left a message.

He'd check his emails while he waited. The Toronto Police Commission sent him one. His heart jumped with excitement. Did he get the job as a detective on the Guns and Gang Division?

Patricia was in her office, Hassam taking a call, and Sergei out. He moved forward, shielding the screen with his body, and opened the email.

Detective Lecavalier,

Thank you for applying for Detective, Guns and Gang Division with the Toronto Police Commission. After much consideration, we have offered the position to a more qualified candidate with solid—

Armand closed the email and fell back against his chair. He didn't have to read more. He lost yet another opportunity with a big city police force because he didn't have enough experience in thefts or drugs or gangs and so on.

How could he get real theft or gang or drug

experience in King Court? How could he make it to the big-time police forces if none of them gave him a chance to prove himself? If he stayed in King Court much longer, he would turn into Sergei or Bassam. Comfortably overweight or smugly over-muscled and satisfied with locating wandering cows, bringing drunk teens home by the ears, and investigating petty thefts of insignificant objects. Only Patricia had experience with a big-time police force, and he couldn't understand why she uprooted her teenage daughters and husband over ten years ago to supervise a small police detachment at King Court.

He returned to his report. Ten cars stolen in the last four weeks, a huge spike from their usual one or two a year. None of the cars were found and there were no clues to shed light. Witnesses gave varying descriptions of the thieves—tall, short, fat, skinny, muscular, even roly poly—leading him to believe the thefts weren't the work of one person but of many. A loose military parka, black hat, scarf, and sunglasses was generic. Anyone could buy them at a thrift store. Armand checked the auto mechanic shops in King Court and beyond, but none saw or heard about the cars. All of them were high-end SUVs. He believed they were repainted and shipped to South America or Africa. His spitfire's Camry was a departure. It was a sedan and not an ultra-expensive SUV.

He tried the car rental office again. Mariana still didn't answer.

He moved to the storage room and grabbed a trace evidence collection kit. "I'm going to Roberto's to check the car again and to Halloran's Antiques," he told Patricia. "I'll have my reports for you tomorrow."

Without waiting for a reply, he put his uniform hat on, flung on his parka, and dashed out to his car.

Whether she liked it or not, the spitfire's statement was going to be his ticket to a big-time police force.

Then he'd worry about how sultry and sleek and wonderfully dangerous she was.

Chapter Five

Emily checked the poster-sized sign, hanging on gold-colored hinges from the wooden post. Acadia Inn. Five gold stars were etched below the name. This was it. She trudged down the drive lined with white trailers used for filming on location. The other side had evergreen trees, coated with a thick layer of snow and glistening ice. As she drew closer to the two-story inn, she noticed the parking lot crammed with cars. Probably the film crew. The inn officially closed in January.

At the walkway, leading to the inn, Emily lifted her suitcase and rolled it toward the front doors. But there weren't any front doors. Instead, swinging saloon doors replaced them along with a lopsided wooden plaque over the frame. "Saloon" was inscribed on it

She lifted her foot but abruptly set it down. She thought it was snow, but it was a big white inflated air bag. It covered the ground in front of the steps, leading to the doors. Obscured by the snow, she would have punctured it. Another big white airbag lay on the side of the steps and a third on the veranda.

A tall husky man with silver hair, who reminded Emily of a WWE wrestler, came around the side of the inn, dressed in a heavy parka and carrying a shovel. "It's not a saloon. It is the Acadia Inn."

"Good to know." Emily walked around the airbag.

"Because the day I've had, I didn't want to think I was hallucinating, too."

He placed the shovel against the side. "You're either a lost stunt woman or an appraiser from Kanata Auction House."

"The latter. I'm Emily Atterberry. Katrina Sherrer is expecting me."

The man moved to the walkway. "Yes, she told me you'd be arriving early afternoon. I'm Jerome Beach." He took off his glove and extended his hand.

"Excuse me if I keep my gloves on, Jerome." She shook his hand. "My hands are frozen."

"Quite understandable. We've been in minus double-digit weather since before Christmas. Did you drive or take a taxi?"

"Neither. It's part of my long story."

His eyebrows rose. "A long story makes for a good story. We'll get you inside and warmed up. Katrina and her parents are in Ottawa this morning. Some unexpected business with the sale of the property, but she updated me on everything. I'm helping her and her parents take care of the inn while the film crew is here."

Emily's face softened. "Between you and me, it's the best news I've heard today. I can get myself cleaned up before anyone else sees me—including my colleagues. I was afraid I'd have to sit through a meeting, trying to look respectable and dry."

He took her suitcase. "From what I understand, your associates are arriving much later." He moved around the air bag to the veranda. "We'll get you settled, and you can clean up before anyone arrives."

Emily followed him. "Sounds wonderful. I gather there's a film shoot going on."

"It wraps up at the end of the week. They're shooting a couple scenes in the lobby and out here today before moving to the barns and corral tomorrow for the rest of the week. You and the other appraisers will have the entire inn to yourselves after tonight, but you can get started on the restaurant whenever you're ready." He pushed the saloon doors and held them open for Emily. "Do you watch *Intergalactic Wars*?"

"I've seen bits and pieces. Is that what they're shooting?"

"It is. Captain Borgman, the half-man, half-android who runs the *S.S. Intergalactic* has to go back to the old west. He has to stop a female assassin from the Crystalline planet from killing a mad scientist and a rival female assassin. If she kills them, the mad scientist's frozen sperms—the first ever recorded in history—will not be taken back by the rival female assassin to the planet Luxor. She's the one who starts the evolution of a new race of biotechnical female assassin-geniuses, which could potentially destroy the pure but evil race of female assassins on Crystalline."

"Oh, I love mean girls. I'll definitely catch the episode." Emily walked into the lobby, stumbling on a trolley with a camera. People moved around either packing sets in large crates, viewing film behind cameras, adjusting lights, or wearing old west gunslinger, cattlemen, or barmaid costumes. The rustic opulence of the lobby screamed through the chaos. The wood burning fireplace in the center, surrounded by tables and chairs made of thick oak casks or packing boxes, which characterized the local saloons of the wild west period, was a masterpiece of handmade construction. A weathered oak stand-up bar with smoky glass shelves and wall covering was set up over a polished dark-stained bar with beveled glass curios. The original pieces became visible as the set was dismantled. Everything took Emily's breath away, including the hardwood floor and paneling. She was back in time like Captain Borgman and the female assassins, but to nineteenth and twentieth century Canada.

A man with his face half encased in steel, wires, and a computer processor for an eye threw his hands up in frustration. He rushed toward them, his auburn-colored duster coat with a triangle-shaped *SSI* pin on his chest, flinging open. Emily spied a holster with two revolvers peeking out of the coat. Smith & Wesson type revolvers from the 1880s. The man lifted the processor attached to a wire from his eye, so he could see. "Please tell me this is one of our lost stunt crew people."

"Sorry," Jerome said. "This is Emily Atterberry from Kanata Auction House. Emily, this is my son Lowan, better known as Captain Borgman. He's directing this particular episode."

"And anything that can go wrong is going wrong." But he smiled and shook Emily's hand, taking in the mud and water on her coat and pants. "Are you sure you're not a stunt woman? Looks like you've been doing stunts in muck."

Emily was used to looking up to talk to tall people but Lowan was even taller and broader than his father. He could also be a WWE wrestler. "Let's say everything that could go wrong with my first solo gig as an appraiser today has gone wrong, too."

"Touché. Do you watch the show?"

"On and off. My parents watch it religiously and

my sister wants to marry you."

Lowan readjusted his processor over his eye. It lit up on contact as a computerized eye. "Want a grandchild, Dad?"

"One without a half-cyborg body, please."

A cameraman called and Lowan excused himself.

"From what I can see through the wild west setting, this lobby is Canadiana heaven," Emily said, following Jerome to the front desk. "It's unfortunate everything has to be stripped down and sold."

"It is a gorgeous place. But it lost its value in today's market. The entire inn is going to be demolished and a massive housing complex will take over the property." He led her into an industrial-sized kitchen. A tall, thin woman in her fifties or sixties arranged potatoes in several huge casserole dishes, while a dark-haired woman in the late stages of pregnancy stood beside her, eating a potato.

"Ladies, this is Emily Atterberry from Kanata Auction House. The woman with her hands arranging the potatoes is my lovely wife Theresa. The woman eating the potatoes is my lovely goddaughter Nicole. Nicole's head of Magnum Security and Alarms. They're putting up security cameras. You will probably bump into a few of her people while you're appraising."

Theresa said hello while Nicole, her mouth full of potatoes, wiped her hands clean on a dish towel. She swallowed. "Potatoes are for the baby, not me." Nicole extended her hand, taking in the condition of Emily's coat and pants.

"It's a long story," Emily said.

"Both Theresa and I love long stories—over a cup of hot tea," Nicole said.

"And biscuits," Theresa replied.

"The tea and biscuits sound wonderful, but I need to look respectable first."

"We'll put the kettle on the minute you give the go ahead," Theresa said, putting a casserole in one of the ovens.

Jerome read a text. "One of the saloon doors fell—again."

"I'll show Emily to her room," Nicole said.

"I'll leave the suitcase in the hallway." He carried the suitcase through the kitchen and to a hallway. Then grabbing a potato, much to Theresa's dismay, he left the kitchen.

"Katrina is giving you a room in what was once the servants' quarters and then became the family's quarters," Nicole said, moving toward the hallway. "All her sisters have moved out and the rooms are available to you and your colleagues. She left you a key in the family's office. When you're ready, we'll have a cup of tea and Jerome will give you a tour of the inn. Theresa is preparing the meals for the film crew and for you and your colleagues—unless you'd like to go into town."

"Dinner here sounds wonderful—and cozier." Emily followed Nicole into the hallway. She unlocked the first door, which was a large office. It was packed with boxes, labeled with family photos, Wilhelm's collectibles, Elsa's figurines, and Katrina's plates. A roll top desk made of walnut and brass from the late 1800s was maintained with loving care. A laptop, piles of file folders, and other office paraphernalia resting on the desk along with an ergonomic office chair, made sharp contrasts between the old and the new.

Nicole pulled open drawers. "I thought Katrina left

the keys here, but they might be at the front desk. Make yourself comfortable. I'll be back in a minute."

Emily took off her mud-encased coat and folding it inside out, slung it on the back of the banker's chair. She sat down, exhausted after her morning and the walk to the inn in high heels and was thankful for the thick cushions on the hardwood chair. A calendar on the wall behind the desk caught her attention. The picture featured a man wearing a police hat low over his forehead. He held two sets of handcuffs along with his police belt over his privates. A standard police-issued set of handcuffs and a furry red-lined one for erotic fun. His smile was nothing short of a "come hither woman".

Emily raced behind the desk.

Holy crap! It was Armand the police officer. She read the inscription under his picture. *A six-year member of the King Court Police Force, Armand Lecavalier is a detective, who investigates all crimes.*

Armand Lecavalier. Mr. February. Holding red furry handcuffs. A set adorned the square for February 14, too.

She took the calendar and checked the cover. It was the King Court Calendar of Men. She flicked through it. Did this small town really have enough gorgeous men to fill a calendar? She couldn't believe it.

She went back to February and stared at Armand.

Wow, she knew he was well-built and solid, but this? He was the definition of hunky with a bold but boyish-mischief charm in the come-hither woman smile, which tied all the wonderful and explosive male package together. She wouldn't mind sharing those furry handcuffs with him on Valentine's Day and beyond. *Anytime, Armand Lecavalier! Anytime!*

She heard footsteps. She hung the calendar up and sat down like a prim schoolgirl.

Nicole walked in, holding a note and a key. "All right. Katrina has set you up in room two, which used to be her sister Ingrid's." She led her to the hallway, locking the door behind her. "Your other three colleagues are in rooms three, four, and five," she said pointing to them. "Katrina occupies Number Six, her parents Number Seven, and Theresa and Jerome are in the eighth bedroom. My security crew and I are here, right across from yours. Number One. We're in the middle of setting up cameras in each of guestrooms, the public areas, and hallways. Once everything is listed, we expect a lot of people roaming around even though I know the majority of the auction will be online."

"We do expect a lot of people coming in person to check the items. Security cameras are necessary." But her thoughts were on Armand Lecavalier. Mr. February and the furry red handcuffs. She couldn't get over it—him.

"If you need anything, feel free to find me or Theresa or Jerome. My husband Darryl will take over for me this evening. Darryl will be more than willing to help you out, too. You'll know him when you see him. Full beard and tightly curly hair. Please tell him you hate the beard if he asks."

Emily could only smile. "I have someone from the car rental agency dropping off a car."

"You didn't drive?"

Emily grabbed her suitcase. "That's part of the long story to be told over a hot cup of tea and biscuits."

"Sounds like the tea may need to be spiked. I'll let you know when the car arrives."

"Thank you." She looked forward to evaluating everything and becoming a full-fledged furniture and art appraiser. She never wanted to see Detective Armand Lecavalier again, but she wouldn't mind going back into the office and taking a long and leisurely look at his beautiful semi-naked self. It was safer. She couldn't do any damage by just looking and dreaming about him and the furry handcuffs. This way he would never know about her illicit thoughts and activity. She was on the wrong side of the law just like the girl who stole her car.

Chapter Six

After checking the inside of the stolen Camry for prints again, Armand gave up. He hoped once he was clean and thinking straight again, a second check would yield clues. But the car was cleaned to a polish by King Court Car Rentals before leasing it. Other than the imprint of a size seven female Dr. Martens pair of boots, which everyone wore, he didn't have much else to go on—until, of course, he located his elusive spitfire.

He took more photographs of the outside of the car when Roberto, the owner of the shop approached, wearing his usual blue mechanic's uniform. Roberto was the same age as his sister Nicole, in his early thirties. She had a monster crush on the man she used to call her gladiator in school, but Roberto's only love back then was his race cars. He won several major titles, the Belgium Grand Prix, the Indy 500, the Daytona 600 but an accident during the Monaco Grand Prix kept him sidelined. He turned his father's mechanic shop into an exclusive racing car body shop. But he continued to work with the police as his father had. In the garage were several Ferraris and Mercedes, a couple Aston Martins, and a cross between a Lamborghini and a rocket, all in various stages of repair or innovation.

Roberto extended his hand. "You're back to

wearing a uniform?"

Armand shook it. "I got all muddy going after the Camry this morning."

"Yes, I noticed the mud in the tires." He moved to the front. "I haven't had a chance to check but offhand there doesn't appear to be much damage, except for the fender." He indicated a minor dent over the license plate. "The air bag didn't deploy. I don't think the thief sustained any injuries."

"I noticed, but I'll have to call a couple walk-in clinics and see if anyone came in with whiplash or some other car-related issue just to make sure."

"Is tomorrow okay for a report?"

"Tomorrow's great. Great looking Ferrari."

"It's my old racing car. I'm trying to make it run again."

"It's still a beauty." He shook his hand again. "Don't let me catch you speeding."

Roberto laughed. "Even if you're sitting in the passenger seat?"

Armand pushed back his hat. "Even if I'm in the driver's seat and you're in the passenger's."

From Roberto's Pit Stop, Armand moved to Halloran's Antiques. While Mrs. Halloran asked him question after question about the car theft and especially about the cute pushy lady, whose car was stolen, he dusted for prints and took photos. But nothing was out of place there, either. He had the shoe print and soon would have the spitfire's statement and possibly a description of the car thief, but he had nothing to go on for the theft of the wooden horse.

He dropped the kits and camera off at the station and headed for home, the bottom floor of a three-story

Victorian house. He checked his cell several times and twice called the car rental agency, but he and Mariana kept missing each other. He left another message, asking her for the information about the woman who rented the stolen and barely scratched, silver Camry.

He changed into a pair of jeans and a long-sleeved T-shirt, topping them off with a heavy jacket and headed to the Acadia Inn in his black Jeep. He found a space between two film trailers and strode toward the front doors. It was dark but massive lights were set up to illuminate the entrance. Swinging batwing doors replaced the solid wood front doors of the inn and a "Saloon" sign hung lopsided above them.

Lowan came out of the swinging doors wearing some Wild West coat minus the half-wire face of Captain Borgman. He saluted Armand as he would the crew of his spaceship by standing with his feet together, touching his forehead with the tips of his fingers, and directing them toward Armand. "Civilian."

Armand did the same. "Captain."

"I hear you're on deck this evening."

"Yes, but I have to work." He stumbled on an airbag on his way to the veranda. "No partying." He leaped onto the veranda and gave Lowan a fist punch.

"We'll have to see about that, Civilian. What happened to your nose? Looks a little black."

"Compliments of a woman who decided to use me as her personal toboggan."

"Was she good-looking at least?"

His smile was sly. "One of the best I've ever given a free ride to."

"You will have to tell me the whole story over a beer later. But right now, how would you mere civilian-mortal like to do a little stunt work?"

Armand's eyebrows lifted. "I'm listening."

Lowan moved to the saloon doors. "Our stunt crew is stuck in Toronto and we need to film a quick shot before we strike this set down."

"You know I'm all for stunts. What do you want me to do? Leap through a burning sky deck? Take on five Borgbots single-handedly? Wrestle the beautiful princess-assassins on Crystalline before bedding them?"

Lowan put his arm around his shoulders. "Something similar." He pushed open the saloon doors and led him into the lobby crowded with cameras, wires, lights, and people, some in costumes. "I've found our sheriff's stuntman," Lowan told a man holding a tablet and another man talking on his cell. "And he's in law enforcement, too."

The man on his cell disengaged and grabbed a clipboard. "Wonderful." He handed Armand the clipboard. "Sign the waiver. We're not responsible to any damage you do to yourself."

"Am I going to do damage to myself?" Armand asked Lowan.

"That woman roughed you up more than this stunt ever could," Lowan said. "You won't suffer a scratch—as long as you land on the airbags outside."

Armand signed. "Do I get paid?"

"You'll get as many beers as you want, a credit the size of a pinpoint, and free access to our canteen."

"I always have access to your mother's food."

"I'll throw in a big favor." Lowan directed him to the woman standing in front of a rack of costumes. She handed him a black suede duster jacket with a silver sheriff's badge, a black vest, silver dickie, red bow tie, and riding boots with spurs. "Put these on and get ready for your big break." He indicated a partition behind the bar.

Armand did what he was told. He came out. "How do I look?"

Lowan handed him a black cowboy hat and pistol. It was over a hundred years old and weighed at least a kilo. "Now you look perfect."

"So what do I have to do? Do I have superhuman powers?"

"Nope, only me, bro. I'm the star of the show, remember. All we need you to do is keep the pistol in your hand and stand with your back to the saloon doors." Armand did as he was told. Two men who could get jobs as bouncers but were dressed in cowboy outfits came on each of his sides. "These two big puppy dogs are going to pick you up and throw you out the saloon doors. If all goes well, you will land on the airbag outside."

"If all goes well?"

"There are several airbags. One on the veranda and one beside the steps, but you should land on the airbag at the bottom of the steps. You just fly, bro. These guys know how hard to throw."

Armand took both in. "Physicists?"

"Sure."

"Are the doors going to crack?"

"The doors are made of sponge. We'll edit in the sound later. Ready?" He lowered Armand's hat over his eyes. "Look mean and tough. Police mean and tough."

"Not a problem." Armand stood with his back to the saloon doors and bulked up to appear formidable.

"Whenever you're ready."

Lowan moved behind several cameras. "On my cue, guys." A woman snapped the clapperboard in front of Armand and moved aside. "Action!"

The men picked Armand up and threw him out the saloon doors. He landed on the airbag at the bottom of the stairs, staring up at the beautiful but surprised face of his elusive spitfire.

Chapter Seven

"The revolver you're holding is a Colt Walker used at least forty years before the Wild West era and almost two centuries ago," she said. "This little town can't afford modern guns or up-to-date uniforms?"

Armand pushed his hat off his forehead to get a better look. "You know your revolvers. You *are* a dangerous woman."

Lowan came out onto the veranda with the two cowboy-bouncers and the woman with the clapperboard. "How was it?" His eyebrows rose at the woman hovering over the airbag.

"The revolver doesn't cut it," Armand said.

Lowan pushed aside the airbags and rushed down. "What do you mean the revolver doesn't cut it?"

Armand indicated the spitfire and she told him.

"You've got to be joking?" Lowan turned to the woman. "Call Halloran's Antiques before it closes. We need the right revolver. A," he turned to the spitfire. "What do we need?"

"At least a Smith Wesson Model 3 from the 1870s to early 1900s."

"Did you get it?" The woman ran inside, pulling out her cell phone. "Armand didn't hurt you, did he?"

"I'm fine."

"I'm good, too," Armand said. "Thanks for asking."

His spitfire's smile was warm but seductive. She gave Armand a gloved hand. "May I, Detective—excuse me, Sheriff?"

"Are you going to punch me or scrap me or knock me down again?" He eyed her high heels. "You're wearing your weapons."

"I can't speak for the fates or elements, but I promise not to do any more damage."

Armand didn't need her help, but he took her hand anyway.

Lowan eyed them with interest. "You know each other?"

Armand indicated his slightly bruised nose. "We had the pleasure of meeting this morning."

The corners of Lowan's lips curled, and his eyes lit up with amusement.

A cameraman pushed open the saloon doors. "Good shot, Lowan."

"Not good," Lowan said. "We have the wrong revolver. We're doing it again with the right one. I also want to get a shot from outside. You up for a couple more shots, Armand?"

"Always."

His spitfire moved past him. "Nice seeing you again, Detective."

"Hey, not so fast—again." Armand moved toward her, but his spurs ripped the airbag. A whoosh of air burst through.

"Great," Lowan said. "One more mishap to contend with today."

"Dock it from my pay." Armand bounced off the airbag, creating a bigger hole and another burst of air, and to his spitfire.

"You're not getting paid," Lowan shouted.

"Exactly." He hopped onto the veranda and moved in front of her as Lowan bellowed for someone to patch up the airbag. "You disappeared on me before I finished with you."

"Had a meeting to keep. You're quite the Renaissance Man. Detective, stuntman, sheriff, and Mr. February with an intriguing set of handcuffs. Wasn't sure which set was more formidable. The metal ones or the furry ones."

Armand's smile went sly. "It seems you know me and saw a little more of me. The red handcuffs added *intrigue and danger* to the metal ones—and me. I unfortunately don't have the pleasure of knowing you." His cell rang, and he pulled it out of his trousers.

"They didn't have cells back then either—Sheriff."

"Noted." King Court Car Rentals. "Looks like I'm about to find out who I have the pleasure of seeing again. Hi, Mariana. Yes, I know we've been missing each other. Yes, I need the young woman's information. Great." His gaze rested on Emily. "Emily Atterberry. Toronto. Expensed to Kanata Auction House. She's staying at the Acadia Inn. Appreciate the info. Can you scan the leasing agreement? I'll look it over tomorrow. She's rented another car? A white Toyota Camry this time." Emily pointed to it in the parking lot. "Thanks. Have a good evening." Armand put his cell in his pocket and extended his hand. "Well, Emily Atterberry, appraiser from Kanata Auction House based in Toronto. Nice to meet you."

Emily shook his hand. "Nice to meet you, Detective. Sheriff. Mr. February. Renaissance Man."

"It's Armand Lecavalier."

"It's Armand Lecavalier only if you're not going to press me for a description of the person who stole my car. I told you everything. I didn't see the person."

"Then, why aren't you looking me in the eyes?"

"My weapons aren't high enough to look you in the eyes."

Nicole pushed open the swinging doors and came onto the veranda. "You're here, Armand, good." Her smile turned wicked. "And I know you met Emily this morning."

Armand should have been annoyed at Nicole's playful jab at his morning escapade with Emily but wasn't. He was about to spend the evening with his lovely spitfire. He wanted to sing and dance.

Emily was confused. "How did you know it was him?"

"Because she heard," Armand said.

"Who didn't hear?" Nicole didn't suppress a big smile. "Emily told us the story over tea and biscuits but not the *whole* story. She didn't know who she used as a slide, but Theresa and I had our ideas—especially after she mentioned a GQ suit. Mom called me, then Grandma, followed by Mrs. Halloran, and even Patricia." She laughed. "I'm sorry, Emily, but—"

Emily waved it off. "Don't worry. I'm close to laughing about it, too. You're related?"

"Armand's my brother," Nicole said. "And my dear brother is watching things here at the inn until my husband arrives."

"How nice." Emily's smile was tight.

"Isn't it?" Armand's smile was huge. "I may be here the entire night if my poor brother-in-law's plane keeps getting delayed."

Nicole opened her mouth "Darryl said—"

"—Darryl called me, too, Nicole—when he couldn't reach you." His voice was loud and effusive. "He's stuck in Toronto, poor guy."

"Montreal."

"Yes, and Montreal."

"Well, thank you for the update." Nicole came down the stairs and handed Armand a large set of keys. "If Emily and the other appraisers want to start on their work, you'll need these to open the rooms. Thanks again, and," she glanced at Emily, "have a good evening."

Armand took the keys, wanting to flash them in front of his spitfire. "For sure." Nicole moved to the parking lot. "So here we are. Together again, Emily."

"And on our feet." She moved around him to go inside but he stepped in front of her again. "If you'll excuse me, I have to start on my work."

He dangled the keys. "How about you show me how you appraise things and I convince you to ID the thief?"

"No." She moved to the right.

He moved to the right, too. "No? No to the ID or no to me seeing you appraise things?"

"No to both."

"How heartbreaking."

"I'm sure you've had more intense heartbreaking, Detective."

"Yes, Alexis in grade six, Maia in grade twelve, and we won't talk about Candice in Psych 101." She moved to the left and he moved too. "How about we work on one and then on the other? We can start on the ID and then work on the appraising."

"No."

"All right. We'll start on the appraising and then on the ID."

Emily laughed.

"Oh, come on. I'm going to be bored simply opening doors for you and your colleagues, walking around an empty inn, and watching monitors of rooms full of furniture. They aren't going anywhere unless they're magical or haunted."

"You have your stunt man job."

"All of five seconds of work." He held up the prized set of keys. "I also have the keys to the rooms in the inn. The rooms you need access to appraise the furniture."

"So you do."

"I knew I could convince you."

"I never said I was convinced."

"Close enough. Why don't you get yourself ready to start appraising? Take off your nice new coat, put on boots or shoes or runners without weapons, and I'll shoot my five-second scenes of fame. Then I'll open any door you want and observe you." That didn't come out right. "I'll observe *how* you appraise. Think of me as a student."

Her eyebrows rose as she caught his slip. "What do you know about eighteenth and nineteenth century Canadian furniture and artwork?"

"I'm about to learn everything." He held one of the saloon doors open and lifted his cowboy hat. "After you—ma'am."

Chapter Eight

Emily hung the cashmere coat Mrs. Sonberg from King Court Dry Cleaners lent her from her stock of unclaimed items. Emily planned to return the wooden horse once her colleagues and everyone else in the inn were asleep, but how could she if Armand stayed the evening and followed her as she worked? She thought she wouldn't have any problem leaving the inn and coming back unseen, especially since her associates were still in transit from Toronto. But Armand ruined her plan.

She needed to return the wooden horse at night. The other appraisers would not only be at the inn after tonight, making it difficult to leave without telling them why or where, but she would be too busy appraising the furniture.

Taking a deep breath, Emily slung her Kanata Auction House ID around her neck and changed from her boots to a pair of heels. She checked the full-length mirror on the closet door. Along with her coat, she left her muddy suit at the dry cleaners and changed into another. It wasn't one of her severe suits Isla said made her look like a forlorn novice lawyer. This one was a skirt suit and it hugged her well.

Armand ruined her plans, but he was escorting her around the inn. She wanted to look good. He was sexy as hell in whatever outfit he wore. As the ultra-professional but also ultra-GQ detective in his cashmere coat and charcoal suit, even after they became soiled and muddy. As the badass sheriff in the black Wild West outfit for the film shot and, of course, as Mr. February with only the police hat, belt, red and non-red handcuffs, and come-hither-woman smile. That was her favorite.

She undid a button on the jacket. She still resembled a forlorn novice lawyer. She removed the jacket. The skirt was pencil thin and her light blue blouse was V-necked, showing off her black hair and— she opened one more button—some skin. Why not? Mr. February Detective couldn't arrest her for showing a little cleavage. Correction, no cleavage. Her identification badge covered it up.

She checked her makeup. No runny mascara or bleeding lipstick. She ran a brush through her hair. All in place. She grabbed her iPad and returned to the lobby where the film crew packed up sets. Armand waited for her at the bar, still wearing the sheriff's outfit. He smiled and jumped off the stool. Her heart leaped in excitement. His smile was just for her.

How would she focus on the furniture and not on him when he was so bad boy sexy and a simple smile melted her professional reserve?

Armand took off his hat in real, old-fashion gentleman etiquette. "So where do you want to start?"

She hugged her iPad to her chest as though to keep her attraction at bay. "I'm scheduled to start here in the lobby, but I'd rather wait until the filming finishes and the sets are removed. How about a quick tour of the inn first? I'd like to see what's in store for me."

"Not a problem. We can begin with the restaurant.

Right this way." He led her to a set of double doors, unlocked them, and held one open. He flicked on a light and Emily's mouth all but fell open. The restaurant combined the rustic with the modern and the opulent with the welcoming.

"Wow." She sauntered around the tables. "I've been transported to some English countryside tea house." She ran her hand over the tops of the tables and chairs. "For the most part, the furniture is nineteenth century."

Armand ambled in, holding the hat, and looking bewildered. "I guess you like what you see."

"Like?" She stopped in front of a secretary. At first glance it could be from the early nineteenth century. A two-door cupboard caught her eye. "A pie safe. It's in mint condition."

"A what?"

Emily was surprised to find him standing beside her and stepped away. "A pie safe or pie cupboard." She opened the cupboards, putting a door between her and Armand, and ran her hand over a shelf. "It had other names, but it was largely used in the eighteenth and nineteenth centuries to keep mice out of food. It's beautiful." She closed the cupboard doors and moved to a table. She pulled out a chair, examined it, removed the other three chairs, and put them between her and Armand.

He sauntered closer. "Interesting?"

"Very. These chairs are individually handcrafted." She glanced around the vast restaurant, taking in the other chairs and tables. "I think I need to spend a little more time in here. Maybe more than a little. How about leaving me and coming back in an hour or so? You must have a lot of work monitoring the inn. I don't want to keep you from it."

He held up his cell. "Can monitor right from here. I'm all yours, ready and eager to learn all about appraising eighteenth century tables and chairs and pie safes."

That's not what Emily wanted to hear.

"So how does it work?"

Emily pulled out another chair. "How does what work?"

"Appraising furniture—and revolvers. You identified the revolver with one look."

"Can you keep a secret?"

His eyebrows rose with devilish intrigue.

"I saw the revolver on Lowan earlier and thought it wasn't the right time-period piece. I Googled it."

"Your search proved you right."

"It did but I didn't have to give it a monetary value. Here I do. I'll have to look at the item's age, style, size, origin, and condition. Look at these chairs." She lined them in a row.

He came around them for a better look. "They're the same style."

"At first glance, yes, but they were all individually hand crafted. Canadian furniture took its lead from French, German, and British styles in earlier centuries. Even now to some degree. These chairs look like they were influenced by Louis XIV." She ran her fingers down the back. "They're curvy with rope shaped frames," she touched the seat, "and upholstered in brocade with a floral design. But the wood is walnut, the design is of muted leaves and not florals, and the rope shape of the frames is softer. These tell me they're

Canadian." She moved to the second chair. "This chair looks the same but if you check the rope design, you'll see they're slightly different than the first chair. Even the brocade and stitching are different. Offhand, I'd say they should each go for a pretty penny. I have to suggest a starting bid and it takes research."

"Interesting." He moved to the bar and held out a stool. "These stools don't look the same either. They don't look like the chairs."

Emily moved to the bar and pulled out another. "Incredible. A Hepplewhite, shield-back dining-room chair with a needlepoint seat reinvented as a bar stool."

"Hepplewhite? Doesn't sound like a name from Louis XIV's time."

Emily couldn't help but smile. She didn't want him around, but he was an intuitive and engaging learner. "George Hepplewhite was an English cabinetmaker from the late eighteenth and early nineteenth centuries and not a king. He created an elegant and streamlined style of chair. The chairs have a wide shield-shaped or heart-shaped back, sometimes oval, with rounded front seats." She examined the stool closer. "This wood was picked apart and put back together brilliantly." She checked another. "This one too." She straightened up. "Wow, wow, wow. From what I can see everything is in astounding condition. Some completely authentic, others put together from genuine pieces with amazing craftsmanship."

"The Sherrers restored the furniture with help from master craftsmen from a First Nations reserve just north of here. Lowan's dad is a deputy commissioner with the RCMP, but he helped out, too."

"They maintained the furniture with a lot of love—

as artists would."

Armand sat on a stool and put his hat on the bar. Emily wanted to slide in next to him but kept her gaze on the stools.

"You like what you do?"

She moved to a buffet next to the front doors in case she did slip in beside him. "I wouldn't be doing it if I didn't."

"How did you get into it?"

"I got my master's in art history two years ago from the University of Toronto with every intention of working as a curator at the Louvre in Paris or the Uffizi Gallery in Florence. But of course, those are the idealistic jobs of any art historian. I was always fascinated by antiques and applied for the appraisal training program with Kanata Auction House. I've been in training this past year and this is my last gig. I get through this and I become a full-fledged furniture appraiser. Art appraising will be next on the list."

"You must be an artist, too."

She opened the drawers of the buffet. It was lined with velvet to hold cutlery. "I can draw, but I wouldn't call myself an artist."

"Draw me a picture of the car thief you saw this morning, and I'll be the judge."

Emily shot him a glance. "You are one smooth talker, Detective Lecavalier." She shut the drawer. "You made me believe you were interested in appraising."

"Oh, I am interested in you—in *what* you do."

Emily heard the slip and her heart raced with pleasure. "Then you led up to it with real finesse."

Armand's smile was as sexy as it was sly.

"Actually, I didn't work up to it. It fell into my lap when you said artist. You saw the thief, didn't you? You saw her?"

Emily moved to the other side of the doors. She wanted to take a look at the secretary hutch and more importantly put distance between her and Armand. "Her?"

"There were shoe prints in the snow, leading from the passenger side and into the trees. The shoe prints were a women's size seven Dr. Martens boots. The heels of your weapons or boots as you call them, were there, too. If you recall, you also said "she" this morning." He slid off the stool and ambled toward her. "Therefore, Ms. Atterberry, I deduced you saw the thief. Did you send me in the opposite direction to put me off her trail? If you did, I might have to arrest you for misleading an officer of the law."

Emily wanted to run but was glued to the spot. His amble made her forget what she wanted to say and just watch him. She tore her gaze away and opened the doors of the secretary, focusing on the shelves, which held nothing, not even a speck of dust. "There was movement in the trees. You saw it, too."

"There was."

She sensed him drawing nearer and inched closer to the shelves.

"Saved by movement in the trees, Ms. Atterberry. You're off the hook. I can't arrest you for obstruction of justice."

Emily had no place to run and kept her gaze on the shelves. "I didn't see her." She gulped her lie.

"But you saw enough to know it was a she." He held a cabinet door open and gazed inside, too. "I think this morning's thief was not only female but a kid. I think they're all kids who are stealing the cars. What do you think, Emily?"

Emily? Her name rolled off his tongue like he said it all the time. Like they knew each other well. Intimately well. She moved away but the wall stood on one side and he stood on the other. If she looked up, she'd be right in his face—and swimming in his dreamy, topaz green eyes. "Like I said. I didn't see the thief. I don't know if it was a she or a he." She crouched and opened the bottom drawers. "Were any of the other cars recovered? Are they stealing them for fun?"

"None of the cars were recovered and no, they're not stealing them for joy rides. The only car we recovered is yours. Either the thief became scared and decided to ditch it and run or she is an inexperienced driver and couldn't control the car. Your car is also a departure from the others. The others were luxury SUVs. We think these SUVs are going to an auto body shop, revamped, and sold overseas. If they are, then there's a mastermind behind them. We find the thieves, we find the source, and bring it to a stop. We also help the thieves—again, I'm working on the theory they are kids. No one was as close to a thief as you were."

"I'm afraid I can't help you." She closed the drawers and moved behind the bar. She couldn't be beside him. He made her blood heat both in excitement and apprehension. "I told you everything. I think it was a she because the body looked female, but I couldn't tell you for sure. That's why I said she."

"Can we maybe sit down so I can question you further?" He strolled to the bar. "You'd be surprised what you remember when you're being questioned."

"You mean interrogated?"

"I interrogate suspects. I question victims."

"Are you questioning or interrogating me now?"

His smile was boyish. "Maybe a little bit of both."

She smiled at his honesty. "Sorry." Three paintings on the wall caught her eye. One was of a female servant in a long skirt and bonnet, cooking at a fireplace of an eighteenth-century kitchen. Another was of an Indigenous woman, also in a long skirt and bonnet, holding a basket and picking herbs from a garden. The third was a portrait of a young woman with a bonnet. There were three red dots under each painting, which indicated the Sherrers weren't offering them for sale.

Armand sat on a stool and twirled the cowboy hat on the counter. "More remarkable stuff?"

"Yes, these paintings." She moved closer for the artist's name. "Marie-Anne Couture. She painted all three. I've never heard of her, but her strokes are remarkable. Impressionist style with rustic notes. I could stare at them all day."

"Do you think they have value?"

"I'm just a furniture appraiser and still in training too but the Sherrers don't want to sell them." She moved away unable to pull her gaze from them. "I'm going to show these to my supervisor when she arrives later this evening. She knows more about paintings than I do. They really are beautiful." She noticed a curio hidden in the corner next to the buffet and went to it. It contained figurines of kitchen utensils, chairs, baskets, tables, food, and forest animals, all of which had red dots. They were made of basswood, the same as her little girl figurine.

She opened the doors to take a closer look. Her heart missed a beat. They were familiar but she was sure she'd never seen them before. Probably online from the photos taken by her supervisor when she checked the Acadia Inn a few weeks ago.

But she had seen them before and more than a few weeks ago. It was like a dream she couldn't fully recall.

Jerome stuck his head around the door. "Excuse the interruption, but my son, the aspiring movie director, has asked me to tell you the right revolver has arrived, and he'd like to borrow his sheriff's stuntman to do some re-shooting."

Armand jumped off the stool and put his cowboy hat on. "Duty calls." He winked at Emily. "I'll be back."

"I'm sure you will."

Jerome walked to the curio as he left. "What do you think about the furniture in the restaurant?"

"The woodworking is all original and custom made. The condition is remarkable."

"A lot of the furniture was made by Wilhelm Sherrer's ancestors. Indigenous craftsmen from a reserve north of King Court helped them. Wilhelm is a master carpenter himself or should I say artist and continued the tradition of maintaining the furniture and hiring only the best craftsmen, also from the reserve."

"Armand said you're one of these craftsmen."

"My father was, not me. He trained me, but I only do it as a hobby. Wilhelm and the artists from the reserve do it as a vocation."

She indicated the basswood figurines. "These little gems are beautiful works of art."

"They are, aren't they? They're intricate and

mesmerizing."

"Probably why the Sherrers don't want to let them go. Were they made by craftsmen from the reserve, too?"

"They were made by First Nations artists but from different reserves around Ontario. The cradle was made by Oliver Fines. Have you heard of him?"

"I know of a few First Nations artists but not him."

"He trained a lot of craftsmen. Some were brilliant and went on to do different things, some big, some small, some functional, some not. Canoes, furniture, kitchen cabinets, carvings, totem poles, and more. Furniture brought in the money. Artwork didn't, so they're few and far between."

"Do you know any of these craftsmen's names—especially those who made these collectibles?"

"Oh, there have been many over the years. I remember a Meneses, who was brilliant with furniture, especially bed frames. He moved to Europe and made a fortune. A Saul or Sam crafted wonderful canoes, but I think he died some time ago. There was one who disappeared after making incredible cradles and toys. An older woman focused on mythological creatures and another woman on Madonna and child figurines. Some of them even created coordinating pieces, like a horse and carriage with passengers or a cradle with babies and toys. Often these pieces had scenes detailed in the basswood, telling the story of the artist's life or of someone in his family."

"How interesting." She moved toward the paintings. "Do you know anything about Marie-Anne Couture and her paintings?"

"Marie-Anne Couture painted more than those

three paintings. There's one of her paintings in almost every room of the inn. She was a maid here. Wilhelm's grandmother found them in the servants' quarter at the turn of the twentieth century and put them up around the inn. There must be about thirty of them. Those three are Katrina's pride and joy. She has no desire to part with them, but the others are available for the auction."

"I can understand why. They're captivating. Were they ever appraised?"

"I don't think so." He moved to the bar. "Do you think they have artistic worth?"

"We'll find out tomorrow. I'll see if Detective or should I say Sheriff Lecavalier will show me the other paintings. If they're as stunning as these three, then I will make a point of showing them to my supervisor." She moved to the curio. "If you remember any of the artists' names of these collectibles, do you think you could send them my way?"

"Of course, but Wilhelm would remember. He worked with them and paid them. You can ask him when he returns from Ottawa."

"I will." She had to. She couldn't shake the feeling she saw the figurines before, possibly even touched them, but didn't know where or how.

Chapter Nine

Emily gazed at the collectibles. Armand appeared at her side, startling her.

"Sorry," he said.

Emily took him in. He had changed from the badass sheriff's outfit to impeccably fitting jeans and a tight long-sleeved T-shirt, opened with three buttons at the throat. The casual look was as eye-popping as his other ones. "I didn't recognize you."

"No badge or revolver on me. I'm off duty. More or less."

Whether he was or wasn't, she still needed space. He was disarming. She took a step back. "Is your claim to fame over?"

"It is. We shot one scene from inside the lobby— with the right revolver—and one from outside. Jerome is now putting the front doors back on and the production crew is moving everything to the barn. Do you want to spend more time here or do you want to see the rest of the inn?"

Emily wanted to stay, pick each figurine up, and stare at the three paintings longer but she did want to see the other paintings by Marie-Anne Couture. A tour of the inn would also show her the locations of the security cameras. If she had the chance to return the wooden horse, she needed to avoid them or risk Armand seeing her. "A tour of the inn would be better.

Jerome told me there are thirty more paintings by the same artist. I'd love to see them. And I promise not to drool."

"Over me?"

Yes, she almost blurted out but managed a discreet smile. "Over the paintings."

"I'm heartbroken. Can I interrogate you while I act as your personal escort?"

"I told you everything I saw of the thief."

"Will you leave that to me?"

Emily sauntered to the doors, leading into the lobby. "Do you have more detective interrogation tactics to try out on me?"

"Possibly. And detective *questioning strategies* not *interrogation tactics*."

"Should I be afraid?"

"Do you have something to hide?"

She laughed as she opened the door. She had a lot to hide. More than he knew. "If I say no will it stop you?"

He reached over her head and pushed the door wider. "No, I'll just have to move toward strategies of the *finesse* kind."

The thought intrigued her, and a small smile gave her away. "Then finesse away, Detective."

"You can start by calling me Armand."

"What will it say about me if I do? I am a witness—and a victim."

He locked the doors. "It'll say you'll have a *working* dinner with me after giving me a description of the thief."

"A *working* dinner?" This was getting better and better—and worse and worse. "How interesting. So, if there is no description while we're on the tour, I'm to assume wining and dining might produce something?"

"What if I promise to call a truce during our working dinner?"

She scowled.

"Oh, come on. Give me a break. Otherwise, it'll be lonesome me and a whole lot of cameras and monitors and inanimate furniture."

Emily sighed. Her face softened. "I'm afraid it might just have to be you and cameras and monitors. I should have dinner with my colleagues. They're arriving soon and will probably want to know what I've been up to on company time."

Armand conceded with a not-so-happy nod. "If you change your mind, or your colleagues are a bore, you know where to find me."

The lobby was chaotic with the film crew packing equipment and sets in boxes, but Lowan got their attention. Probably because he stood at least a head taller than most. He had removed his duster and the half-computerized face of Captain Borgman and his heritage came through. As Theresa told her, he was half First Nations from Jerome's side of the family and half Scottish from her side, which explained the mellow black hair, olive skin, and electric blue eyes. He still wore a holster over black canvas pants and shirt, making him formidable. He held up the revolver. "Right one, Emily?"

She gave him a thumb's up sign.

"Good." He motioned them over. Emily and Armand picked their way around boxes, costumes, cameras, and wires. "Can I leave these things with you in the security office? Mrs. Halloran is picking them up tomorrow morning. She needs to ship them off to Toronto for another shoot." He placed the revolver in a cloth-lined box and handed it to Armand. Then he indicated a set of cast iron handcuffs in a velvet-lined box and a black ball and chain used to restrain prisoners in the eighteenth and nineteenth century in a cushion-encased crate.

Emily moved closer. "Those are the real deal."

"How much does the ball weigh?" Armand asked.

"Not much."

Armand was about to put the box with the revolver down when Emily took it. He picked the crate up easily enough but glared at Lowan who laughed. "At least thirty pounds."

"Try building a railway with it attached to your weak ankle, while chained to a few other of your comrades, who are also wearing these beauties," Lowan said.

"I'm on the right side of the law, bro. I'd be the one holding the rifle and issuing the commands."

"Always the model of police enforcement. Don't forget this." Lowan placed the box with the handcuffs on the crate. "Next beer is on me."

"Can we make a pit stop at the security office?" Armand asked Emily.

"Not a problem." She followed him to the security office. Monitors filled the room, showing different parts of the inn. This was better than a tour. Emily saw where all the cameras were without walking through the inn and inspecting every nook and cranny.

Armand put the boxes in a corner and the revolver on top.

"This is a sophisticated set up." She ambled to the

twelve monitors fixed against a wall and over a large desk with two chairs. "Nicole said cameras are going up in each room."

"So far, they're only in the public areas." He moved to the desk and indicated the cameras. "The restaurant, lobby, kitchen, banquet hall, exercise room, and of course, the hallways, except the family's quarters, have cameras. I can show all angles of a room on one screen." He touched the screen of the monitor, showing the lobby and several angles appeared. "Or I can focus on one." He touched the lobby monitor again and one angle came into view. "There are also cameras over every door leading outside except, of course, for the door of the family quarters. Cameras were set up in one of the barns and the corral today, but I don't see either." He touched the screen of another monitor. Nothing came on. "They're not working. Lowan is storing his film sets in there tonight. There are two security guards taking care of them, but the cameras should be working here. I'll have to ask Nicole."

"What about the guest bedrooms? Any cameras in there?"

"Not yet. They should be installed in time for the auction. The parking lot also has cameras." He touched the monitor, showing the parking lot and zeroed in on her white Camry. "Yours I believe?"

"It is. Is the company Nicole's?"

"Hers and her husband's. They were both police officers until they started up the security company two years ago. Most of their business is in Ottawa, but they've done a few places here in King Court. Not enough as I would like. I can't get any of the stores to install alarm systems. If some in our downtown section had any, I would have arrested the car thief or thieves a long time ago."

"It's a safe town."

"Compared to most, yes, but the car thefts, and now a very unusual theft of a small item at Halloran's Antiques, is changing King Court's colors."

"This makes more work for you."

Armand's face shut down. "If only."

Emily was surprised. "It's not?"

Armand fiddled with controls to bring the camera up. "Not at all. Just a bleep. The car thefts are the biggest thing to hit the town. Otherwise, it's always mundane crimes."

"It says a lot about the town. It's safe or well policed."

Armand's grin was dry, which told Emily a lot.

"You want more action?" she asked.

Armand pulled a chair out as he continued working the keys. "I want a lot more action. I'm coasting here, sometimes rotting."

Emily sat in the other chair. "Have you applied to other police forces?"

"Many times. The Ottawa and Toronto police forces, the OPP, and the RCMP. Jerome has tried to get me in, but they want more experience. I have what no one wants to tell me. Small town policing experience. It doesn't make the grade."

He brought an image of the inside of a barn into view. Several of the film crew were dropping off sets. The image went black.

"You think solving the car thefts will give you more credibility?" she asked.

"It certainly wouldn't hurt."

Emily focused on the monitors. She was a fraud. She could identify the car thief and bolster his chances of getting a job on a big police force, but she couldn't live with herself if she did. The girl's future would not be the same if she identified her and Armand arrested her. The girl would be different. Emily would not be standing here with two art degrees to her name if the policewoman from ten years ago hadn't given her the chance to go straight and backed the decision to her supervisors. The chance she gave the girl by letting her run would be as constructive.

Her phone vibrated. It was a text from her supervisor Marilyn. She and the other two appraisers Lubna and Tatyana wouldn't arrive until later in the evening. They couldn't even give her a time.

Emily grimaced. Returning the wooden horse was becoming more difficult. If she didn't know when her colleagues would arrive, she couldn't chance going out during the middle of the night and coming back to explain her absence. She could only do it while they slept. She also had to make sure Armand didn't see her leave. Then, of course, she had to make sure no one was downtown, and the stores were closed.

"Everything okay?" Armand asked.

Emily brushed away her thoughts and cleared her face of emotion. "My colleagues are stuck in Toronto. Planes are delayed because of snow. They don't know when they'll leave let alone arrive."

"Then we're on for dinner? Our *working* dinner?"

Emily opened her mouth to say no when Armand jumped in. "I knew you'd agree. I have to go to the barn and check the camera or Lowan can't store his sets. Then I have to make a quick check of the grounds. I'll meet you in the kitchen in," he checked his watch, "an hour or two?" He dangled the keys in front of her. "I'll even give you the keys to the city. You can check any of the rooms and drool over the paintings of Marie-Anne Couture."

How could she say no when he gave her carte blanche to look at the furniture, the paintings, and the rooms? She took the keys and indicated the screens. "Come and find me in an hour or two."

"Will do. Then I can continue questioning you about the thief?"

Emily laughed. "You can give it your best shot." Should she, or shouldn't she? Why not? "*Armand.*"

His smile turned sly. "See. My finesse is working on you. No more Detective Lecavalier."

Emily wanted to make him happier than simply calling him by his first name. She wished she could tell him everything she knew about the car thief and help his chances of making it to a big-time police force. But she had to give the girl a chance. She could also tell him a thing or two about the theft of the wooden horse—and even present him with it. It would close the case, but she would be in a whole lot of trouble.

She had to watch herself. Carefully. Or she and Isla, and the young girl-thief were going to wear matching orange jumpsuits and share a prison cell complements of the gorgeous detective, who was going to wine and dine her.

Chapter Ten

What was supposed to be an intimate meal with Armand, turned out to be a fun-filled dinner with Lowan, Theresa, and Jerome, followed by Katrina Sherrer and her parents Elsa and Wilhelm. Katrina reminded Emily of Isla. Tall, blonde, willowy, and beautiful. While Isla was all attitude and could blow you down, Katrina was soft-spoken and reserved. Before dinner and in a whirlwind, Emily saw all the paintings by Marie-Anne Couture and told the Sherrers they could prove valuable. But other than acknowledging interest, Katrina didn't show any emotion. She was sad. Emily assumed it was over the sale of the inn and restaurant, but it went deeper. She brought up the basswood figurines and asked about a visit to the artists' studios. Wilhelm said he'd check his old files but most of the artists worked out of their garages or basements and didn't have public studios let alone websites.

After a wonderful meal of salmon and roasted root vegetables, followed by crème caramel and espresso for dessert, everyone went their separate ways. Theresa and Katrina stayed in the kitchen and planned the next day's menu for the film crew. Jerome checked the lobby to make sure everything was back in place, and Wilhelm and Elsa packed the items they didn't want to sell. Lowan left to meet some of the film crew at Koffee &

Tez while Armand put on his coat and checked the cameras in the barns again. Sometimes they worked and other times they didn't.

Emily went to her bedroom just after nine. She wanted to return the wooden horse but didn't know how. Armand would see her leave and return during the middle of the night. He'd wonder where she went when she didn't know the town or anyone in it.

She unpacked her suitcase and noticed her jogging outfit and runners. That was it! She'd jog to the center of town, return the wooden horse, and jog back. It couldn't be more than three or four kilometers both ways and she always did five kilometers back home even in below freezing temperatures. She walked a couple kilometers in the morning, but she was always up for a jog.

She put her outfit on including her running jacket and thermal top, pants, hat, and gloves. She slit the inner pocket of her jacket larger, put the wooden horse, and a couple picking utensils snugly inside and secured it with masking tape. As always, she put her figurine in her pocket. She never went anywhere without it, even jogging.

In the hallway, the door to the security office opened and Armand came out. "Going out for a run?"

"I am. Been a long day. Need to exercise."

"You mean the walk in those high-heeled weapons from the ravine to the inn wasn't enough this morning?"

"I ate far too much at dinner, including the crème caramel."

"You're jogging around the inn?"

"I thought I'd go a little farther. I tend to do about

five kilometers every day. I want to jog to the downtown section of King Court and come back."

"It's more than ten kilometers to the downtown core."

Emily's eyes rounded as her expectations deflated. "I guess I won't be jogging to the downtown area after all." But it had to be now. She had to return the wooden horse. "Maybe I'll drive into town and jog around there. Seems a little more interesting than around the inn. It's also better lit."

"You want company?"

Emily held back her surprise—and dismay. "Aren't you working?"

"Nope, Darryl just pulled into the parking lot." He indicated the parking lot monitor. A man in a parka got out of a pick-up truck. "My shift is over. I'm on my way home. How about I come with you?"

No! "You're a jogger?" The words came out as though she was forced to eat three plates of broccoli.

"Yup. I just have to stop home and put on my gear. Why don't you follow me in your car? You can wait at Koffee & Tez. I shouldn't be more than ten minutes. We can jog and then have a coffee or tea."

She swallowed her panic. "Sounds great."

The instant Darryl walked in, Armand gave him a quick rundown and threw on his jacket. He walked Emily to her car, got into his Jeep, and led her to Koffee & Tez. A number of cars were parked in front. Emily made a U-turn and parked in front of Halloran's Antiques, where she wanted or rather needed to be.

Armand's Jeep moved down the road and disappeared into the night. She was terrible. He was so nice, and she was so bad. But she needed to return the wooden horse and it had to be tonight.

She stretched her leg muscles against the side of Halloran's Antiques, which gave her a close-up view of what she was up against. Koffee & Tez across the street was well lit. Lowan sat at a table with several of the film crew. Jessica laughed as she poured coffee into their mugs.

Jessica worked long hours, but she was composed and fresh. She spied Emily and opened the door. "How about a coffee instead of a run?" she shouted

"Later," Emily said. Nodding, Jessica moved back inside.

This was her chance to return the wooden horse before Armand returned. She jogged to the end of the block. When no one was outside, she dashed behind the stores and to Halloran's Antiques' back door. It was exactly as Isla described.

She removed one of her picking keys, and in a couple of seconds, the door opened. She left her runners outside and sneaked in. She moved through the store like a silent breeze to the tallest curio. Top shelf, smack in the middle between a wooden train car and a totem pole.

Emily opened the curio, unwrapped the wooden horse, and placed it in its spot. The train car caught her eye. It, too, was made of basswood like her figurine and had a place where the engineer sat.

A cold jolt went through her body. She had seen this train car before just like the collectibles in the curio of the Acadia Restaurant. Another blow made her flinch. Could her figurine sit in the engineer's seat?

She removed the train car and placed her figurine inside.

She covered her mouth to stop from crying out. The figurine fit perfectly. The store was dark, but both the figurine and train were made from the same piece of basswood. Her figurine belonged to the train car. Emily always thought the cap was hair, but it was an engineer's cap. Even the overalls etched on it made sense now. It wasn't a jumper as she assumed but a uniform.

On the side of the train car were fine etchings. Evergreen trees and the side of a house. On the house were swirls, but the image wasn't complete. She remembered what Jerome told her about the collectibles and sets. Her figurine and this train car were part of a larger set. The swirl would continue on another train car. If she found the other pieces, they would show her the complete picture. It would reveal something about the artist or someone in his family. It could lead to her biological family.

She held onto the curio handle. The thoughts swirling through her head made her lightheaded.

Was her biological family First Nations or did they have some First Nations in their blood? Her hair and coloring suggested it as a possibility.

Tears sprang into her eyes. She didn't know what to do. If she came back to buy the train car tomorrow, after the mysterious return of the wooden horse, the owner and, of course, Armand, might suspect her of stealing the wooden horse in the first place.

This was not what she wanted to do. This was not what she thought she would do again. But she had to do it. She didn't have a choice. Not if she wanted to find her biological family.

She padded to the cash register and found a packet

of heart-shaped Post-it Notes and a pen. In big block letters she wrote, *Sorry, will return it. Honest.*

She put the train car in her inside jacket pocket, sealing it shut with the tape. She pressed the note in the curio in the place of the train car. As deftly and silently as she came in, she moved to the back door, checked to make sure no was outside, and left, locking it behind her.

Her heart thumping wildly, confusing her thoughts and making her tremble, she slipped her feet into her runners and jogged across the back of the stores to the end of the block. On the street she saw Armand going into Koffee & Tez. She would leave the train car and her utensils in the Camry under the mat and meet Armand. She hoped her face or eyes wouldn't show anything because she wanted to cry in sadness and fear as much as in joy and hope. She hoped she could talk logically. Her mind was muddled.

The lights of her car switched on. She was sure she turned them off.

Her car engine started.

Why was—holy shit! Her heart thundered in her chest. Was someone stealing her car? *Again?*

"Stop!" She raced to the car and pounded on the trunk and side to the driver's window. "Get out of my car!"

The driver faced her. The car wasn't lit, and the windows were tinted but it was the same girl as that morning. The girl was as surprised as Emily.

"No." Emily breathed out. "I gave you a chance."

"Sorry," the girl mouthed.

Armand came out of Koffee & Tez with Jessica, Lowan, and the film crew.

"Emily?" Armand shouted.

"My car is being stolen! Again!"

Armand raced across the street to the driver's door. He tugged at it, but it was locked. The car sped back, forcing Armand to loosen his grip and Emily to jump out of its way.

Armand grabbed Emily's arm. "Are you hurt?"

"I'm fine but—"

The car jumped onto the sidewalk and back onto the street. It screeched forward and skidded on a patch of heavy slush. Black snow and mud flew onto Emily and Armand.

Armand shook the mud from his face. "Holy shit!" He held onto Emily, who cleared her eyes of snow. Shouts and exclamations came from the café, too. But Emily was too paralyzed to say anything or move.

The car zoomed onto the sidewalk again, back on to the street, and skidded again on ice and slush. More slush hit Emily and Armand before the car roared down the road.

Emily refused to cry. "This cannot be happening."

Armand swiped the mud from his mouth. "I have to call this in." He pulled out his cell.

Jessica and Lowan ran across the street. "Are you guys hurt?" Lowan asked. He took a step closer but stopped.

"I'm okay." Emily flung mud off her sleeves. "But my ego." She used her glove to clean her face but only smeared it. She held onto her tears. "Two cars in one day." Her smile trembled. "Can you believe it?"

"Did you see who it was?" Armand asked.

Could she tell him? If she told him the truth, he'd know she lied about not seeing the thief in the morning.

"No. I saw the lights and raced over. It was dark inside."

"I didn't see the person either. I saw a hood and scarf and nothing else."

"We didn't notice anything or anyone," Lowan said.

"Do you think it could be the same person as this morning?" Jessica asked.

Tears rolled down her face. It was all too much. Her figurine fit in the train car, and another car stolen.

Armand put his arm around her. Emily turned into him, wanting the comfort of his arms but his jacket was so filthy she pulled away.

"Here," Jessica handed Emily her apron. She took it and cleaned her face and tears. She handed it to Armand, and he cleaned his face but only smudged more on it.

A police car stopped. The passenger window rolled down.

Armand peered in. "The car headed down the road. White Camry. License plate," he turned to Emily, but she only shrugged. "Call Mariana at King Court Car Rentals. It was rented out to Emily Atterberry."

"The same Emily Atterberry as this morning?" the police officer asked.

Emily turned her face away.

Armand nodded, and the police car drove off after the car.

"Do you want to come inside and get cleaned up?" Jessica asked.

Emily shook her head. "I'd make a mess of the place. I think I'd better get back to the inn and clean up there."

"I have to get my car," Armand said. "I left it at home."

"I'll drive you back," Lowan said. He strode across the street and jumped into a pickup. He made a U-turn and stopped beside them. "Hop in." Armand and Emily moved to the passenger door. The locks on the pickup clicked shut. Lowan powered down the window to reveal a pearly white interior. "Sorry, but this isn't my car. It's the executive producer's and you two are a mess. Sorry, Emily."

Emily nodded and with Armand sat in the bed. Armand closed the tailgate and banged the side. Lowan drove off. He put his arm around her, and she cried again.

"Hey, everything will be all right." He removed his hat, turned it inside out, and placed it on his shoulder.

Emily placed her face on it. His sweet gesture and kind words—his warmth and compassion—only made her cry more. She didn't care if he thought her a wimp or a baby. It had been a long but momentous day. She not only found an impossible lead to her biological family but a wonderful man she could never be with.

Chapter Eleven

Emily allowed Armand to help her out of the back of the pickup. She could have jumped off on her own, but she wanted his warmth and compassion around her for as long as possible.

"I'll walk Emily to the inn and be right back," Armand told Lowan, who also stepped out of the pickup.

"It will be okay, Emily," Lowan said, giving her a thumb's up.

Emily gave him a thumb's up sign too. "I don't have any more cars to be stolen, so I guess it will be."

Lowan smirked and got back in the pickup.

She held onto Armand's arm. "You don't have to walk me to the door. I'm fine now."

"It's not a problem. I'll text Darryl and he'll let us in without ringing any doorbells."

But the motion sensor lights came on and Katrina opened the door. Her eyes rounded. "I'm afraid to ask."

"We haven't been mud fighting," Armand said. "Emily's car was stolen."

"Wasn't it stolen this morning?"

"That was her first car. Her second car was just taken, too. We happened to be on the back end when it squealed away."

Katrina moved aside. "You need a hot toddy, Emily." Emily stepped into the hallway as Armand stayed outside. "Why don't I take your jacket and get it cleaned for you?"

"Not to worry." Emily removed her runners on a mat, white peeping through mud. "I have to pick up my other coat and a suit from the cleaners tomorrow. I'll bring this in, too." She faced Armand. She knew her eyes were puffy and red, and she was filthy, but she needed to face him. She had to show him she was truthful, even though she hid something that would make him despise her. "Thank you for seeing me home."

He made a move forward but backed up. "You'll be all right?"

"Yes, thank you."

"We'll take care of her," Katrina said.

"I'll see you. Maybe tomorrow. You have to give another statement."

"I didn't give one this morning."

"Two statements." He lingered.

She didn't want him to go, either. She went on her tiptoes, cleaned his cheek with her fingers, and kissed him. "Take care of yourself, too."

Armand still didn't move. Then with a deep sigh, he left and jumped into the back of the pickup.

"Lowan is making him sit in the bed?" Katrina asked. "Did he make you sit in the bed, too?"

"We're a mess, and it's not his pickup. It's all pearly white inside."

"I don't care." Katrina stepped outside. "Lowan, you dog!"

Lowan shot his hand out the window but drove off.

"Wait till I get a hold of him tomorrow." She locked the door. "Do you want a hot toddy, now?"

"Don't worry about me, Katrina. I'll probably just make an herbal tea and keep the hot toddy in mind. You've had a long day. Get some sleep."

"I'll be in my room but up if you need me. These days, I'm always up for a hot toddy."

"The sale must be difficult."

She thought about it. "Yes. And more." She moved off to her room.

Emily was surprised at her reply. She was right. There was more to her sadness than the sale.

In her bedroom, she locked the door, unzipped her jacket, and from the pocket removed the train car, figurine, and picking tools. She set the train car on the table and placed the figurine inside the engineer's seat.

Tears filmed her eyes again. She couldn't believe she found a piece of her past. The discovery now forced her to find the other pieces. The scene engraved on the other train cars could lead to her biological family.

But she did what she thought she'd never do again, what she hadn't done in over ten years. Steal. She should have left the train car, gone back the next day, and bought it. She shouldn't have worried about how it might appear. But at the time she wasn't thinking clearly. She could have wandered into the store, looked around like the furniture appraiser and art historian she was, showed some interest in the train car, and purchased it—even though it sat next to the wooden horse, which miraculously reappeared. She'd inquire about the other pieces. The owner of Halloran's Antiques or Armand might wonder if she had anything to do with the theft of the wooden horse, but she could say it was for a client or a collector or even a birthday present for her father. She could make up an excuse.

Now it was too late.

She was foolish, and in a lot of trouble. She shouldn't have taken it, no matter how much she wanted it. *Period.* It made talking to Armand more difficult.

If Isla hadn't stolen the wooden horse and she hadn't returned it, she could have enjoyed any kind of relationship with Armand. Professional or otherwise. Now, it was impossible. She was a thief. He was a police officer. The two didn't go together.

She moved the train car, the wheels turning.

Maybe she could mail Halloran's Antiques the money. That's it! It wouldn't clear her of the crime but at least the owner of the store would get the money owing him. She could even leave it in the store when no one looked. It wouldn't make right her wrong. It wouldn't make right the fact she stole something from the store. But her conscience would be allayed. She'd leave more money to make amends. Then she would look for the other piece or pieces to locate her biological family. How could she not look for them now? How could she ignore this when the fates gave her the opportunity?

She put the train car and her picking utensils in her luggage and locked it. The figurine she put in her purse as she always did. She found a big garbage bag, went into the bathroom, removed her jacket, and put it inside. Her workout jacket and T-shirt were clean, but her hat, gloves, and jogging pants were filthy. She took them off and threw them in the bag, too. She took a long hot shower and put on her pajamas. She thought she'd feel better clean, but she didn't. The theft of her two cars was a problem, but it was the furthest thing from her mind. The theft of the train car poked holes in her conscience.

Nothing would be right anymore. She broke into a store and stole an object. What made it worse was Armand was so sweet and considerate. How could she keep up a pretense of innocence when she knew who stole her cars, and she'd stolen something, too? How could she be coldhearted when she knew how much it meant to Armand to find the car thief and get enough credibility to move to a bigger police force where his skills as a detective could be challenged?

Armand was kind and good. She wanted to stay in his arms and against his chest all night. She didn't care he was filthy. He was warm and compassionate, and he cared about her.

But whatever he felt and whatever was starting between them, it had to stop. It wasn't right. His feelings were honest and sincere. Hers were too, but she wasn't. She wasn't what he thought. Under the furniture appraiser exterior was what she never thought she would be again. A petty thief.

If only she'd met Armand in another context. If only she hadn't allowed herself to steal again, no matter the circumstances.

She took out the train car, sat on the floor, placed her figurine in it, and stared at them. She picked up her cell. Her supervisor left a message. She, Lubna, and Tatyana arrived an hour ago. She wanted to have a short meeting at breakfast. She texted her back. She would see them in the morning and show her the paintings of Marie-Anne Couture. She didn't want to see her tonight. She didn't want to talk to anyone tonight. Except Isla.

She called her sister's cell, but her voice mail kicked in. "Isla. It's me. Call me when you get this message. Anytime. I returned your package. But you won't believe what I found. You won't believe what I did. I can't believe I did it. I can't forgive myself." She held the phone for a long moment. "I met a very nice man, too." She didn't hide the sadness in her voice. "I'll tell you all about him when we speak. Just my luck. I met him right before Valentine's Day." She took a deep breath. "But, once again, there's no Valentine Day celebration for me this year."

Chapter Twelve

Armand went back to his place, dropped his filthy clothes onto a plastic mat, took a shower, and pulled on a pair of track pants and a T-shirt. He called the station about the car and thief, but Sergei'd lost them.

He threw his cell phone at the sofa. Two car thefts in one day and still no closer to identifying the thief—or thieves.

He dropped onto the sofa and turned on the TV. He flicked through channels, over and over again until he gave up and moved onto his game console. He played an old video game but couldn't concentrate and gave up halfway through. A shot of gin and an old *Sherlock* episode on TV didn't settle him either. Thoughts of Emily disheartened and crying in the back of the pickup broke into his thoughts.

He called Darryl. "I'm coming over."

"What?"

"Go and stay with Nicole. I can't sleep. I'll spend the night at the inn."

"Aren't you on duty tomorrow?"

"I am but I've pulled all-nighters before. I shouldn't be more than ten minutes."

"Actually, I wouldn't mind going home. Carli showed up two hours after curfew. Nicole called her friends, but no one knew where she was. She's in her room now and doesn't want to talk."

Armand strode to his bedroom. "Where did she say she was?"

"She said she fell asleep at the library."

He grimaced. "Didn't we all use the library excuse at one time or another?"

"I did, but she didn't have any books in her knapsack when she arrived home."

He pulled a sweat top out of his dresser "You think it's some guy?"

"If it is, neither Nicole nor I are ready for the boyfriend thing."

"I'll surprise her tomorrow and see what I can sniff out."

"Appreciate it."

He threw on the sweat top and his police parka, his only clean coat, got into his Jeep, and drove to the inn. Darryl waited for him at the back door with his coat on. "Thanks again." He dropped the keys in Armand's hand and rushed to his pick-up.

Armand locked the door and headed to the security office. The hallway was dark, but a faint light came from under Emily's bedroom door. It was almost one, but she was awake. He stopped in front of her door, ready to knock.

Maybe she fell asleep with the light on.

No, he couldn't risk waking her up. He moved into the security office, closed the door, and slumped in the chair in front of the monitors. No movement on the screens, in the hallways, in the lobby or kitchen, and no one looking like Emily anywhere. He wished they had set up a camera for the family quarters but the Sherrers refused it.

In the corner sat the boxes containing the revolver,

the cast iron handcuffs, and the ball and chain. He checked out the foot shackle, the chains, and handcuffs. All were big and clunky and made of heavy metal. He picked up the handgun. It was a Smith & Wesson, model 3 from the late eighteenth century. He pulled out a card and recognized Mrs. Halloran's perfect script. A 44 caliber American single-action six-shooter. She always kept precise notes. It was twice as big and heavy as his Glock pistol.

Emily. He worried about her. Two cars stolen under her nose. She must feel awful and vulnerable.

He put the gun on the table and took out his cell, ready to call her. But what if she was asleep? He opened the door. The light in her bedroom was still on.

He couldn't. Maybe she wasn't sleeping but she needed her rest.

He closed the door and put his cell away. He returned the weapon to its velvet-lined case and fell into the chair and swirled back and front, side to side, and around several times.

This was going to be one long badass night.

He put his arms on the table and rested his head when he heard a door open in the hallway. He zoomed up and pulled open the door. Emily closed hers, a throw blanket over her pajamas.

She gasped. "I thought you went home," she whispered.

"Couldn't sleep," he whispered back. "Thought I'd let Darryl go home." He took a step into the hallway. "I see you didn't have much luck with sleep either."

"No. Long and difficult day." She pulled a wry grin. "I'm making some chamomile tea. It's supposed to induce sleep. Can I offer you a cup? Or is herbal not your thing?"

"I'd love one."

"I'll bring it to you."

"Thank you." He wanted to follow her but at the risk of looking too eager, he sat back and focused on a monitor. He saw her on screen. She turned on one small light, put water in a kettle, set it on the stove, and opened cabinets until she found the tea and two mugs. She moved heavily as though something weighed on her mind. She was sad, too. But then both her cars were stolen in one day. One was enough to upset anyone. Two was unheard of. It didn't help he pushed her for an identification of the car thief.

About ten minutes later she came into the security office with two mugs of steaming tea.

"I didn't know how you wanted your tea. I don't take anything in mine."

"I'll give it a taste first." He closed the door and pulled out a chair. "Did your colleagues arrive?"

"They did but I didn't get a chance to see them." She sat down, pulling the throw blanket tighter. "They're probably fast asleep now."

He took a sip of the tea. It wasn't bad. "Those are the most interesting pajamas and slippers I have ever seen."

Emily's laugh was soft. "What you're saying is ugly. It's a family tradition to give something ugly or tacky for Christmas." She lifted her legs and pointed out her slippers. "My sister gave me the Mona Lisa pajamas. My parents gave me the paint brush slippers. I had a wonderful Sistine Chapel robe, but my sister took it by mistake. She spent the weekend with me in Ottawa."

"Your family must know you love art."

"You think?" She smiled and so did he.

"You have only one sister?"

"I do." She took a sip of her tea. "I'm lucky to have her and my parents. I'm adopted."

His eyebrows lifted. "Really?"

"Yup. I was one year old when they adopted me, and you'd know if you saw me with them. My family is tall, blonde, and fair-skinned. Pure Anglo-Saxon roots through my dad and pure Irish blood through my mother. I'm the complete opposite. Most people guess at my roots. I get everything from Persian to Mexican to Egyptian. I, unfortunately, don't know."

"Ever try to find your family?"

He touched a raw nerve because she averted her gaze and took a while to answer. "Isla, my sister, thinks I should. She thinks I'm dying to know my roots. My parents support any decision I make, but me…" She shrugged.

"You don't want to?"

"I'm a little afraid of what I may find."

"That's understandable."

"Is it just you and your sister, Nicole?"

"Samantha, Nicole, and me. I'm the baby brother."

"They must spoil you."

"They've spoiled me, used me as their excuse when they went out with boyfriends, forced me to put their stuff away or they'd report anything I did wrong to the folks—the usual stuff. Both are married now with kids. Samantha has two nine-year-old, twin boys and Nicole is expecting her first child, a girl. She also has a sixteen-year-old stepdaughter from Darryl's first marriage. They think she's having boyfriend issues now—she's supposedly at the library when no one can locate her and she's hours late. It's my duty as her wonderful and understanding uncle to see what's up with her. I'll be cornering her tomorrow and trying to get some information."

"Will you be questioning or interrogating her?"

Armand raised his cup to her. "Touché. Probably both."

"Sixteen is a rough age." She snuggled into her blanket. "You've lived here in King Court all your life?"

"I have. My parents and grandparents still live in the house they bought when they first got married and Nicole is here, too, but with most of her business in Ottawa, it won't be long before she moves there. Sam's been living in Ottawa for over twelve years now."

"Is Ottawa where you'd like to be, too?"

"Quite honestly, I have my eyes set on the Toronto Police Force. Their Guns and Gang force intrigues me."

"Sounds dangerous."

"Sounds challenging to me. But I just received my third, "thank you for applying for the position with Guns and Gang," letter today. I'm not moving any closer to getting in with the Toronto Police Force or the Ottawa Police Force or any other big-city police force. I find this car thief and break up what I believe is a theft ring, and I should have enough credibility to get my foot into any of these big-city police forces and the department I want."

"Is that why you want me to identify the thief?"

"I want you to identify the thief mainly because I think he—or rather, she is a youth. We can set this young person straight before stealing becomes a way of life. But yes, on a more personal note, I do want you to identify the thief, so I can crack this criminal ring and get a good chance of making it to the big-time forces."

Emily took a sip of her tea but kept her eyes averted. "You're right. It was a girl." She took a deep breath. "And the same girl stole my second car, too."

"You saw her both times?"

"Clearly this morning and only slightly this evening, but it was the same girl. She raced out of the passenger side of the car this morning, and her hood and scarf fell off. Then her sunglasses flew off. I didn't tell you because I wanted to give her the chance to go straight. I wanted to show her compassion and understanding." She took a sip of her tea. "I was in a similar place as the young girl ten years ago. I could have gone the wrong way too if a policewoman hadn't shown compassion and understanding and let me go. I," she searched for the right words. "I chose to go the right way. This girl didn't. Is that understandable? I'm sorry. I lied."

Armand nodded. "It's understandable, and there's no need to apologize."

"I thought the girl would think better as I had, but it was her again tonight. She was terrified, Armand. She cried."

"She's probably being forced to steal."

"Possibly." She took another deep breath. "She wasn't tall. Maybe a couple inches taller than me. I think she's skinny. The military parka hung loosely on her. A white golf shirt peeked out of her collar and she wore black school-uniform pants. I recognized both because I wore the similar white golf shirt and black pants in high school. The pants had the high school's logo on the shin. Do you have a paper and pencil?" Armand found both in a drawer. She drew a logo. "This logo. It's her school."

The logo had an italicized S over two M's and an A. "Saint Margaret Mary's Academy. It's here in King Court. What about her face? Can I call in an artist to sketch it?"

"Detective Lecavalier," she said, lifting her chin high. "Under my furniture appraiser exterior, I'm an artist at heart. I may not be a master but I'm not an apprentice either." She extended her hand for another paper. She rolled the chair closer to the table and sketched. Armand wanted to bring his chair up to her and breathe down her beautiful neck into the slope of her back, maybe even kiss it while she drew, but he sat back. He even distanced himself by rolling his chair away and sipping his tea. He shouldn't think of kissing her neck.

He thought of kissing more than her neck.

This wasn't good. She was the victim of two crimes he was investigating. He had to be professional. He *had* to think professional. Not about kissing her neck and more.

He played with the controls of the monitors and zoomed onto a family of raccoons moving through the cars in the parking lot. He was glad when she handed him the sketch. The girl had long straight hair, parted on the side, and framing her face. Her facial features, eyes, cheeks, and lips were well defined with heavy makeup. She looked like a doll. But the eyes stood out. Emily captured fear in her eyes.

"You're very good."

"Thank you. If I had colors, I could give you a

better picture. Her hair was flaming red, the kind you only get from a bottle. Her eyes were heavily lined and shadowed, and she had on fake and thick eyelashes. They were popular a few years back but are still used today. Her eye color was flat. Blue violet. I'm sure they were tinted contact lenses. I've never seen eyes that shade before. She had thick foundation on. A deep suntan color, which is the rage now with young women. The lipstick was a brownish red. The hair and makeup were professionally done. She looked ready for the stage or a performance. Unless the girl is a hair and makeup stylist, both were professionally done. I don't think she was more than sixteen or seventeen, but she looked twenty-five."

"I'll show this to my supervisor tomorrow and stop in at Saint Margaret Mary's Academy and make inquiries."

"I'm sorry I didn't tell you earlier. But you know why. I'm not proud of what I did ten years ago and not telling you earlier."

"You have nothing to be ashamed of." He glanced at the picture again. "It's unfortunate this girl looks like some cut-out doll or story-book princess. Who knows what she actually looks like? Hopefully, we can save her, too."

"She probably won't think so."

"Unless she's being forced. Then she'll thank you for giving her the chance to help out. She isn't the only one, Emily. There were others stealing cars, and I can bet they were all teenagers, too."

"My apologies again." She took a sip.

But even with telling him about the young girl, she was down. No smile and no emotion in her eyes. "Don't let the robbery—the robberies bother you. Neither was your fault. You just happened to be at the wrong place."

"Twice in one day?"

Armand laughed. "It was a bit of a coincidence or a crazy fluke."

A soft laugh came out of her. "Right."

"I think Mariana is afraid to rent you a third car."

She shook her head. "I have no intention of renting car number three. I'll get someone to drive me around or call a taxi."

"You didn't get hurt, that's the main thing."

"Only my ego."

"And mine."

Both laughed and Armand sat taller. He made her feel better.

She spied the revolver, handcuffs, and ball and chain. She picked up the thick handcuffs and opened and closed them. "Anyone could pick this lock and escape."

"Probably, but if you had this tied around your ankle," he picked up the ball and chain, "you weren't going anywhere." He took the shackle of the ball and chain and put it on his ankle. He stood up and could barely walk to the door. "Definitely, no jogging with this baby on." He took the handcuffs and put one fetter on her wrist and the other on his.

"Is this my punishment for not telling you earlier?" she asked.

"That's right. You're keeping an eye on these monitors with me tonight."

"I'm afraid I have to leave you the pleasure. It's time to sleep. Busy day appraising tomorrow. Thank you for understanding and especially about my little run-in with the law many moons ago."

"What run-in with the law?"

She acknowledged with a wry smile. "Again, my thanks—Detective Lecavalier."

He rummaged around the boxes. "Do you see the keys for these things?"

Emily checked, too. "Maybe they fell on the floor."

Armand pulled the boxes away from the wall and checked. He moved around the room, dragging the ball, and forcing Emily to go with him. "They have to be here. Maybe they fell behind the table"

They both looked but saw nothing.

"Behind the monitors?" Emily asked. "Let me see. I'm smaller." She threw off her blanket and crawled under the table. But with the handcuffs on both of them, she pulled him down with her. She backed out, bumping her head against his. "Are you sure there were keys?"

"Of course. The film crew used them to unlock the actors." He opened drawers, checked beneath the table, and monitors again, dragged Emily to all corners, and back to the chairs.

"Do you think they fell through the boxes when we brought them here?"

Armand shrugged. "I have no idea. Looks like you have the pleasure of watching these monitors with me this evening, after all." His smile turned wider and wider, and slyer and slyer.

Could life get any better?

Chapter Thirteen

Emily could easily pick the handcuffs with either of her tools or the hook of a pen. But if she did, Armand would know a whole lot more about her—the whole lot more part she didn't want him to know.

But, if she were honest, she liked being with him. Being *bound* to him was the unexpected bonus.

Who was she to argue with the fates?

Armand had a devilish smile, and his eyes sparkled with mischief. "Whatever shall we do? I'm an officer of the law, sworn to serve and protect."

Emily knew she shouldn't want this. She knew she shouldn't get involved. But—her petty crime and past be damned! She wanted to be with Armand. She wanted him. "I guess you have to serve and protect me."

Armand's eyes widened in excitement. "Oh, it will be my pleasure." He picked her up, sat her on the desk, and slid his hands into her hair.

But her hand came up, too.

She shook the handcuffs and laughed. "Is this telling us we shouldn't?"

He moved against her, spreading her legs around his hips. "This is telling us we must."

"It's a challenge." She shimmied closer, pleased he was hard. Pleased she made him hard.

Armand's groan was long and low. "I love challenges, Emily." He kissed her. Short and fleeting at first, a taste of her lips, of her. But she wanted more, and she wanted it now. She wanted to taste his balm around her tongue, and the heated moisture of his mouth on hers. She wanted to melt or sizzle as his warm hands flowed along her cool skin or his flesh pressed against hers. She darted her tongue between his lips and showed him what she wanted. Armand understood. He rubbed himself against her as his bound hand went deeper into her hair.

Emily pulled herself back. "My hair feels nice, Armand." She could barely talk. "But I want to use my hand to feel yours." She threaded their handcuffed hands through his hair.

"Enough?" He was impatient.

Emily laughed. "No, not enough." But she dropped her hand and plied it against his chest. She froze. "Can others hear us?" she whispered. "My supervisor is in the next room."

He pulled her to him. "We romp quietly."

She brushed his lips but pushed him away again. "What about conflict of interest?" Could the fates be so cruel as to bound them together and then force them apart?

"What do you mean?"

"You're investigating the theft of my car—excuse me, my *cars*."

"Shit!" Armand kissed her palm, sending delicious sparks of fire shooting through her body. "I've thought of you and only you since you jumped into my car this morning and glared at me with those silvery eyes. And now you remind me of conflict of interest?"

Emily kissed his palm and thread her fingers through his. "You have?"

He moved closer, his breath caressing her cheeks and inflaming her. "You haven't thought of me?"

Her lips brushed his. "I went through the entire color scheme for green for your eyes. Topaz green," she whispered as though telling him a secret. "And browns for your hair. Espresso brown-black."

He smiled in satisfaction and kissed her. Her lips, her chin, her jaw, her throat. Emily forget everything except him.

She remembered he didn't answer her question. Crap, she had to stop him.

She averted her face. "So *is* there?"

"What?" He licked the hollow of her neck, making her lift herself as though about to take him inside her.

"A conflict of interest?"

Armand stopped, his frustration visible in his eyes and face. "Of course, there is. And I'm so upstanding I can't believe you made me forget."

"I'm flattered, Detective."

"And I'm confused—and angry! Where's my cell?" He spied it at the end of the desk. "Don't move." He rushed toward it, but the ball and chain pulled him back. "Shit." It was fettered around his ankle. "This challenge is a nuisance." He pulled the chain until the ball rolled to the end of the desk, stopping it with his other foot before it smashed into the wall. He rushed toward his cell but pulled her over by their bound hands.

"Hey!" She put her free hand over her mouth, remembering her supervisor was next door.

He kissed her over and over again. "So far, this is the only way to keep you quiet, so your supervisor doesn't hear."

"I'm never quiet, Armand," she whispered against his ear.

Armand's eyes rounded with anticipation. "My kind of woman. This romp is happening." He carried her toward the cell. "Did I tell you your pajamas are hot?" He set her down and grabbed his cell. "But I can't wait to take them off."

Laughing, Emily kissed his neck. He smelled wonderful as though he showered in fresh mountain snow.

Armand put their bound hands on her lips. "I have to speak to my supervisor." He slid his hand away and gave her a quick kiss, then another and another until Emily heard a voicemail message check in. He put his hand back on them. "Patricia, this is Armand. It's late. Past one or two. I'm off the car theft investigation. It's all Bassam's or Sergei's. I'll work on parking tickets." He dropped the phone. "Conflict of interest put to rest." He brought her handcuffed hand with his as he unbuttoned her pajama shirt. "And no more clothes either. You aren't cold, are you? We have to keep the temperature lower here with the monitors."

"I'm steaming." With want of him.

"Oh, we've only begun," he sang. He flung the shirt aside, grazing her breasts and pressed her against the monitors. He licked her nipples, took one in his mouth, and sucked it until it was hard. Emily threaded her fingers through his thick hair as her knees came up to hold him to her.

She wanted him to keep sucking her breasts, but she tore his mouth away and pulled the pajama shirt off her free hand. She wanted nothing between them and flung it off. But it hung limply over the handcuffs.

"We may be romping with baggage," she said.

Armand unzipped his track jacket. "Feels like we're doing it in the back of a car."

She slid a sleeve off his arm, but it draped over her pajama shirt and the handcuffs. "Can't say I've ever had the pleasure."

"Just name the time."

"Don't have a car—and don't want one either. Might get stolen with us in the back."

"I do. Anytime, Emily. Any. Absolute. Time." He couldn't remove his T-shirt. "Shit."

"Allow me." She lifted the T-shirt with her free hand, pulled it over his head, and flung it over the other clothes and handcuffs. She took him in. He was all muscle, all hard and lean and glorious muscle like the fine and chiseled strokes of Realism paintings. She ran her fingers down the steep curve of his breastplate to the waistband of his pants. Armand groaned in pleasure. "Sensitive?"

"All other."

She reached deep into his track pants. Her fingers grazed his hard and thick tip.

He groaned. "Everything has to come off." He pulled his pants down and stepped out of one leg, but they hung over the cuff shackled to his other leg. Emily didn't care. She saw every inch, and the picture of him as Mr. February didn't do him justice. His flat stomach was taut, covered with a fine brushing of hair, while his hips tapered to thick thighs and long muscular legs. He oozed strength and vigor. He grew harder as she rubbed him. She leaned back seeing all of him, and he was beautiful.

Emily took him in her hand. He was strong and

stiff, but she wanted him throbbing. For her. She stroked and caressed, kissing him on the neck and chest, wherever her mouth landed until he groaned and pulled her hand away. "But—" She didn't understand.

"You first, Emily."

He set her on her feet. Crouching, he pulled down her pants, kissing her flat belly, her hips, her groin, the inside of her thighs, all the way down to her shins. Emily swooned and braced herself. She never knew how sensitive she was. She wanted to close her legs tight but take him in at the same time.

She kicked off her slippers and pants, wanting only her skin against his. Armand grabbed her pants, lay them on the desk, and sat her down. As she shimmied to the edge, he went down on his knees, spread her legs, and held her by the hips.

At the first touch of his tongue, she gasped in delight. He lapped the sensitive outside, and then inside her, over and over again. She grew weaker and hotter with each kiss while her body became tighter and stronger. She threaded her fingers through his and gripped his other hand, but Armand was relentless, expecting more from her. Her body shook. Then it exploded with such intense pleasure she almost screamed in joy.

"You were quiet," he said.

"I," she couldn't talk. "I don't want. Don't want. To get fired."

Armand laughed, but she couldn't. She was breathless, and she wanted him inside her now. She lifted his head and kissed him, tasting her sweat and liquid on his lips and tongue. "Now, Armand. I want you inside me, now."

"No, my love."

My love? Did he call her *my love?* Tears pricked at her eyes. She knew it was in the heat of the moment, but still. No one had ever called her *my love* during lovemaking—or otherwise.

Armand went down and started lapping at her once more. Her body exploded again and this time she stopped a muffled scream.

"Still too quiet," Armand said.

"Wait. When." How could he talk when she couldn't? "When we're alone. Then. I won't be quiet. I promise. And neither will you." But now she wanted him in her. There was no more waiting. She was beyond satisfied and ready for him. "Now, Armand. Please. Now."

He grasped her by the bottom, and she wrapped her legs around his hips. He reached down with his free hand, opened her, and slid himself in, groaning in delight as she swallowed him up. "You feel me?"

"Oh, I feel you, Armand. I feel you."

He thrust but stopped. "Please tell me you're protected."

"Yes, yes, yes. Now, go, go, go!"

Armand smiled as he thrust into her, again and again. Emily cherished every thrust, every groan, every bead of sweat between them. He moved faster and deeper as she took him in. Then with one low groan he released himself inside her.

Emily held him as he pushed into her. With a sigh, he eased himself out. He placed her on the desk and kissed her, slowly and deeply. He wasn't ready to separate himself yet and neither was she.

Sweat lined his back, but she ran her free hand over

it. He oozed out of her, and she was thankful he placed her pajama pants on the desk.

Something dug into her back. A monitor. "Armand?" His name came out in one low almost inaudible note.

"Yes, Emily?" He had her in his arms, their sweat binding them.

"Are there cameras in here, too?"

Armand pulled his head back, his beautiful topaz green eyes shimmering. They both laughed quietly until they couldn't anymore.

Chapter Fourteen

Armand tossed the blanket around Emily as she drew closer. The floor was uncomfortable, but the blanket was big enough to lay beneath them and throw it around themselves like a cocoon. The clothes hanging over the handcuffs and ankle fetter added warmth if also bulk.

"Do you think the phone call to your supervisor will get you off the case?" Emily asked.

He thought about it. "No."

Her laugh was soft. "Really?"

"Quite frankly, I don't know what she'll say. I've never been in this situation before. I've been the model constable and detective. No one has ever broken through the hard skin of my incredible scruples."

"Was a piece of cake for me."

"Except you. My outstanding scruples took a direct hit and went for cover."

"Should I consider it a compliment or an insult?"

His arm went tighter. "An accomplishment."

"I'm sorry, Armand."

"Why?"

"The car thefts were your ticket to the big-time police force. Now you're back to parking tickets."

"Emily, I'm the only one investigating the car thefts. I'm the entire criminal division of the King Court Police Force. I'd be very surprised if my supervisor didn't put me back on the case."

"So, you won't lose it?"

He traced the curve of her back, enjoying her squirm. "First off, my captain will be shocked. Supremely shocked. I never break rules. Then she'll ask me if I've had an encounter of the third kind. When I tell her I'm still here and she gets over her surprise, she will do her duty and give me a lecture on police and witness and police and victim relations. She'll tell me I compromised you and you can't be called as a witness. She'll reprimand me. Since we're not a big force, she'll send me to a corner—where my desk is already to ponder long and hard on my transgression."

She kissed his chest. "Still, I'm sorry."

"Then, why stop? The damage is done." He moved on top of her and placed their handcuffed hands over her head and the other one, too. He ran kisses down both her arms, to her throat and took one of her nipples in his mouth. She squirmed. He wanted to sink himself inside her again. "You are gorgeous, Emily Atterberry."

"I can say the same about you, too, Armand Lecavalier." She flipped him onto his back and straddled him.

He was surprised. "And strong."

The blanket slid off her hips and thighs but with only the monitors giving off light, he couldn't see her the way he wanted. Touching her would suffice tonight. He stroked her thighs to her hips and across her flat belly, wanting to dip his fingers inside her and bring on her excitement again. He wanted her again. He knew he broke the rules—and with his eyes wide open—but he didn't care.

"You do more than jog," he said. "You're tight all

over."

She threw her hair off her face and around one shoulder. It was a simple act but a big turn on. He gripped her tighter. He was hard and wanted to thrust himself inside her wet heat again.

"My family is big on fitness," she said. "I did lots of gymnastics and yoga while growing up thanks to my mother who is a yoga master. My father on the other hand is into boxing."

He fingered the ends of her hair with his free hand. Her hair was like cool water. "Boxing? You are a woman made from my vision."

"My dad insisted my sister and I learn how to protect ourselves. I was never interested in it, but I played along. My sister won a couple local championships until she became bored and moved onto something else. I do a little kick boxing now and then just to make him happy."

His fingers moved down her arm. "Does he still box?"

"For fun, my dad and uncle square off, but it turns into a pushing match toward the coffee and cake. The only real boxing he does now is with a baby-sized punching bag on his desk."

She dragged her handcuffed hand over his arms and chest. She appraised rather than caressed him. "Bench presses?"

"And boxing, too."

"Oh, a man made from my father's vision." She tapped his abs. "Tight abs, too. You do crunches, don't you?"

"I do the old boxer's routine. Rope skipping, crunches, pushups, everything. My father is a high school physical education teacher. He coaches everything from boxing to hockey. I either helped him out or ran practices with him for as long as I can remember. We still run the occasional marathon together. My mother and sisters are joggers but prefer the aerobics of the day."

"I hate crunches. They're boring."

He ran his hand over her smooth belly and down her thighs. "The yoga and gymnastics are serving you well. You're as tight and strong as anyone who does crunches. You and I will have to go over to Tristan's Gym and do a little boxing together."

"It's way above my comfort level."

"Then you can show me what you've got, and I'll show you what I've got."

"I thought we already did," she murmured.

He kissed the palm of her hand. "Yes, but there's so much more I haven't." He pulled her down by the handcuffs. He wanted her again, but he didn't want to hurry it this time. He wanted to touch her now, explore her, and enjoy all her responses, however minute or explosive.

He massaged her into the contours of his chest. "Are you into skiing or skidooing? There are great trails around here. In the summer dirt bike racing is spectacular."

"I'm only here for a couple weeks at the most, Armand." Her breath was warm against his neck. "Then I'll be back for the auction."

The heat drained from his face and his arm went tighter. He forgot she didn't live in King Court. He forgot she would leave. "That's not long enough to do what I want to do with you." He inflected lightheartedness into his tone, but he was upset at the thought of not seeing her let alone not being with her. "I might have to get a subpoena to force you to stay here."

Emily's laugh was soft, her breasts jiggling against his chest. "You don't need any subpoena. Right now, all I want to do is stay right here." She raised herself and shimmied down his hips and legs until she was over his knees. "And right now, all I want to do is forget about conflict of interest and everything else."

She took him in her mouth and moved up and down, kissing him, licking him, sucking him, and making him hard again. When he was about to come, he grabbed her by the hips. She slid him inside her and pushed down on him. He raised his knees and as she held onto them, he moved her up and down. Emily's eyes closed, and her mouth parted until she stilled, and he heard a deep sigh of satisfaction. He kept his eyes on hers and thrust her up and down until he came, too.

Emily's eyes opened, and she smiled. It was a smile of deep satisfaction. Good. It was what he wanted.

She slid off and plied herself against his chest. The veil of sweat on her skin bonded her to him.

Armand was silent for a long time, threading his fingers through her hair and listening to her breathing.

"Armand?"

"Yes?"

"We're in a lot of trouble."

Armand massaged the fine curve of her back. "I know. Emily. I know." But he was more upset at the thought of not seeing Emily after she left King Court than losing the case that would propel him into the big-time police force.

Chapter Fifteen

What was all the ringing? Armand shifted but Emily was in his arms. They were in a tangled mess of track pants, T-shirt, Mona Lisa pajamas, and throw blanket.

He jumped into a sitting position, tugging her with him and jolting her awake.

"Armand?"

They'd fallen asleep on the floor. The handcuffs bound them together and the ball and iron still shackled his ankle. "It's my cell." He picked up the blanket and clothes. Where was his cell?

Emily slid back down on the blanket, her tousled hair, and bare shoulders a turn on. Who cared about his cell? He fell back and kissed her. "Good morning."

"Good morning." This time she jumped into a sitting position, bringing him with her. "Did we fall asleep?" Her voice was a whisper as she took in her surroundings to get her bearings.

"We did." He caressed her back. She was warm and soft, and he ran kisses along her spine.

Someone knocked on the door. "Armand?" It was Nicole. "Why is the door locked?"

Emily's eyes rounded and so did his. He was a teenager again, when whatever-was-her-name's parents came home earlier than expected.

Emily put her hand over her mouth to stop from

laughing.

"I'll be out in a minute, Nicole," Armand shouted.

"Mrs. Halloran is here to pick up the things Lowan borrowed for the shoot yesterday. She also wants to speak to you."

Emily lifted their handcuffed hands and shook her head vigorously.

"I'm sort of getting dressed, Nicole."

"Dressed?"

"I got hot during the night."

There was silence on the other side of the door. "Really?"

He cringed. "Make yourself a coffee and one for Mrs. Halloran—make me one, too, if you don't mind, and I'll be out soon."

Footsteps became faint.

Emily zoomed up, the blanket falling off. She was gloriously naked except for her pajama top and his shirt, which still hung from around the handcuffs. "What are we going to do?" she whispered.

"You'll just have to come out with me in your lovely Mona Lisa pajamas and paintbrush slippers and meet Mrs. Halloran. She'll love you. She's into art history, too."

She pulled up his T-shirt and track shirt to get to her pajama shirt. "I have a reputation to preserve."

He pulled his T-shirt over his head. "I don't."

She smirked as she helped him with his jacket. "My colleagues will see me."

She pulled her pajama shirt over her arm, around her shoulders and slipped her other arm through. He didn't want her covering herself up and moved closer, plying his free hand over her breasts and stroking.

"Armand, we can't." She pushed him away and buttoned the shirt up.

"We can make it a quickie."

"Armand!"

He could watch her all day and not get his fill. He made a dramatic sigh. "If I must." He pulled on his jacket and grabbed his pants from around the shackle.

She found her pants hanging on the desk. "Do you always go commando?"

"No. I was ready to go to sleep when I decided to come back. It worked in my favor." He gave her a quick peck on the lips. "And in yours."

Once they were dressed, she held up the handcuffs. "What do we do about this?"

"I'll call Lowan. He or one of his crew must have the keys to unlock them."

"He'll see us."

"He's covered up for me before. It was always reciprocated by the way. We were on the wild side in high school."

"I thought you were law-abiding."

"I was—except when it came to girls and such."

"And such?" She shook her head. "Lowan's not staying at the inn. He'll have to get here pretty quickly if Mrs. Halloran wants to speak to you."

He found his cell phone in his track pants. "Let me call Nicole. I'll involve her, too."

"What will she think?"

"She already guessed."

"But she doesn't know it's me."

"She'd think you couldn't resist me—like all the other women in my life."

She punched him in the arm. "Or I took advantage

of the detective investigating both of my car thefts. I'm without scruples."

He shook his head. "No one would ever believe it. I can't be swayed, remember? I'm incorruptible."

"*Were* incorruptible."

Armand kissed her. "No one knows you're the exception to the rule. My downfall."

She punched him again. "Downfall?"

"It's a compliment." He found Nicole's number and called. "Listen and just nod okay?"

"One of those mornings?" Nicole replied.

"A much better one." He pulled Emily to him using the handcuffs. "Best I've ever had."

"I'm intrigued but Mrs. Halloran needs to speak to you."

"No—"

"Armand, this is Mrs. Halloran."

"Mrs. Halloran, good morning," he said breathlessly. Emily glided her feet into her slippers and stopped. "I was going to bring the revolver and the other things to you personally this morning. They're heavy and you can't carry them inside the store by yourself."

"Not a problem, but it's not why I came. I came to let you know the wooden horse was returned."

"The wooden horse?" It took him a second to understand what she said. "The wooden horse was returned? You mean the stolen one? When?"

Emily pulled out a chair and sat down. She was wonderfully disheveled.

"Probably during the night. I went to the store earlier this morning, and it's back in its original spot."

"I'm sorry, Mrs. Halloran." He put the cell on the

table and put it on speaker, so he could adjust his clothes. "Are you telling me the thief broke in again and returned it?"

"Seems so. But a wooden train car is missing now. There was another note with the same big print. It said, *"Sorry. Will return it. Honest."*

Emily's eyebrows raised. "Wow", she mouthed.

He found one of his runners and put it on. "You're kidding?"

"Have I ever kidded, Armand?"

He moved a chair in search of the other runner. "Did you touch or move anything?"

"Nope. I left everything exactly the way I found things and came here."

Emily found his missing runner under the desk and pushed it toward him.

"Okay, I need to do a few things here, and I'll be there shortly. Oh, do you by chance have a spare key to both the ball and chain and the handcuffs?"

"There's only one key for each. Why? Did you put them on yourself and now are stuck?"

Emily's lips pursed as she tried not to laugh.

"Of course not."

"Lowan, then? You two always were pranksters."

"No, not Lowan either. One of the stuntmen. The keys went home with Lowan but he's on his way. I just thought you might have extras."

"Sorry. Your partner in crime will have to unshackle you."

"Not *me*, Mrs. Halloran. The *stuntman*. The *stuntman* is shackled to them."

"Of course. The *stuntman*."

"Exactly. Can I speak to Nicole?"

"Armand?" It was Nicole.

"Are you on speaker?"

"No."

"Good. Don't let Mrs. Halloran near the hallway."

"Coffee, Mrs. Halloran?" Nicole asked before she hung up.

He closed the phone and scrolled through his contacts.

"Mrs. Halloran and your sister know you well, Armand."

"I told you I had a reputation. I need to call Lowan. He has to know where the keys are."

Emily moved toward the door, pulling him with her. "I have tools in my room I can use to open up these things. Sometimes we need to unlock old cabinets. They might work on these locks, too. You have to come with me, but you can't come into my room."

"I can't come into your room?"

"It's a mess."

"I've seen messes before."

"I know but I'm not usually disorganized and you certainly aren't. I made you all dirty yesterday and," she held up their bound hands, "last night. Your place is probably perfectly organized—like your nice suit yesterday. I don't want you to think I'm not together. Professional image to uphold."

Armand's eyebrows knitted. "Believe it or not, I think I understood you, but really?"

"Really. You have to wait outside. I'll be quick. It's just behind the door."

He picked up the ball. "Holding this?"

"Do you want to drag it? You have to go first and make sure no one's out there. I can't have any of my

127

colleagues see me—especially my supervisor."

"Fine." He went to the door and peered out. "Ready?"

She nodded.

He opened the door and she dashed to her room. Armand waited outside in the hallway, holding the ball with one hand, his other hand stretched behind the door with Emily. He looked both ways for anyone who might come out of the other rooms. Should he whistle like in old movies?

"Okay. Got it." Emily dashed into the hallway and the security room, pulling him behind her. She opened a black, rolled-up canvas bag. Inside were an assortment of picking tools and keys in sleeves.

"Looks like you're ready to pick a lock."

"All the appraisers have them. But this will be the first time I've ever used one."

"If this doesn't work, then you either have to let me call Lowan or you come with me to Halloran's Antiques in your Mona Lisa pajamas and paintbrush slippers. Mrs. Halloran will have enough gossip to last a week or two."

"What about Jerome? He could use a saw or wrench."

"I thought you were concerned about your reputation?"

"I am, but I forgot my supervisor expects me to meet her for breakfast very soon for a quickie meeting. I can't wait for Lowan." She checked the fetters and grabbed something looking like a dentist's cleaning hook. She shrugged and inserted it in the hand cuffs. Nothing worked until a lock clicked open. The handcuffs dropped from their wrists.

"Well, well, well, Ms. Atterberry. Can you do the same for my big round friend on my ankle?"

She checked the shackle, pulled out another hook, and did the same until it clicked open. "I should have thought of this last night."

"Really?" He pulled her up and gave her a big kiss. "We wouldn't have had a ball."

"Terrible simile, Armand."

"I know. Tonight again?"

"We broke a lot of rules, Detective. Are we going to continue?"

"Are we going to stop? The damage you inflicted on my irrefutable code of honor is done. Yours, however, is safe."

She put the hooks in the bag. "I may be working. It's what I'm supposed to do here, remember."

"All day and all night?"

"No, but my colleagues are now here. Might be difficult to get some time on my own."

Armand scowled. He wanted to see her again. Hell, he didn't want to be parted from her.

"Are you going to Halloran's Antiques right away?"

"I need to load these things into my car and stop off and shower and change. I also need my bat mobile with my own official work kits to do my job."

"Can I catch a ride in about an hour or so? I need to pick up my coat and suit from the cleaners and drop off my jacket. I'm also curious to see what Halloran's Antiques has. Occupational hazard."

He kissed her. "My pleasure. I should also bring in my coats and suit to Mrs. Sonberg. I only have my police parka."

"I'll fill in my supervisor and be ready and waiting when you call. Can you check to see if the hallway is clear again?"

Armand opened the door. "Clear. Go."

She passed him, but he held her and gave her another kiss. Smiling, she pulled away and dashed into her room just as Nicole appeared at the end of the hallway holding two mugs of coffee.

Nicole turned back around. "I'll go and get a third coffee."

Chapter Sixteen

Emily plied herself against her bedroom door.

What did she do? She told herself to keep her distance from Armand and then spent the night with him. Worse, it was the most wonderful night of her life.

Thank goodness Armand didn't come into her bedroom. The train car and figurine were where she left them. On her bed. Otherwise, another kind of handcuffs would be around her wrists. Authentic ones, compliments of the King Court Police. She'd be hauled off to a cell in the town's police station by the very man she made wonderful love with. The very man who was supposedly incorruptible.

She put her lock picking kit in her briefcase, thankful Armand bought the reason why she owned it. But she had to stop whatever was developing between her and Armand from becoming a relationship. She was sure it would go that way if she didn't nip it now. It felt right with Armand. *She* felt right with him. Comfortable and secure and peaceful, as though she'd known him her whole life when she only met him twenty-four hours before.

But she was a thief. She was a criminal. He was a detective. He only knew about her one incident with the policewoman ten years, which put a stop to her life as a bona fide thief. There were other times, and she didn't want to remember them.

Last night, she went back to where she never thought she'd go again. She broke into Halloran's Antiques to return the wooden horse but took the train car. Worse, she had no intention of returning it. She stole again but this time for keeps. She had to distance herself from Armand before she let something slip or he learned who she was.

She put the train car and figurine in her suitcase and locked it. She raced to the bathroom and threw off her clothes.

Armand would be back soon. She wanted to check out Mrs. Halloran's antique store and go to the dry cleaners, but also to learn about the train car. If it was part of a set, then Mrs. Halloran might know where the other pieces were. She needed to know. The fates put the train car in front of her, and now she couldn't stop until she found the other pieces and located her biological family.

She stepped into the shower.

Why couldn't she have met Armand another time? Why was he wonderful? Why couldn't she stay away from him as she wanted? Why, why, why? And why, why, why couldn't she wait to see him again?

This was bad. Really bad. So why did bad feel so good?

An hour later, Emily sat in Armand's Taurus. She purred. He wore his police parka over an impeccable dark blue suit.

"Does the police parka turn you on?" he asked.

"*You* in the police parka turns me on." She wanted to strip it off of him, followed by the impeccable suit until he wore only the satisfied smile.

He placed his hand over hers. "Well, we'll have to

do something about it. Maybe I can locate those furry red handcuffs."

Emily wondered how she didn't nod in agreement. "No, you won't. And no we won't." She removed his hand. "We have to be professional from now on. I have work to do and you have work to do and there cannot be any police parka or furry red handcuffs interfering." She faced forward and sat up primly. "Snazzy suit by the way. Very sexy. You have great taste, Detective Lecavalier."

"I certainly do." He squeezed her hand and drove to Halloran's Antiques. She stepped out of the car, holding her jacket in a plastic bag, and waited as Armand removed the boxes with the revolver, handcuffs, and ball and chain. She held the door open as a slight woman in her sixties peeked out from behind a massive cash register. Emily recognized her. She was the woman with Armand the day before when her first car was stolen. She assumed this was the formidable Mrs. Halloran.

"The keys miraculously reappeared?" Mrs. Halloran asked.

Yes, she was formidable.

Armand maneuvered around counters, curios, and shelves. "They did. One of the other stuntmen had them."

"Of course, he did. You can put those boxes behind the counter. You've brought a friend?"

"Mrs. Halloran, this is Emily Atterberry with Kanata Auction House. She's appraising the furniture at the Acadia Inn but is an art historian like yourself. Emily, Mrs. Halloran, forever my history teacher with no first name."

Mrs. Halloran squeezed Emily's hands between hers. "A woman cut from the same cloth as me. I love everything historical—art, music, furniture, except men, of course."

Emily laughed but Armand managed a "I'm not amused" smirk. He placed the crates behind the counter and spied a chair. "Hepplewhite chair," he told Emily.

Her smile was furtive. "It is."

Mrs. Halloran's gaze moved between them. "You're learning about furniture styles, Armand?"

"I'm picking up a couple things here and there as I help Nicole with the security."

Mrs. Halloran glanced at Emily. "Of course, you are. From Nicole." Emily suppressed a smile. The woman was no fool.

Armand moved to the curio where the wooden horse sat next to the Post-it Note she wrote the night before. "*Sorry. Will return it. Honest,*" Armand read out loud. "Fascinating. Such a conscience."

Emily turned to another curio filled with miniature Inuit sculptures. "I hope you don't mind if I look around while you two do your business."

"Take your time, Emily," Mrs. Halloran said. "I have things here I don't even remember."

"And it all looks wonderful." Emily ambled toward a wall covered with paintings and photographs, but her ears were on Mrs. Halloran and Armand's conversation.

"The object this time was a wooden toy train?" Armand asked.

"I don't know if it was a toy train, but it was a train car also made out of basswood. It has been on the right side of the horse since I bought it years ago. Now, the lovely heart-shaped note is in its place."

"I need to get my camera and fingerprint kit." He left, winking at Emily.

"How long have you been collecting antiques, Mrs. Halloran?"

"Forty-five years. My husband and I opened the store when we got married. He managed the store while I taught, but I've been here since retiring. He's at an auction this week in North Bay. I always get a thrill when he returns with some treasures from the past."

"Those of us who think things from the past are treasures are few and far between."

Armand came back with his camera and a briefcase. He took a few pictures of the curio and note. Wearing latex gloves, he removed it and inserted it into a paper envelope.

"You saw the train car missing this morning when you came in?" he asked.

"I did. I walked in ready to dust and was surprised to see the horse returned and the train car gone. This is the fact sheet and a photo."

Armand took both. "Front train car, basswood, bought twenty-five years ago at a garage sale for five dollars. If it's worth five dollars, why are you selling it?"

"It's not worth five dollars. It's worth several hundred dollars on its own but other pieces go with it. Two other train cars and a figurine, which I never saw. You see the design on the train car in the photo?"

"It looks like trees and the side of a house or porch."

"Exactly. The other two train cars continue the engraving. It probably tells the story of the artist or someone he knows. I don't know what the figurine shows."

"There's no artist listed?"

"None I could find, which is unusual. The artist always leaves a logo or initials. My guess is it's on one of the other train cars or the figurine. I bought this train car from George and Gilda McEnrole."

Emily moved to a glass case of Victorian teacups, saucers, tea pots, and cake platters. The figurine was a girl wearing overalls and a cap. She knew now it was an engineer's cap, but she had no idea of its significance.

"I don't know them," Armand said.

"You wouldn't. They've both been gone for twenty-five years. Their children sold off the house and everything in it. Can't remember where they lived but possibly near Hewett Equestrian."

"Do the children still live here in King Court?"

"None do. I think the oldest moved to Newfoundland, their youngest son is in California, and the middle child I believe passed away. There was only the one train car left when I arrived at the garage sale, but they did tell me they sold two other similar pieces. They obviously didn't know they were a set and valuable. I know one of the people who bought a train car. I don't know who bought the third one. They told me about a figurine. Like I said, I never saw them."

"Who bought one of the other train cars?"

Emily moved toward a case of coins, surprised several were Napoleonic gold francs, waiting anxiously to hear who owned another train car.

"Colm Saunders. He collects toy trains."

"Jessica's grandfather collects toy trains?"

Emily picked up a velvet pouch and removed a Georgian silver serving spoon with a Celtic star design, trying to control her racing heart. Jessica was the barista at Koffee & Tez and the photographer of the incredible portraits hanging in the shop.

"Jessica's grandfather can't get enough of trains. I'm surprised you don't know since your grandparents are on the same bowling team as the Saunders."

"I knew he had a collection but not a massive one."

"It's so massive Colm renovated one of his barns to hold the collection. It's impressive, believe me. We have a little bet going. Whoever finds the third train car of this set gets the other one. Been years now and neither Colm nor I have had any luck finding it."

Emily needed to connect with Jessica and sooner rather than later. She'd call her this week and set up a day when Jessica could shadow her as she appraised the furniture. Then maybe she could get information about her grandfather's train collection.

"They're in Florida now, aren't they?" Armand asked. "Won't be back until the spring like all the snowbirds?"

"I believe so."

Emily's heart beat so rapidly she couldn't hold the spoon and set it down. She needed air. She had more information about the train car, and it frightened as much as excited her. "You have a wonderful shop, Mrs. Halloran. I could spend days looking around."

"Once you don't have your hands full with the Acadia Inn come by and spend as long as you'd like. I'll show you my private collection of porcelain figurines from England and France from the 1600s. I will never part with them."

"I'd love to." She glanced at Armand. "I'm going to drop off my jacket and get my coat and suit back.

Would you like me to drop off your coats," she was about to say "Armand" but decided against it. "Detective?"

"Thanks, but I'll drop them off myself later. I'll bring you back to the inn. I just have to take a few photos here."

"If it's not too much trouble, I'd appreciate it."

"I heard about the second stolen car and right in front of my shop again," Mrs. Halloran said. "Heard it was rented out to you too, Emily."

"It was quite a day. One I want to forget." She walked out of Halloran's Antiques and toward King Court's Dry Cleaners located at the end of the street. Her cell rang. Isla.

"Who's the guy you supposedly aren't spending Valentine's Day with," were her first words.

Emily's smile was bittersweet. "He's the detective investigating the car thefts. My car, actually both cars I rented, were stolen from under my nose yesterday. He's also investigating the theft of the wooden horse and now," she lowered her voice, "the train car I took."

"Are you shitting me?"

"Have you ever known me to do that?"

"Describe him."

Emily should have known Isla was more interested in the man than the train car. "He's gorgeous."

"Gorgeous can look like a lot of things. Send me a pic."

"I'm not taking a picture of him. You could locate one. He's Mr. February on the King Court Calendar of Men."

"Is it online?"

"Don't know. Check. By the way, I met Lowan

Beach."

"You met Captain Borgman?"

"He's filming a couple scenes at the Acadia Inn for his series. Seems he and Armand are best buddies."

"Armand? Is that the name of your detective?"

"He's not my detective but, yes, it is his name." She waited at the curb for the streetlights to turn green. She could walk across, there were no cars, but decided to wait.

"Holy shit, the pictures are on online. January—Marc Johansen of the Montreal hockey team. Yummy, yummy. February—oh my, your detective is delicious. Clean cut and all together, your type—with just the right amount of spice. Love the furry handcuffs. You would look good in red. And the other months. The town is not so sleepy after all. I'm coming back."

"No, you're not. You're staying there and writing those exams."

"You did it then? You did what you said you'd never do again and even took it one big step forward? You're keeping it?"

"I couldn't leave it. I may return it, but not now. My figurine sits perfectly in it, and it was made from the same piece of wood. It also has an engraving of what looks like a house and some trees on the side. Isla, I learned there are two more train cars. They continue the scene and could tell something about the artist." Her throat tightened with emotion. "The scene could lead me to my biological family."

"I knew stealing the wooden horse wasn't for nothing."

"I shouldn't have done it. But it would have looked awkward after the return of the horse if I strolled in and bought the piece next to it."

"Do you know where these other two pieces are?"

"I know where one is. I have to figure out how and when to get it. The third piece is a mystery. If I'm lucky I'll find the middle train car with the majority of the etching and won't have to look for the third." She paused. "I may be putting my future on the line for nothing."

"You have to try, Emmy. You know you do."

Emily knew she did and didn't like it.

"Are you telling Mom and Dad?"

The light turned green and Emily crossed. "I will eventually, if I get a name or location but not now. I told them I wouldn't steal again, and I haven't in ten years. They'll be disappointed in me."

"They'll be over the moon if you find what you're looking for. You know they're all for finding your biological family."

"But not happy for how I'm doing it. I'm not happy about it—especially with Armand involved. He's a great guy, Isla. I want to get to know him better, but I can't. It's not right."

"Are you telling me he's the kind of guy you'd bring home to me, and of course, Mom and Dad?"

"I'm not bringing him home."

"Hypothetically speaking?"

She didn't answer. If she did it would be "yes."

"Move onto to Mr. March, Emmy. He's the bartender and owner of the Coyote's Hole. Best ginger I've ever seen."

"I'm not moving onto anyone else." She wanted to stay with Armand. But she couldn't.

"Want me to come up this weekend and see if I can

help you find those other train cars?"

"No, I'll figure it out." The ATM in the bank caught her eye. She had to leave money for the train car. "I have to go. I'll call later." She put her cell away. That's what she'd do. It wouldn't make up for the theft or the breaking and entering but at least Mrs. Halloran would recoup her loss financially.

She withdrew five hundred dollars, money going toward a holiday with Isla. It was more than Mrs. Halloran said the train car cost, but it was priceless—to her if not to anyone else. As a set it could be worth so much more. She would mail the money to Mrs. Halloran with a little note explaining it was for the train car.

She moved to the cleaners. Mrs. Sonberg heard of the second car theft and would have the jacket ready for her as soon as possible.

Emily gave her back the loaned coat and put on her black one. She took her suit and headed back to Halloran's Antiques. But Mrs. Halloran and Armand weren't anywhere. She called out to them, checked the back room, and saw them across the street at Koffee & Tez.

Quickly, Emily grabbed a tissue, used it to take an envelope from the counter, and slid the five hundred dollars inside. She took the gel pen she used the night before and using the tissue, wrote on another heart-shaped Post-it Note, "*For the train car. Sorry for breaking in.*" She placed the note on the envelope and slid it under a pile of mail and packages. She hurried toward the front door just as Armand and Mrs. Halloran came in.

"Got you a coffee." Armand held it up.

"The Valentine's brew," Mrs. Halloran all but sang.

Emily's eyebrows shot up as she kept from laughing.

Armand's lips twitched. "Didn't know how you took it, so I brought cream, milk, and sugar."

"Just cream. Thank you." She put the cup on the counter and stirred in two creams.

"I'm ready to go, Emily."

"Nice meeting you, Mrs. Halloran."

"You too, Emily. I'll look forward to our next visit."

"So will I." She followed Armand to his car and waited as he put his gear in the trunk.

"You were the news about the car thefts but now you're the gossip," he said as they got into the car. "It won't be long before Mrs. Halloran calls my grandmother who will call my mother who will call me."

"Why?" She put on her seat belt. "Because you bought me a coffee? The Valentine's brew?"

His cell rang. He pointed and laughed. It said, "Mom". "Right on cue." He pressed accept. "Hey, Mom."

"What's this about Hepplewhite chairs, Armand?"

Chapter Seventeen

Armand drove to the police station, a big smile on his face. He'd wipe it off if the long arm of Mrs. Halloran's gossip reached his colleagues.

He walked in and Patricia zoomed out of her office. Tall and solid she was intimidating. "You!" She pointed at him. "Into my office. Now."

Armand walked past Sergei and Bassam, whose eyes rounded with curiosity.

"Is our poster boy in trouble?" Sergei asked.

"That can't be," Bassam replied. "He's never in trouble."

"Good morning, Constables," Armand said in a good little boy's tone.

Patricia held the door open and shut it when he sat down. She strode behind her desk and plied her hands on her hips. "What do you mean you're off the car theft cases? You're the only one investigating them. Did you have one too many beers last night after being showered with snow and mud? Or did you have one too many beers with our victim and our only witness? I heard you were with her last night when the robbery occurred."

"No beers. Only tea. Chamomile."

"Chamomile? You expect me to believe it?"

"It's the truth."

"So, what the hell—" Her eyes rounded as

realization struck her. She plopped into her chair. "I've heard through the town's various grapevines, she's quite attractive. Please don't tell me you've *tampered* with our one and only witness."

"Tampered?" He rolled it around in his thoughts. Interesting word. He did more than tamper and loved every second of it.

She raised her hands and shook them. "No, don't tell me. You're going to say nothing, and I'm pretending I didn't complete the thought in my mind. I'm going to pretend it was beer and a lot of it and not chamomile. Beer and lots of it made you phone me during the middle of the night and leave the message I didn't hear. Beer, Armand. Beer. Got it?"

"Can I say what happened before the *tampering*?"

"If it's foreplay, no."

"Not really foreplay—"

"I didn't hear that!"

"Fine, before," he thought about, "Let me phrase it in *innocent* terms."

"I didn't hear that either!"

"Fine. During the time I sipped chamomile tea with our witness, I swayed her in the right direction."

"*Sway* is not a good word, either. Only wise police questioning techniques. Now, tell me about your *wise* police questioning of our only *witness* as well as our *victim*?"

Armand took out the picture Emily drew from a large envelope. "Emily—" Patricia's eyes went stern. "Ms. Atterberry drew this for us. It was the girl who stole both her cars, a young girl."

Patricia put on her reading glasses and took the picture. "This does not look like a young girl. She looks about my daughters' ages, early to mid-twenties. Actually, she looks like a made-up doll. She could be anyone under the fake face."

"Em—Ms. Atterberry said the exact thing—fancy hair style, lots of make-up, both professionally done is what she said. She could be any girl. But she is young. High school age as a matter of fact." He removed another paper from the envelope. "She wore pants with this symbol."

"Saint Margaret Mary's Academy?"

"Yup. Em—Ms. Atterberry saw the collar of a white golf shirt. Said she wore a similar one when she was in high school."

Patricia leaned forward. "Do you think all the thieves were high school kids, too?"

"It's a gut feeling. I'm going to the high school to show the picture and see what I can get out of the principal and guidance counselors. I'm sure if they are youths, their behavior has changed radically. If not their behavior, then their grades for sure."

"You realize we won't be able to call Ms. Atterberry as a witness to identify this thief if it goes to court?"

"I'll get you enough evidence to make up for it."

Patricia's stern gaze made him squirm. Under the hard as rocks exterior beat a compassionate heart, which he admired. "You crossed the line last night, Armand. Never expected it from you. Was it really chamomile and not beer?"

He held up his hand. "Scouts honor."

"She must be special if she managed to do that to you."

Armand shrugged. "She's nice."

"Nice? Not if she made you drop the case. I know how much you want to get solid experience to move to a big police force."

"All right. She's more than nice."

Patricia shook her head, a small smile shaping her lips. "There was another theft at Halloran's Antiques?"

"Yes. The original stolen object, a wooden horse, was returned and a train car taken. Another note was left, too."

"The thief didn't like the horse?" He took out the envelope with the Post-it Note and showed it to her. "Such manners. Did you dust the place for prints?"

"I did but found nothing. I do have some information on the train car and want to do some digging into it. There are a few other pieces belonging to it. Might lead to who would want to take it and the lovely notes this thief leaves."

"You have a full day ahead. Now get out of here and solve these car thefts. And lay off the chamomile."

Armand opened the door. "Easier said than done."

"I didn't hear that!"

He got into his car and headed to Saint Margaret Mary's Academy. He spoke to both the principal and the guidance counselors and showed them the picture, but they couldn't provide any details or identify the girl. The youths were in the throes of hormone changes, so erratic behavior was normal. They took photocopies of the picture and would show the teachers.

Armand left the guidance office just when the last class let out. Some of the youths knew him and either gave him a fist punch or greeted him. Some of the girls huddled together and twittered as he walked past. They saw his spread as Mr. February.

He sat in his car and kept an eye out for his niece Carli who took a school bus home. As he waited, he checked out the boots the girls wore. Most wore Dr. Martens. Solving the car thefts wasn't going to be easy if most of the girls in the school wore them. He went through his messages, too, until the last bus left.

Did his niece miss school today? He headed in the direction of Nicole and Darryl's home when he saw Carli, dragging her feet through snow on the shoulder. Her coat flew open and her knapsack hung over one shoulder. She was by herself, too. He could not remember a time when she wasn't with her gal pals, twittering away. She didn't look like his smart-talking, don't-give-me-any-shit niece.

Armand stopped his car and rolled down the passenger window. "Miss the bus today?"

Carli glanced at him. She usually wore her long curly hair loose to cover up the acne on her face but today it was pulled back in a ponytail. "No."

There was no attitude or witty smart talk back. This was not the Carli he knew. "How about a lift home?"

She looked behind. "No thank you. People will recognize you."

"And?"

"And I can't be seen with a police officer."

"I'm a detective."

"Is there a difference?"

"I have a better wardrobe."

"Ha, ha, ha. Where was one of your suits when you posed nude? You completely embarrassed me. All the girls in my class and even girls I don't know in higher grades keep asking me about you. They drool over you like dogs in heat."

"First of all, I wasn't naked, and second, it was for a noble cause. We raised a lot of money for the kids' hospital."

"Right. Having your ding-dong wear your duty belt while you wear just your cap classifies as naked to me. And as far as I know, the furry red handcuff is not part of your uniform. I can't wait until the month is over and they can pin you back forever."

He'd had his privates called many things, but ding-dong was a first.

She pushed through knee-high snow. She wore Dr. Martens too, probably filled with snow now.

"I'm not taking you home because I'm a detective or Mr. February. I'm taking you home because I'm your uncle."

"My step-uncle."

Armand grunted. "Well, well, well. You haven't called me your step-uncle since you first met me. I believe you were five years old and flexing your mouth-muscles."

"So, I'm calling you step-uncle now. Live with it." She pulled her knapsack over her shoulder and continued on.

What the hell was wrong with her? He drove at a crawl. "Get in the car, Carli, or I'm coming out and putting police-issued handcuffs on you."

She stopped, and her face turned white, surprising him again. "You wouldn't dare?" A note of panic was in her voice.

"You know I love a dare." He parked the car, stepped out, and pulled his handcuffs from his belt. "Maybe I'll throw you into the back, too. Complete the picture."

He should use these handcuffs on Emily—and join her in the backseat. He might bring then tonight to the inn.

Damn, he promised Patricia he'd lay off the chamomile. And he knew better.

But…

No, buts. He'd keep on his side of the law and Emily would stay on hers.

"Fine." Carli pushed up her eyeglasses, threw the hood over her head, sat in the passenger seat, and slouched down.

Armand got behind the wheel. "Seat belt, please."

She huffed and pulled the seat belt on.

He drove off but even when they were out of range of the school, she kept her hood on and remained slumped.

"So, what's up?" he asked.

"Nothing."

"You are going home, aren't you?"

"Where else would I go?"

"Just wanted to make sure." He needed her to come down from her miserable state before he questioned or interrogated as Emily put it.

He pulled out a pack of Dubble Bubble and handed it to her. She took one and gave him one, too. Both started chewing. When she blew her first bubble, Armand knew he could start the questioning or interrogation. "Your parents are worried about you."

"Which ones? My father and my step-mother, your sister, or my mother and her wife, my second step-mother?"

"My sister, your first step-mother, and your father. I'm sure your father or first step-mother has told your mother and second step-mother they're worried about you."

"There's nothing to worry about."

"Why aren't you with your friends?"

"Do I have to be with my friends all the time? Can't I walk home alone?"

"You don't walk anywhere let alone by yourself. It's wheels or nothing. And usually your gal pals are with you."

"So I wanted a change."

"Is one of them bothering you?"

She averted her face. "No."

He gave her a few moments of silence. "How was the library last night?"

She turned on him. "Your sister spoke to you?"

"My sister, your first step-mother, is worried and so is your father. Quite honestly, I am, too. You're not your usual self. No attitude, no smart-talking, no energy. Are you getting boring on me?"

She stared out the window and remained silent.

"It's me, Carli. I may be your step-uncle as you now call me, but you're my niece—blood or no blood—and my go-to girl."

Carli took a deep breath. It meant he broke one barrier.

"Boyfriend issues?" he asked.

"No."

"Girlfriend issues?"

She turned on him. "I'm not a lesbian."

"It would be fine with me if you were."

"Posters of K-Pop boy bands you have never heard of are on my bedroom walls. I'm straight—Uncle Armand."

"How would I know what's in your bedroom? There's a big "no trespass" sign on your door with "on pain of death" written in bold underneath."

She blew another bubble and stared out the window.

"If you're in trouble you can tell me."

She kept her head averted, which told him she still wasn't telling him anything. He changed the subject. "How are the driving lessons going?"

She flinched. "I'm not taking them anymore."

Armand was surprised. "Really, why? Has the instructor made a move on you?"

"The instructor is a woman and no, she hasn't. I just don't want to learn to drive, okay. It's slippery when it's icy and scary. Winter is not a good time to learn. End of story, and I don't want to hear about driving lessons or boyfriends again. Got it?"

"Got it." What the hell could he speak about now to get her to open up? He smiled slyly. "I met a nice woman."

Carli sat up. Stirrings of a smile pulled at her lips. "Define nice woman, Step-uncle Armand."

He grinned. "Well, Step-niece, Carli, she's gorgeous."

"That's it?"

"No, that's not it. She's artistic, too. She draws, and she's smart. She's has a master's degree in Art History and is training to be a furniture appraiser with her eye on becoming an art appraiser in the future."

"And this smart, artistic, and gorgeous woman likes you?"

"Is there something wrong with me?"

She shrugged. "I guess someone will find you all

right. You'll finally have a date for Valentine's Day on Sunday."

"What do you mean finally? I've had dates on Valentine's Day before."

"Really? Name one when you weren't at our place for dinner, so Grandma and Grandpa didn't know?"

He thought about it. She was right. He hadn't had a date for Valentine's Day since high school. Maybe he would have one for this Valentine's Day. He just couldn't tell Patricia. Shit, he wasn't supposed to think about Emily, let alone be with her on Valentine's Day.

"What's her name?"

"What's your boyfriend's name? We can double date on Valentine's Day."

"Spiderman."

"Wonder Woman."

"You're not going to tell me her name?"

"You're not going to tell me your boyfriend's name?"

"There isn't a boyfriend."

"Then I can't tell you her name. And she's not my girlfriend." Yet. Because he couldn't indulge in chamomile anymore—unless he found another witness. If the witness issue weren't a problem, he wanted Emily to be more than his lover. He wanted to know her and see where that would take them.

"I'll get her name out of your sister."

"She doesn't know." But Nicole saw Emily coming out of his room in the morning.

He gave his thoughts away because Carli laughed. "Oh, yes she does. She'll tell me without me even asking her."

"Well, at least you're still talking to her."

152

She slumped in the seat and pulled the hood over her forehead. "What were you doing at the school?"

"Trying to see if your principal or guidance counselors knew anything about the car thefts in the area."

"The car thefts?" She sat up with interest. "What about the car thefts? You think it's a student?"

"We have reason to believe it could be."

"I don't know anything."

"I didn't say you did."

"You're thinking it."

"No, I'm not." She was back to a foul mood. "But if you do hear any rumblings—"

"If I do, it's gossip, and I don't listen to gossip or spread it." She turned her back. "I want to chew my gum in peace now."

Since he couldn't think of anything else to talk about to draw her out or not upset her, he remained quiet. At her home, he drove onto the driveway.

Carli rushed out. "Thanks for the ride." She strode to the side door, pulling out her key.

He rolled down his window. "Carli?"

She gave him a cursory glance. "What?"

"You can talk to me anytime."

Her shoulders slumped. "I'll speak to Spiderman instead."

Chapter Eighteen

The instant Emily stepped inside the Acadia Inn she didn't have a moment to herself. All she wanted to do was return to the privacy of her bedroom, put the figurine in the train car, and find Colm Saunders' home. But she returned to the Acadia Restaurant and appraised the furniture. At lunch, she headed to her bedroom, but her supervisor Marilyn was eager to see the paintings by Marie-Anne Couture. Emily showed her the three in the restaurant, followed by the other twenty-eight located throughout the inn. Some were in guest bedrooms, others in hallways, and a couple in the tea salon. Marilyn was intrigued and contacted an expert in Canadian eighteenth and nineteenth century paintings from Ottawa to evaluate them. Before Emily realized, it was early evening and time for a dinner meeting with Marilyn and the other two appraisers.

She hadn't heard from Armand. As much as she wanted to hear and see him, she hoped he was too busy to bother about her. Otherwise, she wouldn't resist and sneak into an available room with him. Worse, she imagined sneaking him into her bedroom and, once again, trying not to make noise while her colleagues slept next door.

If he didn't come, she would check where Colm Saunders lived and possibly his barn full of trains. But just before dinner, Armand surprised her by popping into the restaurant. He held up her jacket in a King Court Dry Cleaners plastic bag. "Special delivery."

Emily sat at the bar, downloading photos of the inn's furniture onto her laptop. As much as she tried to hold her emotions back, her smile and delight gave her away. "The police force delivers dry cleaning in this small town?"

He ambled toward her. "Only this one police officer and for special clients." He handed it to her.

"Well, thank you, Detective Lecavalier." She took it and stuck out her hand to shake.

He came closer. "Really?"

She put the jacket against his chest to hold him back. "We're supposed to be professional, remember?"

Armand scowled, took her hand, and kissed it. "If we must."

Emily's defenses fell apart and she pulled him in for a quick kiss. "You have to stop this." She shook her head. "*I* have to stop this."

Armand swept her into his arms and gave her a big kiss. "Stop what?"

"Whatever you're doing to me."

"What am I doing to you, Ms. Atterberry?"

"Making me forget what I am here to do and what you're here to do."

"I came to deliver your dry cleaning."

"We're both going to get fired if we don't stop this illegal affair."

Armand's arms dropped from around her. "Yes, I've already been spanked." His eyebrows rose. "Spanking. Now there's a thought. I really have to find those furry handcuffs."

"No!"

He laughed. "I guess I'd better solve these car thefts and fast or we're going to keep breaking rules." He gave her a quick peck on the lips. "For the road, so to speak." He sat on a stool. "So, how goes the Hepplewhite chairs and basswood small stuff and Marie-Anne Couture paintings?"

Emily draped the jacket over the bar counter. "Slow but steady. My supervisor called in an expert in eighteenth and nineteenth century Canadian art. She's coming here tomorrow to look at the paintings."

"Does this mean you discovered an artist and may be skipping over furniture to art appraisals?"

"They're allowing me to tag along and listen tomorrow. I'm lucky they are. It'll be a first for me. Marilyn is in charge." She had to ask the question. "Will you be moonlighting tonight?"

"Do you want me to moonlight?"

Emily's gaze went stern. "I thought we decided against any more wrong doings."

Armand took a deep breath. "No, I won't be moonlighting tonight. Darryl will be here. Are you working through the evening?"

"Until about eight. Then my fellow appraisers and I are having a dinner meeting at the Coyote's Hole."

"It's a great bar. Try the coddle or Irish stew and the Working Class Craft Lager. It's the pub's latest brew. The distillery is right behind the pub. Call if you finish early. Call even if you don't finish early."

"Armand…"

"We can just talk—away from a bed, of course."

"There was no bed in sight last night."

Armand nodded. "Okay, I guess it might not work."

It definitely wouldn't work. She wanted to stay away from him, but she was ready to throw him over the bar, rip his clothes off, and make love with him below the three paintings of Marie-Anne Couture. "Any luck with the picture I drew you?"

"I visited the school and spoke to the principal and guidance counselors. They're going to get back to me tomorrow after some inquiry with the teachers. Drastic drops in grades are a sure indicator something is going on in a student's life." His cell rang. "It's my supervisor. Have to take this." He leaned forward as though he was about to kiss her when he stuck out his hand. Emily shook it, and he left.

Emotions flooded her as her body deflated. Armand was so wonderful. He wanted to be with her as much as she wanted to be with him, but they couldn't. Both realized it but at the same time it was difficult pretending she felt nothing.

What exactly did she feel for him? It certainly wasn't love. Love didn't happen in twenty-four hours, did it?

She went back to her photos but saw nothing.

No, love didn't. It couldn't. She longed for Armand. That was it. Longing was like lust. It would go away. She could help it along by distancing herself from him. He was investigating the theft of both her cars, so the relationship was professionally inappropriate. It would turn downright disgraceful if he learned that under her appraiser title, she was a petty thief like the criminals he arrested.

She remembered the train cars. Putting aside the downloads, she did a Google search of Colm Saunders' home. It wasn't far from the inn. Under two kilometers.

If she had the chance after returning from dinner, she would go for a jog and check the house and barn. She didn't know if she would break in. She didn't want to but the thought of finding another train car holding answers about her biological family overrode her desire not to steal it. If she did decide to take it, maybe she'd be lucky, and it would be the train car with the design leading to her family. Then she wouldn't have to look for the third one. If it wasn't, she was at a dead end. She had no idea how to find the third and final train car.

She'd take out some money from the ATM again, just in case she found it.

After a late dinner at the Coyotes Hole with her colleagues, they returned to the inn. Marilyn, Lubna, and Tatyana sat in the lobby, enjoying a night cap with Elsa, Wilhelm, Theresa, and Jerome but Emily excused herself. She barely stepped inside her bedroom when her cell rang. It was Armand.

"Are you at the inn?" he asked.

Emily wanted to lie and say "no", but she couldn't. "I am, but I'm going straight to sleep."

There was a knock at her door. "Hold on." She opened it to find Armand, wearing his complete police uniform under his parka and holding his cell in one hand and a bottle of wine in the other.

"Night cap before you put on your Mona Lisa pajamas and I tuck you into bed?"

Chapter Nineteen

Emily wanted to tell him to leave. She wanted to tell him she was tired and going straight to sleep. Or, she had to download photos and write blurbs. Or, the truth. It wasn't right. Anything she could think of. Instead, she looked up and down the hallway, grabbed him by the coat, and kissed him.

Armand pulled her out, slammed her door shut, moved into the security office, and locked the door.

After a heated kiss, making Emily swoon, she remembered herself and pushed him off. "This isn't right, Armand. You're going to get fired and to save you I'll have to play the part of the femme fatale and admit without an ounce of remorse I set out to corrupt you and sway you from your focus on the law." She said it all in one breath and now breathed out.

He took her in his arms again, the corner of his lips raised in amusement. "Sounds like a lot of old movies I've seen with my grandparents."

"This isn't a movie." She shimmied out of his arms and against the door.

"How about this scenario. I met you in the hallway." He took a step toward her. "We started talking," another step forward, "and I invited you into my office," he butted himself against her, "for a nightcap."

"So, what would you call what I did to you outside

my door and what you're doing to me now, pinning me to the door?"

He pulled his lips from side to side as he thought. "You slipped and fell against my lips, and I held you up until you were stable."

Emily punched him in the chest, then placed her hand on it. He wore a bulletproof vest. "I'm stable now."

He didn't move. "Are you sure?"

"I'm sure."

He took a deep sigh and stepped back. "I'm here if you're not."

"Duly noted." Emily hurried to the monitors and leaned against the desk. She needed to put distance between them or fall to his appeal. "I thought you weren't working here tonight."

"I wasn't until Nicole frantically called Darryl and Darryl urgently called me."

She got excited. "She went into labor?"

"If she did, she's one month early. He brought her to the hospital just in case." He pulled off his jacket and slung it over a chair. Even with the bullet-proof vest over his police uniform he screamed muscle as much as authority. He was tantalizingly seductive as he always was in whatever he wore or didn't. "You are such a devilish sneak."

Armand laughed boyishly as he removed his hat and plopped it on her head. "You don't like me in my uniform?"

She pushed him into a chair and sat on him. "You're corrupting me."

"Is it working?"

"No."

"Then why are you sitting on me?"

"Because I tripped and fell on your lap."

He put his arms around her waist. "Sounds reasonable to me."

"You're very sexy in your uniform, Detective Lecavalier."

"You're soliciting a representative of the law, Ms. Atterberry. I'm going to have to take you in." He pulled out his handcuffs and dangled them. "Still trying to locate the furry ones."

Voices came from the hallway. Emily covered her mouth, trying not to laugh. Armand put one cuff around her wrist and one around his.

"No," she mouthed. "That's my—," she listened, "Marilyn, my supervisor," she whispered. "And Lubna and Tatyana and the Sherrers." She put her fingers on his mouth to signal silence, the cuffs hitting his chin.

Armand pushed the handcuffs aside to kiss her fingers. "Haven't you ever wanted to do it when your parents were in the same house?" he whispered.

"I went to a Catholic school," she whispered back.

"So did I."

The people conversed outside the security office door about the various four poster beds in the guest bedrooms. Emily shook her head and placed her forehead against Armand's.

"They're talking about beds," he murmured against her lips.

"Canopy or four poster eighteenth and nineteenth century beds," she whispered and kissed him slowly and sweetly, enough to elicit a groan of pleasure.

"Were they more conducive to love-making?"

Emily ran her lips along his jaw to his ear. "In

medieval times they gave lords and ladies privacy. Their guards often slept in the same room."

He tickled her neck with the tip of his tongue. "So, it was the same as having your parents sleeping next door?"

She squirmed. "You want me to corrupt you, Detective Lecavalier, don't you?"

"I'm testing myself." He was breathless. "Want to see if I can be corrupted a second time by the same woman."

She smiled in satisfaction as she felt his arousal. "It's not working."

"Not at all." He dove in for a kiss, but she put her hand over his lips. The handcuffs hit his again, making him flinch. "Why aren't these working in my favor like last night?"

"Because we know better tonight. We have to stop. Now." She sighed in frustration. "Couldn't they have the conversation in the lobby?"

Armand pulled her hand away and kissed the palm. "But I never had the chance to do it with my parents in the same house. I was robbed of an adolescent experience."

"Because I don't do quiet." She bit the tip of his ear lobe, and he groaned in pleasure. "Not well, anyway. And you're killing me. You have to stop. *I* have to stop."

"I thought you did quiet very well last night." He kissed her again, but she averted her face. "You have to prove me wrong."

"You do want to get me fired." She dangled their handcuffed wrists. "What about this?"

"We managed very well last night."

"We were clumsy."

"Wonderfully clumsy. Uniform on or off or partially on or off? I'm easy."

The people outside dispersed. Footsteps echoed and doors opened and closed.

Emily stood up and plopped his hat on his head. "Yes, you are easy. As much as I want to—would love to—with and without the uniform," she lifted their handcuffed hands, "and with or without these, we can't. Not until the car thefts are solved and I'm neither a witness nor a victim. You've already put your job on the line for," she wanted to say sex, but it wasn't just sex. It was more. "For me. We have to at least try to be honest."

"Even if the harm is done?"

"Yes, even if the harm is done."

Armand took a deep breath. "You're an honorable woman, Ms. Atterberry. But the instant these car thefts are solved, I'm bringing out this uniform again."

"The whole package," she said slyly. "And I'm undressing you."

"You're killing me, Emily."

She laughed softly as she held out her free hand for a handshake. Armand took it and kissed the inside of it. Emily's blood boiled hot with desire. "That was a no-no, Armand."

"Sorry." He held up the wine. "Nightcap and some talk instead? I'm all by my lonesome here tonight again."

"Wine and chatting are acceptable. I think."

But one glass of wine mingled with lots of talk of her work and his work, and her family and his, led to another glass and to another until the bottle was finished. The chairs were uncomfortable. Armand set his parka on the floor and still handcuffed, they sat down next to each other and sipped and talked. Darryl texted Armand just before midnight. Nicole had false contractions and was home again. He would head over, but Armand told him to stay put. He would bite the bullet and spend the night.

Emily shook her head in dismay. She hoped she could distance herself, but she was very wrong. The lovemaking the night before was wonderful but the talking and sitting was just as wonderful. This wasn't about lust and sex anymore. This was about lovemaking and longing and friendship. It had all the makings of love.

Holy moly, this couldn't be about love! She had to steel herself against him and keep this to lust. Not even friendship was good. Friendship with lust led to longing and could lead to what was impossible. He was an officer of the law and under her appraiser front she was a petty thief. The relationship had to end here and now. Right this very moment. He drew closer. She let him and even snuggled into his embrace.

How the hell would she pull away when her heart and soul pulled her in? She couldn't listen to her heart or her soul. She had to listen to her head. There was no scenario between her and Armand that would end up well for either of them.

Chapter Twenty

Emily woke up the same way she did the night before. On the floor but this time sitting against the wall, fully clothed, one arm around Armand, the other handcuffed to him.

She stared at him a long time, wanting to run her fingers through his hair and kiss him until he stirred. Earlier, she succeeded in not ripping off his uniform and making love with him but the talking and the cuddling were just as nice. Tender and loving.

But it stopped here. It couldn't go further, and it started from this instant. She would work around the clock until she left King Court. She wouldn't have time for Armand, and he couldn't sway her. It was the only way to drift apart.

Not to be with Armand or to see him was emptiness. But she would be devastated if he found out she was a thief. Whatever good he thought of her would be no more. He'd never want to see her again.

She checked her cell. It was just after one. Too late to scout out Colm Saunders' barn with his train collection. She'd set her alarm for early in the morning and go out for a jog in the direction of the barn. She'd bring her tools and money in case no one was around to see her if she went in.

She checked Armand's coat pockets for the handcuffs' key. Nothing. She spied his key chain on the farthest corner of the desk. But, if she stood up, she would drag Armand with her, and he would wake up. He drank more of the wine than she did and now slept peacefully. She didn't want to disturb his sound sleep.

She took a pen from his jacket and picked the lock with the metal hook. The handcuffs clicked open.

She removed the cuffs from around her wrist and Armand's and put them on the table. She moved his key chain closer, so it appeared she used the key, and sneaked out. In her bedroom, she set her alarm for five and got into bed even though she wished she could go back and lay against Armand.

Emily woke up before her alarm went off. She changed into her track outfit and put her tools and the money in her inside pocket. She was at the back door, leading outside when Theresa and Jerome came out of their bedroom.

"Good morning," they said.

"Good morning."

"You must be an avid jogger," Theresa said.

"At least five kilometers every day. Even in below freezing temperatures."

"We did too, once upon a time, didn't we, Jerome?"

"Now we're living happily ever after with extra mileage on our waists."

Emily smiled. "You still start your day pretty early."

"The film crew will be here in an hour and we want to get breakfast going." Jerome held the door open for her. "Enjoy your run."

"Thank you. I will." She went outside. It was dark and cold, and she wished she didn't have to check the barn. If all went well, she would attempt to retrieve the train car.

She warmed up and headed out of the inn. She jogged along the street, following the directions to Colm Saunders' home on her cell's GPS until she came to a group of old but well-maintained, red-bricked farmhouses, separated from each other by at least an acre or two of land.

The homes were lovely with wrap-around verandas, shutters, and decorative moldings. Even though she was a city girl, she could see herself living in one of those Victorian homes.

She wondered if Armand lived in one—no, she had to stop thinking of him. She wasn't setting up house with him. She would go back to Toronto when her job at the Acadia Inn was over and he would never know about her little side job as a thief.

She found Colm Saunders' house. No one was on the street. There weren't even any lights on in the other homes.

She jogged onto the driveway. If anyone saw her, she'd say she heard someone in distress.

Keeping away from snow or mud, so she wouldn't leave shoe prints, she jogged along the side of the house and to the back. Several barns stood in various stages of repair. She peeked into the windows until she came to one barn. It was fully renovated and freshly painted with a picture of a train on the door.

She peered inside but couldn't see much. She moved around the barn to check for a security or alarm system, but she couldn't see anything—no wires, no panels, nothing to indicate there was one. That wasn't to say there wasn't, but she was here, no one was around, and it was now or never.

The door was at the back, facing a vast garden extending into a ravine and a forested area. She picked the lock and opened the door, waiting for an alarm. Nothing. There wasn't even a key panel to disarm an alarm.

She slipped out of her runners, leaving them outside and padded inside, closing the door behind her. There were hundreds of trains on tables, on shelves along the wall, in curios and in opened crates, some new, some old, some wooden, and some plastic. She knew nothing about trains but Colm Saunders had an impressive collection and it had to be worth a fortune.

She moved around the tables, looking at all of them with the flashlight of her cell. She checked curios and crates until she came to a worktable. Several wooden trains were on shelves above it. She spotted the one she looked for, and her heart pounded in expectation and fear. It was at the very end of the first shelf and had the same design as the first train car she found at Halloran's Antiques.

She took it down. It wasn't the middle train car she hoped it would be but the end one. It had a similar design as the train car she had. Trees and the other side of the house. This side of the house however had a tricycle in front.

On a piece of paper, she wrote, *Sorry. Will return ASAP.* She folded the sheet, put five hundred dollars inside, and placed it on the shelf, exactly where the train had been.

She put the train car in her inside pocket and left. She locked the door and put her runners on. It was still dark, but it wouldn't be long before the sun came out.

She turned around and gasped.

A girl stared at her with her mouth opened. "Now I know why you wanted me to run. You're just like me. A thief."

Chapter Twenty-One

Emily couldn't move. Except for the policewoman ten years ago, no one ever saw her leave a store after breaking into it. Until this moment and this girl.

She said she was a thief, too. Who was she? Her eyes widened. This couldn't be. "Are you the girl who stole my cars?"

"Don't recognize me? Good. Don't have on my model look today. Too much time and work. High maintenance and everything else."

She wore a toque, covering up her hair but behind the dark-rimmed eyeglasses were chestnut colored eyes and not some blue violet shade. "It's not what you think," Emily stammered.

"Really?"

The girl adjusted a big knapsack and pushed the toque off her forehead. Without the heavy makeup she not only looked like a different person but her age. Sixteen or seventeen as Emily thought.

"You don't look like the cleaning lady," she said. "I saw you take a little train."

"I left money for it."

"Yeah, it threw me off. Why?"

"Because it's not right."

"Then why did you take it?"

Emily had to tell her the truth. "If I tell you, will you tell me why you stole my cars?"

She dropped her knapsack on the mat in front of the door and sat down on a bench. "You first."

Emily sat next to her. "I need this particular train car. It's part of a larger set. It's worthless to Colm Saunders but it means the world to me."

"You couldn't buy it from Mr. Saunders?"

"It's a long and complicated story."

She settled on the bench. "I don't have an appointment to keep."

Emily took a deep breath. "Three train cars make up a set. I have the first train car and need the other two. There is a scene etched on the three cars. When you put them together, they tell a story or show a place. The story or the place may lead me to my biological parents."

She pushed back her glasses. "You're adopted?"

"I was adopted when I was one year old. I had a wooden figurine of a girl on me, and I've had it ever since. My figurine fit perfectly in the first train car I— the first one I borrowed, too. I have every intention of returning them, after I find the middle one. The middle train car has the majority of the scene. The artist's signature may also be on the middle car."

"You want to know who your biological parents are?"

"I have reservations." She may as well be honest. "Fears, actually, but this is an opportunity I can't pass up. It's not every day a chance presents itself to find out about your past and your biological family."

"How did you come across the first car?"

"Well, that's an interesting story, too. My sister stole a wooden horse." The girl's eyes widened. "When we were younger, we used to dare each other to see who could break into a store without security cameras or alarms, take something, and then return it. We didn't do it for ten years until she came across the wooden horse and decided to see if she still had it. I sent her packing home and told her I would return the horse. Then I saw the first train car."

"Wow. Interesting way of getting over boredom—and trying to get your sister into trouble."

"It wasn't boredom. It was stupidity. We were good and thought ourselves invincible."

"How did you learn to pick locks and do ninja-quiet moves?"

Emily toed the snow around her. "My parents and other professionals taught me."

"What?" She almost laughed. "My parents teach me how to do the laundry."

"My parents are master locksmiths. They can crack any lock. They taught me, and I taught my sister. I could have ended in juvenile court if a policewoman hadn't stopped my extra-curricular activities."

She leaned against the wall to get comfortable. "Is that why you let me go?"

Emily shifted, too. "I saw myself in you. I saw what a policewoman saw in me ten years ago. The chance to make amends and go straight. It wasn't like I was keeping what I stole. It was a stupid but dangerous game between me and my sister. You're not keeping the cars, are you?"

She averted her gaze and shook her head.

"You're also not doing it for kicks, are you? Like my sister and I were?"

"No." She fiddled with the straps of her knapsack. "I had to."

The sun was rising. Emily had to get back to the inn, but this young girl needed an ear and a friend. "Had to?"

"I screwed up with your first car by crashing it into the ravine. I had to bring them another one." Tears jumped into her eyes and she pointed to a garbage bin at the side of the barn. "They killed my dog. I put him in a bag and in there. The ground is too frozen to bury him." Tears slid down her cheeks. "They were going to hurt my family if I didn't bring them a car."

Emily put her arms around her. The girl moved against her and cried. She needed more than a friend. She needed guidance and support.

"You need to go to the police, sweetheart. These are dangerous people making you do what you don't want to."

She brushed her tears with the sleeve of her ski jacket. "They gave me these things." She opened another garbage bin, pulling out a big bag. She undid the knot to show Emily what was inside. "A Canada Goose parka, Ugg's boots, and Gucci sunglasses. I took them because I really wanted them. All the other girls in my school have them and I wanted them, too." She tied the bag up again. "But when they told me what they needed me to do, I gave everything back, but they wouldn't take them. When I still refused, they killed my dog and said my family would be hurt next. I don't even want to see these things anymore. I don't want them." She threw the bag back in the bin and dropped onto the bench.

Emily noticed the packed knapsack. She was sure it wasn't filled with books. "Are you running away from home?"

The girl wiped her eyes of any lingering tears and averted her gaze.

Emily knew the answer. "Do you think leaving home will make everything better?"

"It'll keep my family safe."

"And you? Will you be safe?"

"I can take care of myself."

"I'm sure you can, but you'll hurt your family just the same as the people forcing you to steal—if not worse. They'll search for you endlessly."

The girl pulled her gloves higher on her hands. "I'm damned if I do and damned if I don't. It will at least keep them safe and me away from those people."

"They would much rather have you with them than be without you, not knowing why you left or where you went." She moved to the edge and put her hand over hers. "You need to go to the police and tell them what you told me. They'll protect you and your family and take these people down."

Her eyes rounded in surprise. "You didn't rat me out?"

"No, I didn't. I did give them a description of you. But you look completely different. The picture I gave is of another girl. I wouldn't have recognized you if you didn't call yourself a thief. Did they doll you up?"

"They did my hair with a color that would wash out and put lots of makeup on my face. I felt big and older. They even gave me colored contact lenses. I liked how I looked. Beautiful. Now, I hate how I looked and what I did."

"Then make it good. Turn the bad into a good. If you want, I can come with you to the police. No charges will be laid if you tell them you were forced to steal the cars. I know about the other stolen cars. The people forced to steal might also be the same age as you."

She stood up and picked up her knapsack. "I can't."

Emily jumped up and put her hand on the girl's arm. "Will you at least think about it?" The girl kept her gaze averted. "Do you really want to leave home?"

Tears came back into the girl's eyes.

"I'm staying at the Acadia Inn for the next week or so. I'm Emily. Come and see me, and we can talk a little more. This is big, sweetheart. Me stealing a wooden train car with little monetary value is not legal but it's not dangerous. The people who forced you to steal are dangerous. I'm more than willing to come with you to the police. Think about it, okay? Go back home today and think it over. Unfortunately, you told me the story and I have to tell the police, or I'll be in trouble. But I won't do it right away. I'll give you the rest of today, okay? If I don't hear from you tonight, then I will tell the police." The girl didn't move, which told Emily she considered it. "Where do you live?"

The girl pointed at several houses down the street. "Let me walk you home."

Keeping her head bowed, the girl put her knapsack on her back and walked with Emily toward the house. Snow and ice crunched under their feet as they ambled in heavy silence.

"End of today?" the girl asked.

"End of today."

She was quiet until they passed a house. "I won't rat on you, Emily. I owe you big time."

Emily hugged her. "Sweetheart, you don't owe me

anything." But she was grateful. "Just don't leave home, okay?"

They moved to the first house and the girl stopped at the driveway. "This is it."

"I'll see you tonight, okay?"

The girl nodded and walked toward the veranda.

Emily jogged off. When she arrived at the intersection, the girl moved away from the house.

That was one smart but unhappy girl. Emily now was more involved with the car thefts, and with the man she was distancing herself from.

Chapter Twenty-Two

Armand banged his face against something hard. He opened his eyes. It was a wall.

He rolled onto his back, forcing his eyes to stay open. Monitors stared back at him, showing pictures of the inn. His hands fell to the floor. Had he fallen asleep on the floor of the security office, he lifted his arms, and in his uniform?

Well, that was a first for him.

He spied the empty bottle of wine lying next to the garbage bin. And that was the reason…and Emily. She was loosening him, making him forget about rigid rules of appearance and conduct, and he didn't mind in the least.

He sat up. Where was she? He was positive she'd slept beside him.

He grabbed his cell from the desk. It was just after seven. Nicole would be here shortly, and he could go home and shower and change.

The handcuffs were placed around his key chain in front of a monitor. He forgot about the cuffs. Emily found the key and unclasped them.

He just couldn't remember when.

His cell vibrated. It was a text from Emily. "Are you up?"

He texted back. "Yup."

"Quick chat in the kitchen now?"

Chat, now? Was he in trouble? "Be right out," he texted back.

Armand stretched and went into the kitchen. Emily sat at the table, looking fresh. She wore a suit, sipped at her coffee, and checked her phone for messages.

"Good morning," he said. There was a carafe of coffee on the counter along with bagels, muffins, and croissants. Several industrial-sized pots sat empty on the stove. He took a mug and poured some coffee. "Where's everyone?"

"Good morning. My colleagues are in their rooms. Jerome and Theresa made breakfast and are setting it out in the barn for the film crew. They left eggs and sausages in the oven if you'd like some. I haven't seen the Sherrers, but Marilyn and I are meeting with the art appraiser at ten."

"How long have you been up?" He grabbed a bagel and some cream cheese and sat next to her.

"Crack of dawn. Even went for a jog."

"Without me?" He stirred cream into his coffee.

"You were out cold. I had an interesting jog."

"Oh?"

"I ran into the girl who stole my cars."

He stopped spreading the cream cheese. "Was she stealing another car?"

"No. She was running away from home."

He put the bagel down. "You talked to her?"

"I did. She's being forced to steal the cars. When she refused, they killed her dog and threatened to hurt her family if she didn't go through with the thefts."

"Did she tell you her name? Do you know where she lives?"

"She wouldn't tell me her name, but I did bring her

to a house. It wasn't hers. When I got to the intersection, I saw her moving away from it."

"Could you identify the house?"

"Only the one I led her to." She cleared her throat. "I struck a deal with her. I wanted to chat with you about it."

He moved his chair closer. "You struck a deal with her?"

"I told her she had to turn herself in by the end of tonight or I would."

Armand was baffled. He took a bite of the bagel but didn't chew it with relish.

"I didn't want to force her hand, Armand. She was running away from home. She's very unhappy and she's afraid for her family. I took her home, and she agreed to this. Can you honor it?"

Armand swallowed. "You gave her until tonight?"

"Until tonight—sundown. I said I would even go with her to the police station if she needed me, but if she comes before tonight, I don't know if I'll be able to see her. I don't know how long the art appraiser will be."

"If she shows up here, call me and I'll talk with her. Get Nicole or Darryl involved if you have to. They're both ex cops. They'll know how to handle her until I get here."

"Thank you for understanding."

He put his hand over hers, but she pulled it away, looking around.

"Sorry," he all but sang. His phone buzzed. "Mrs. Halloran, good morning. You've been my first phone call or appointment these past few mornings."

"Sorry to wake you up but you won't believe this. I

found five hundred dollars in an envelope. It arrived in the mail—or it was dropped into my mailbox, I'm not sure. There's a sticky note on it. It says, *"For the train. Sorry for breaking in."*

Armand held his mug in midair.

"Are you there, Armand?"

"I'm here." He put the mug down. "When did you find it?"

"This morning. It must have been left yesterday or the night of the robbery because it was under a pile of my mail."

"I'll be there as soon as I can." He hung up.

"What's up?" Emily asked.

"The thief left money for the stolen train car at Halloran's Antiques."

"You're kidding?"

"Nope. This is the strangest theft I've ever dealt with."

After Nicole arrived, Armand went home to shower and change into a suit. He headed to Halloran's Antiques. Mrs. Halloran handed him the envelope with the message. "Five hundred dollars. In fifties and twenties. The thief probably used an ATM."

Armand was about to drop the envelope with the money into a big paper envelope. "You realize I have to take this money."

Mrs. Halloran grabbed the envelope. "No, you're not. It's my money. Consider the case closed."

"You're not pressing charges?"

"The thief came into my store twice, but he left far more money than the train car is worth. He could have taken more valuable things but didn't."

"But it's not right. The thief broke the law. He

needs to answer for it and be punished."

Mrs. Halloran took out the money and handed him the envelope. "You can take the envelope but I'm keeping this. If you find him tell him I said thank you for the sale and for not taking more valuable things. Tell him to use the front door during business hours next time. It will cost him less."

Armand dropped it inside. Then it struck him. If someone wanted the train, wouldn't he also want the other pieces? "Do you know if anyone has the keys to Colm Saunders train barn?"

"Probably Jessica. She's watching her grandparents' home while they're gone. Why? You think the train car that goes with this was taken, too?"

"Only one way to find out." He strode across the street to Koffee & Tez. Jessica ground the Valentine's blend. He recognized the dense but sweet aroma.

"Hey, Armand. Your usual or do you want to taste the Valentine brew? Everyone is buying it. They think it might work like Cupid's arrows."

"Nothing today, thanks." He thought of Emily. "Maybe tomorrow. Do you have the key to your grandfather's barn, the one with his trains?"

"I do. Why?"

"I'm investigating the theft of a specific train set, and Mrs. Halloran told me your grandfather has one of the other pieces. I'm curious to see if the piece is missing, too."

"You want to check now?"

"Is it possible?"

Jessica turned to a young woman. "Can you take care of the shop for about half an hour?"

She put her coat on and sat in Armand's car. They

drove to her grandparents' home and to the barn.

"When was the last time you came here?" Armand asked, following Jessica to a well-maintained barn.

"About two weeks ago."

Armand stopped and put his hand on her arm to keep her from moving forward. "There are footprints here. Two sets." One even looked like the size seven Dr. Martens found at the scene of Emily's first stolen car.

"Neither are mine," Jessica said. "My parents are visiting my grandparents. They're not theirs either."

Armand took pictures of both shoe prints. If the train car was missing, he'd be back with an evidence collection kit and a better camera.

Jessica unlocked the barn door. "What are you looking for?"

He showed her a picture of the train car stolen from Mrs. Halloran's store. "If it's missing, there'll be a note."

"A note?"

"You'll understand if you find one."

They walked around. Armand had never seen so many train sets and from all over the world. It was impressive.

"Armand?" Jessica was at a worktable, pointing to the end of a shelf. Armand went to her. His instincts were bang on. He put on a pair of latex gloves and removed a folded paper. *Sorry. Will return ASAP.* He unfolded the paper. Inside was five hundred dollars.

Chapter Twenty-Three

After Armand left, Emily moved to the restaurant and sat at the bar. She was early for the meeting with the art expert and her supervisor and hoped to continue appraising the furniture.

But the furniture and paintings were the furthest from her thoughts.

She was in over her head with the theft of the train cars. She was putting her job on the line. If those train cars hadn't come into her life, she would be singing high notes of praise. She was about to become a certified furniture appraiser and on the road to becoming an art one thanks to the paintings of Marie-Anne Couture. More importantly, she was on her way to forming a beautiful relationship with a wonderful man.

But all she wanted to do was run away from the Acadia Inn, King Court, and Armand.

She was putting both her career and relationship with Armand in jeopardy. She was stealing. She never stole anything she hadn't returned. She couldn't believe she resorted to theft to get what she wanted. What was worse she couldn't rest until she found the third and final piece, the middle train, which held the complete picture of where she came from.

Why did she even want to know where she came from or who her biological family was? They abandoned her twenty-five years before. She should stop and return the train cars. The girl saw her but promised not to say anything. She was in enough trouble as it was. But if Armand found out, her job and future would be ruined and so would Isla's and her family's. Her story would come out. Her family's story would come out. It was ancient history, but it could catch up with them.

Armand would be hurt. She knew he felt the same about her as she did about him. Hopeful. Eager. Excited about being together. For now, and possibly longer. She didn't want him to think she had deceived him. How could he ever forgive her or himself for experiencing emotions for a petty thief?

"Everything okay?"

Emily jumped. Katrina was at the end of the bar, putting down a tray of coffee and mugs. "I'm sorry, I frightened you."

"No, I was far away. Lost in thoughts."

She moved closer. "You looked sad."

Emily managed a wry smile. "Have you ever had everything wonderful happen to you and know it could turn bad at the same moment?"

Katrina pulled out a stool and sat down, tucking her skirt under her. She was also making the rounds with the art expert and wore a suit. A deep blue blouse added some color to her pale skin. "Unfortunately, yes." She indicated the restaurant. "I had all this, and I blew it. Blew something even more important, too. A relationship with a wonderful man. It's not a good situation."

"No, it's not."

"Armand?"

Emily laughed. "How did you know it was Armand?"

"Well, let me count the ways." She crossed her legs and leaned back. "He runs here every chance he gets and can't stay away from you or the security office, which is in front of your room. He can't stop being close to you. He looks at you like he's seeing you for the first time. He—"

Emily put her hand on her arm. "He's an open book. I know. But I like it. I know exactly where he stands—unfortunately, so does everyone else. He isn't a fake." Like she was. "We're having difficulty staying in our professional zones."

"It's only until the car theft investigation is over. You should enjoy this stage of the relationship. The dreamy-eyed stage." Katrina's blue eyes lit up. "When the mist leaves your eyes, you'll be back down to earth and it's not nice."

"Seems like you're talking from experience. Like you crashed from the stars."

"I crashed big time, Emily. I lost the inn and restaurant and someone I loved."

"No hope of salvaging the relationship?"

"No." She thought about it. "Not now anyway. I have to focus on the inn and restaurant first and where I'm going after I hand the keys to the new owner." Sadness crept into her eyes. "I chose every one of the chairs and tables in this restaurant. I fought with the painters for the right color on the walls and with the sous chefs who wanted to change what I created. I built this restaurant and the menu from nothing, and I lost everything."

The sorrow—the grief in Katrina's eyes saddened

her. "You don't have to lose everything. I've appraised a lot of the furniture in here, but we can put it all on hold if you want to keep it back."

Katrina remained silent for a long time. "No. It'll bring in good money. We need to sell it. It has to be sold."

"What if you decide to open up another restaurant? The same as you had here? You have the furniture already. You still have your dream—whether you can see it or not. No one can take it away from you—except you. Hold onto it. Why start from scratch again when you have so much of it already?"

Katrina's gaze moved around the restaurant, stopping on different pieces of furniture. She was undecided. Emily put her hand on hers again. "I'm putting a hold on everything in here."

Katrina let out a long breath and a small smile shaped her lips. She made one little nod. "Our secret, okay?"

"Of course." She heard a lot of confessions and secrets today.

"You can appraise whatever you haven't done yet in here, and I'll let you know what I decide before the auction begins."

"Not a problem." She squeezed her hand. "Now, you're back in the clouds and in ownership of your dream again."

"Marginally," Katrina sighed. "But it's a start. Thank you, Emily."

Emily smiled. Katrina hoped again but what about her? If Armand or anyone else found out about her, her time in the clouds and her dreams were also at stake.

Chapter Twenty-Four

Armand sat at his desk at the police station. He updated Patricia on both train car thefts, Emily's unexpected run in with the girl who stole her cars, and the deal they struck. Patricia wanted the girl for questioning now but agreed to wait until nightfall. By this time tomorrow, Armand hoped the car thieves would be in jail and the girl and the others forced to steal safe.

He opened a drawer, and his gaze fell on a key. It was for his handcuffs. He had sets of keys hidden in different places. One in his cruiser's glove compartment, one in his camera bag, and the last one on his key chain. He checked his camera bag. It was in a zippered compartment. He ran out to his car and checked the glove compartment. It was there. He pulled out his key chain. It wasn't there.

He went back inside and slipped the key in his drawer on the chain.

So how did Emily unclasp the handcuffs if the key wasn't on his chain?

He leaned back in his seat. She had her lock picking set, the one she used for the fetters and foot shackles. But did she have it on her when he pulled her into the security office last night? He was sure she didn't.

But she must have. How else could she unlock the

handcuffs?

He took out his cell and called Mrs. Halloran.

"What a pleasant surprise, Armand, but I don't have anything else to add to my statement."

"It's not about the theft. I have a question for you. Do furniture appraisers carry lock-picking utensils?"

She hemmed and hawed. "Maybe. A lock in a buffet may need to be opened with something like a pick if there is no key."

"What do you do when you can't find a key to a buffet or some other piece that needs opening?"

"I call in a locksmith. I get him to make me a key. The piece is devalued without the original key but at least the buyer has something if he or she wants to lock it."

"Thank you, you've been helpful." He closed the phone and Googled locksmiths in Toronto. Many came up. He put in "Atterberry". His heart missed a beat when Regal Master Locksmiths showed the owners as Russell and Claire Atterberry.

Emily's parents were locksmiths. So, what? They made locks and keys and knew how to crack them. If they taught her how to open or rather *pick* locks it came in handy with her line of work.

He didn't want to do it, but he couldn't stop. He plugged Russell Atterberry into the police database, and his name came up. Heat drained from Armand's face. His file, however, was sealed. Whatever he did was pardoned. He tried Claire Atterberry and her name came up too, but the file was also sealed. He needed permission from the Minister of Public Safety to access the files and read about their crimes and pardon.

He moved back against his chair, his stomach

coiling into a knot. Emily's parents had a past with the law. Their line of work made him believe it had to do with picking locks. Possibly breaking and entering and stealing.

No. He moved forward. He couldn't jump to conclusions and assume whatever they did was passed on to Emily.

His heart thumping, he plugged in Emily Atterberry. He let out a big sigh of relief, which made Bassam look at him quizzically. Nothing came up. She had no police record.

A picture of the train car stolen at Halloran's Antiques peeked out from beneath a file folder. He pulled it out.

The wooden horse was stolen Sunday night. Emily had spent the night in Ottawa with her sister when the theft occurred.

The wooden horse was returned Monday night after Halloran's Antiques closed but the wooden train car was stolen the same night. Emily was with him that night. From the time he arrived at the inn, around 5:30 or 6:00 until they went for a jog, around 9:00 or 9:30 and again after midnight. The only time she wasn't with him was when he went home to change into his jogging outfit. He wasn't more than half an hour. He left Emily in front of Koffee & Tez and returned not to find her. A few minutes later he heard her yelling about the theft of her second Camry. Lowan took them back to the inn around eleven. He assumed she stayed at the inn when he returned home to clean up. She couldn't have gone out if she didn't have a car.

The next day Emily went with him to Halloran's Antiques. She walked around the store and left to pick up her dry cleaning while he spoke to Mrs. Halloran about the train car.

Last night she was with him for a while until she unclasped the handcuffs and returned to her bedroom. She told him she went jogging early in the morning and ran into the girl who stole her cars. She didn't tell him where—holy crap!

His sat up straight, his heart thumping like offkey drum strikes. There were two sets of footprints in the snow outside Colm Saunders' train barn.

He checked the photos of the footprints, some falling on the floor in his agitation. One set was the women's size seven Dr. Martens, which were also found at the scene of Emily's first stolen car, but the other set of shoe prints were—he held up the photo. Runners. He recognized the tread. He had a similar pair. The second shoe prints were of runners and the size was small, possibly belonging to a woman.

He covered his face with trembling hands. This could not be. Did the shoe print belong to Emily? Did Emily take the train car from Colm Saunders' barn the morning she told him she went jogging?

This did not make sense. What the hell for? Both train cars were worth nothing. There were more valuable things in both Halloran's Antiques and Colm Saunders' barn. What was so special about the train cars?

He couldn't think rationally. His thoughts raced as fast as his heart.

This could not be right. There was some mistake. He was implicating Emily—accusing her. She was far too good, compassionate, and sensible to steal two worthless train cars. She was the woman he couldn't stop thinking about. The woman reminding him to focus on the moral implications of their relationship.

Dammit, she was the woman he wanted to be with.

He jumped up. He had to look at her runners. It was the only way to clear her.

He raced to his car and to the Acadia Inn. Lowan was filming his last scenes, and the lot was full, but he found a place close to the entrance.

He strode to the kitchen. Nicole was surprised to see him and dropped her sandwich on the plate. "Everything okay? You look like you've seen the ghost of inn pasts."

"Are the appraisers around?"

She balked at his directness as she put her sandwich together again. "Yes, two are in different guest rooms on the first floor and Emily, her supervisor, and Katrina are in the restaurant with some big-time art appraiser from Ottawa."

"And Darryl and your crew?"

"Installing cameras in the top floor bedrooms."

Armand strode to the window, which was almost the entire back wall. The crew was filming a scene with Lowan confronting the female assassin from the Crystalline Planet. He jingled his key chain. How could he get into Emily's room and check her runners?

"Are you sure you're all right?" Nicole asked. "You look tense."

"I'm fine. How's Carli?"

"Same. She hugged both me and Darryl this morning, which scared us at first. It made us wonder what she wanted. But she didn't want anything and went off to school as if nothing was wrong." Her cell buzzed. "Darryl needs me upstairs. Help yourself to a sandwich."

The instant Nicole was out of the kitchen, Armand raced to Emily's bedroom. He tried the knob, but it was locked.

What the hell was he doing? His anxieties flowed out of his body and pooled at his feet. He couldn't believe he thought Emily stole both train cars.

"Hey."

Armand flinched. Emily stood at the entrance. "Hey." His voice croaked.

"I'm not in there."

"No, but I thought I might blow your door down and see if you were. Probable cause. Needed to make sure the appraising wasn't taking its toll on you."

"As you can see, I'm fine."

"You're more than fine, ma'am." He made a move to take her in his arms when she stepped away. What was he thinking? He thought her a thief, promised not to compromise her, but couldn't stop from taking her in his arms and smothering her with kisses.

"Detective Lecavalier…"

"Yeah, yeah, yeah."

She inserted her key and opened the door. "I haven't heard from the girl yet. Both Katrina and I are showing Marilyn and the art appraiser the various paintings around the inn. I asked Jerome and Nicole to let me know if anyone comes looking for me. So far, she hasn't shown up. She does officially have until night fall."

"I plan on being here the instant I'm off work."

"I'm sure you will."

"Dinner?"

Emily's eyes rounded as though she were about to

scold him. "What did we speak about this morning, *Detective Lecavalier*?"

"Yeah, yeah, yeah." He was in turmoil. He was a mess and it was foreign to him. He was never a mess—until this beautiful woman came into his life and deliriously turned it upside down. But now even that was upset in a way he didn't like and couldn't manage. "I remember. You on a break now?"

"I have to grab a file." She squeezed his hand and squealed in delight. "The paintings may be worth more than any one of us imagined."

"It's wonderful news for the Sherrers."

"Exactly, but also for me. I discovered them. I may go from furniture to art overnight."

"Does this mean I'll have to learn more than Hepplewhite chairs?" There he went again. Thinking about a future with her.

He had to clear her name. He wanted to think about a future with her in it. It was all a mistake. That was all. Emily was pure gold.

Emily went soft. She grabbed him by the coat, pulled him into her room, slammed the door, and kissed him.

Armand cupped her face with his hands. "Ms. Atterberry, what is the meaning of taking advantage of an officer of the law?"

She pulled away. "Yeah, yeah, yeah. You were too cute to resist. And I was too happy to resist."

Armand didn't move. "And now?"

She adjusted her jacket. "You're still cute and irresistible but my better judgement is in place again." She moved to her briefcase. "I also have to get back. Just came to grab something. We haven't gone through more than five of the twenty-eight paintings so far."

"I guess I'm in for a lonely night?"

"Lonely nights, Armand."

"Yeah, yeah, yeah, lonely nights. What if I just hang out in your bedroom." He glanced around. "Clean your room and iron your clothes and," he spied her spiky boots and runners on a mat, "buff your weapons?"

She laughed. "Can I take a rain check on all of the above? After we have no professional alliance?"

"Rain check it is."

She removed a couple files from her briefcase. "Even though tidying up my room at this moment sounds wonderful. If you'll excuse me, I need to use the little girl's room." She moved into the bathroom and locked the door.

This was his chance.

His hands shaking, Armand took a picture of the soles of her runners with his cell. He grabbed a paper and drew the shape of the shoe. When he heard the flush of the toilet, he sat down and glanced at the photos of the inn's furniture. "You have a lot of pictures here," he called out.

She came out of the bathroom. "I've downloaded a whole lot more to our website. The auction will also be online." She indicated the door. "Well, thank you for stopping by and making sure I'm all right, Detective Lecavalier."

"Yeah, yeah, yeah." He stood up. "I'll be back later for the arrival of our infamous girl."

"She'll be here. Don't know when, but she'll turn up. I have faith in her." She opened the door, peered out, and pushed him out. "Later, Detective." She locked the door.

"Yeah, yeah, yeah." Armand's false buoyancy deflated. He was scum. But this was the only way to clear her. And he would. He was sure of it.

He returned to the police station and checked the photo of the shoe against the imprint of the one taken in the snow. He measured both. His heart jumped hurdles and he became unsteady. Something was wrong. They were the same. Exactly the same. They were a brand name runner and other female joggers wore them but spots showing wear and a minute indentation where a pebble lodged were visible. The pebble was still in Emily's runner.

He put his head in his hands. Why? If Emily stole both those train cars, why? What was their significance? What was her motivation?

He threw the photos into a folder. There was some mistake. There had to be. He had to clear her and move on to finding the real thief. He could then breathe easily again. He'd get his life and control back. But the only way to eliminate her as the suspect would be to make up a ruse and lay in wait. When she didn't come for the train car as he believed she wouldn't, he could rule her out. He had to rule her out. He was falling hard for Emily. He couldn't be falling in love with a thief. That would be the biggest slap to everything he stood for and believed in.

Chapter Twenty-Five

Emily sat at the bar of the restaurant writing blurbs about the paintings. It had been a long and tiring day. The art appraiser examined all the paintings by Marie-Anne Couture and now it fell on her to write notes and post them on the Kanata Auction House website.

The door opened, and Armand stuck his head in. "Thought I'd find you here."

Emily jumped up, startled.

"Sorry."

She settled herself. "You scared me."

He walked in, wearing the sheriff's costume from his stuntman's job, and holding another costume. "You were deep in your work."

She glanced outside, surprised to see it was night. "How did it get dark so fast?" She glanced at her watch. "Wow. It's almost seven." Now she knew why her stomach growled. She didn't eat dinner. "I lost track of time." She remembered the girl. "The girl hasn't called me or shown up, yet."

Armand nodded. "It's already sundown—ma'am." He sauntered to her, his hand on his hip, showing off his pistol.

"But, Sheriff, I need a little more time. I know my ward will deliver herself to me."

He slung the costume over a stool and lounged on the bar. "There will be consequences to pay if your ward doesn't deliver herself to the law."

Emily flicked his hat off his forehead. "Consequences, Sheriff?"

Armand held up the costume. It was a red and black saloon girl dress, which looked more like a burlesque costume. "This consequence, ma'am."

"Does Lowan know you borrowed two of his costumes?"

"Lowan gave them to me. He asked everyone to be extras in the final scene he's shooting tonight. It's a corral scene—a showdown between Captain Borgman and the female assassin from Crystalline. How about it? Your colleagues are already in costume."

"They're going to be extras?" Conservative Marilyn, stuffy Lubna, and formidable Tatyana agreed?

"Saw them myself. So how about it? It'll be lots of fun."

"I wish I could, but I have to write up the art appraiser's evaluations of the paintings and should I finish, then I have to look respectable and not like a saloon girl when the girl shows up."

"Oh, come on. You've been working since the early morning hours. Give yourself a break." He raised his eyebrows. "I'll even help you write your evaluations."

Emily laughed. "Really?"

"Well, I'll keep the espresso coming so you can write them. Wouldn't know what else to do—except give a little massage here and there."

She stroked his cheek. "The offer is very sweet of you, Sheriff but duty calls."

He pouted. "Will you at least put this costume on and let me see you in it? I'll give the girl until nine o'clock tonight to turn herself in if you do."

Emily shook her head. "This professionalism we're attempting isn't working."

"I'm just asking you to put a costume on."

"Yes, but with a little condition on the side."

"So?"

"Fine. You have a deal. I believe the girl will show up."

He gave her a peck on the cheek. "I can help you in it—and out of it, too."

Emily pushed him away. "Thank you, Sheriff. I'll keep it in mind, but it won't be necessary." She returned to her laptop.

Armand sat on a stool. "Well?"

"Well, what?"

"I'm waiting."

"You want me to put the costume on now?"

"I do. Otherwise, I don't extend my deadline to nine." He indicated the guest bathrooms next to the curio.

Taking a deep breath, Emily took the costume and headed for the bathroom. She removed her clothes and slipped into the gown. The skirt was a little long with a big slit, rising to the top of her thigh. The neckline was low and snug, showing the swell of her breasts. Her hair needed to be done up in some disheveled but lascivious arrangement, but she tucked a red feather behind her ear and slipped on the long black gloves.

She moved to the bathroom door. "Ready?"

"Always, babe, always."

She moved out and struck a pose. "Well, Sheriff?"

Armand pushed his hat back. "You look like a beautiful Valentine gift. *My* Valentine gift. You need to always wear red."

She held up the skirt. "It's a little long for me. I think I need my high-heeled boots, not working girl pumps."

"You mean your weapons? You'd be a dangerous Valentine gift—which of course is fine with me, too. But right now, it looks great just as it is. You look great."

She sat on the stool, crossed her leg, exposing it, and leaned toward him. "Drink, Sheriff?"

"On duty, ma'am."

"Pity." She covered up her leg, surprising him. "I've put it on. Now are you going to let me continue with my work?"

"Not on your life. Come on. It'll be lots of fun. You're going to be on television."

"Work before pleasure." She faced her laptop and removed the gloves.

"I would applaud your work ethic if you weren't depriving me of your company."

She flicked the gloves at him. "Maybe we can borrow these costumes another time and add the furry handcuffs when you find them. Like after the car thefts are solved."

Armand dropped the gloves on the counter and gave her a quick kiss on the cheek. "Deal." He leaned in to view the photographs of the paintings. "So everything went well with the art expert?"

"Better than expected. She appraised all of them and said the style was exactly as I said, but of course I didn't tell her. An unschooled or rustic Impressionist style. They showed the 'perspective of the home-schooled female.' What she wanted to say was the paintings showed the natural talents of the lowly-educated female worker of the late eighteenth century in Ontario."

"From the perspective of someone who hasn't been to an art gallery since high school, it sounds impressive to me."

She turned her full attention on him, making him balk. "You haven't been to an art gallery since high school?"

"Sorry…"

"This has to change, Armand."

His grin was enthusiastic, and he drew closer. "You going to change it?"

"Of course, I am—when the car theft investigation is over, of course." She pushed him back. "We'll start with the Art Gallery of Ottawa. They have a wonderful collection of Canadian art, and then we'll have to go to the McMichael Canadian Art Collection in Kleinburg just outside Toronto and see some of the Group of Seven paintings and Emily Carr's work, and it's just a start. You won't fall asleep on me, will you?"

"Not if you're giving me the tour."

"I'm getting carried away, aren't I? I'm sorry."

He adjusted the feather in her hair. "I'm not sorry. I want you to get carried away." He leaned in closer. "And finally hear you scream," he added in whisper.

She kissed his hand. "But back to the artwork here. The Sherrers agreed to a private viewing in Toronto. More attention and traffic there. All the paintings except those three," she indicated the ones in front of them, "will be shipped off in the next couple of days. And as the junior appraiser on the team, I've not only been tasked with preparing the writeups, which I'm now doing, but to pack them and see they get to our studio in Toronto safely."

"You're leaving?" His voice went higher than expected.

"I'll be back by the weekend. For Valentine' Day, which we may be able to safely celebrate when the girl shows up tonight and you make all the necessary arrests."

"But you'll be gone for a few days."

Emily wanted to dance in joy. He was going to miss her. "This is something Marilyn would normally do but there are some wooden sculptures in the upstairs tea saloon she wants to appraise. It's her forte. She'll leave at the end of the week to set the paintings up in our gallery. They're not excusing me from appraising the furniture here. I'm just making sure the paintings get to Toronto safely and come back."

"Do you at least have time to join the crew and extras for dinner tonight, then?"

"I'll grab something in a little while and bring it here. I have to get these blurbs done by the morning. Then I need to focus on packing the paintings."

Armand twirled in his chair and adjusted the revolver around his belt. He was uncomfortable and it made her nervous. "Jessica may have located the third train car."

Emily kept her expression clear of any emotion, but her heart leaped. "Really?" She added something to the writeup but didn't know what.

Armand picked up her pen and opened and closed it several times. "She spoke to her grandfather, and he said Wilhelm Sherrer bought it."

"One of the train cars is here at the Acadia Inn?"

She said it as neutrally as possible, continuing to type. She couldn't look at him. He would see joy as well as fear in her eyes.

"Seems so." He put the pen down and it rolled to her laptop.

"But I haven't seen any train car in my travels, only the basswood figurines in the curio." She indicated the curio at the end of the bar.

"No, it might be part of Wilhelm's private collection, which he isn't selling. He's packed his collectibles away in his office. I put in a call to him but he, Elsa, and Katrina are on their way to Ottawa. Birthday dinner for their daughter Rebeka. He said he'd check tomorrow morning."

"Well, Armand," she typed a few words but didn't know what. "You might be solving both thefts very soon." Tears jumped into her eyes, but she blinked them away, not wanting Armand to see her reaction. And she might be solving a bigger mystery herself, too. But at the expense of losing Armand. She couldn't carry on with him after so much thieving under his very nose.

Chapter Twenty-Six

Emily closed her laptop and jumped off the stool. "I think I'll move to my bedroom and finish these blurbs there."

"Allow me, ma'am." Armand took the laptop.

"Give me a minute to change." She grabbed her clothes.

Armand put his hand on her arm. "Leave them on."

"But I can't make the shoot."

"And what if you can? Come on, try. I'm sure you can put aside even half an hour to come outside, slip your arm through mine, and cozy up to the sheriff like some wanton female."

Emily smirked. "Won't people talk?"

"They already are."

Emily laughed. "Fine." She gathered her clothes and the black gloves and followed him out of the restaurant, waiting as he locked it. In the kitchen Jerome and Theresa foil wrapped several big stainless-steel pans. Jerome was dressed as a saloon keeper in a white shirt, red vest, black bow tie, pants, and even sleeve garters. A Derby sat on his head. Theresa was a cook in a purple collared shirt and long blue skirt with a pioneer apron over it.

"I thought you were going to be a deputy?" Armand asked Jerome.

"The costume didn't fit. I'm now the saloon

keeper, and I guess Emily works for me?"

"She will if she joins us."

"You won't be joining us?" Theresa asked, surprised. "But you look wonderful. They'll fix your hair, so the hairpiece looks right."

"Unfortunately, as the appraiser in training I have to get some things done for tomorrow."

"Did anyone call for a rancher and his pregnant wife?" From the hallway, Darryl and Nicole came into the kitchen. He wore a red cavalry shirt with a black neckerchief, suspenders, and canvas pants, while Nicole had on a bonnet, shirt, and long walking skirt.

"The beard suits him here," Nicole said, pulling it.

The door leading outside opened and a beautiful woman with long curly black hair stuck her head in. She wore a similar saloon girl outfit as Emily but in red and white. "The director is asking—*demanding* his extras get themselves into the barn for a quickie run-through."

Armand put his hand on Emily's back. "Emily, this is Olivia, Lowan's sister."

"We're both ladies of the night." Olivia walked in and extended her hand.

Emily shook it. "Yes, we both get to be naughty for a couple of hours."

"Don't let it get out of hand," Jerome warned.

"Not to worry, Dad. Those days are over—mostly."

"Mostly?"

"What you don't know can't hurt you."

"Don't say anymore, please. Now, before you turn naughty in my presence, can you carry one of these into the barn?"

"Sure thing." Olivia took a container and left.

Jerome shook his head. "What we do for our children."

"Oh, you're just as excited as am I to be in the film," Theresa said, putting several pans on a three-shelved cart.

Nicole moved to the counter. "Are we going to freeze out there?"

"No. Those massive heaters melted the snow around the corral and will be on full force for the duration of the shoot," Jerome said. "We should be okay. Armand, Darryl, can I ask you to help out, too?"

Armand gave Emily her laptop. "I'll see you later?"

Emily took it and shrugged. She wished she could go out there and join everyone, but she had to do something tonight she wasn't looking forward to. She also had to wait for the girl to show up. It was getting late, but Emily believed she would come.

Armand moved toward the counter. "What can I take?"

"Can you handle this cart of vegetables?" Emily heard Theresa say as she headed toward her room. She glanced at the lock on the Sherrers' office. It was a standard doorknob like the other rooms in the family quarters. The Sherrers upgraded the locks in the guest bedrooms but not these. She could use anything to open it. A hair clip, paper clip, even a credit card. She didn't need her tools. The clip of her hair piece would work well, too.

"Emily, I see you're all dressed up."

Marilyn came out of her room in an emerald and hooped long skirt, black heavy blouse, and coach hat.

"You look great," Emily said.

"So do you. You should see Lubna and Tatyana."

"I won't make the dinner, but I'll try and make it for the shoot."

"I'll see you later."

Emily moved into her bedroom as Marilyn walked past. She put her laptop on the table and slumped into a chair. She wanted to be involved with the film shoot. It sounded like fun. She especially wanted to be with Armand and slip her arm into his. She didn't want to do what she was about to do. She didn't want to break into the Sherrers' office and look for the middle and most important train car. But how could she stop? She couldn't if she tried. She was one small step closer to finding a lead to her biological family. There wouldn't be a more perfect time. No one was around. Everyone would be in the barn having dinner and outside in the corral for the shoot.

It was now or never.

She waited until she heard her other two colleagues walk past, laughing at their costumes. When she didn't hear anyone in the kitchen, she slipped out of her bedroom and checked. She went up and down the hallway, back into the kitchen, the lobby, and the restaurant. The security cameras were set up in all the areas except the hallway of the family quarters and she pretended to look at the paintings again. She rushed to the office door.

She trembled and wanted to cry. She never had any emotion when she broke into those random stores during her youth, took something, broke back in, and returned it. It was how she succeeded. But this theft was different. Armand was paramount in her thoughts and very much in her heart. She would never forgive herself after committing this theft. Worse, she could never be with Armand again. She would have to distance herself from him. She couldn't carry on the pretense of innocence. She was a thief, and he could never know.

There would be no Valentine's celebration for them. Whatever wonderful relationship could evolve never would. And it was all her doing. Her choice for the past instead of the future.

She took the pin from her hairpiece, inserted it into the lock, and within a second opened it. She slipped in and closed the door. The boxes were in the same place as the first day she arrived at the inn—and the very first time she saw Armand posing with just his police hat, duty belt, and the adult toy handcuffs on the calendar. The drapes were opened and the snow outside offered her light.

She moved to the corner. Bless Wilhelm. He was super organized. All the boxes were labeled. Family albums, trophies, and at the very top was a box with collectibles written on the side.

She lowered the box, which was lightweight, and opened it. She went through it but there was only crinkled newspaper. At the very bottom she pulled out a picture of the first train car she stole from Halloran's Antiques

Emily's heart lurched. Something was wrong.

Light illuminated the room. Gasping, Emily swung around to find Armand, wearing his sheriff's costume, sitting in the chair behind the desk, and shining a flashlight.

Chapter Twenty-Seven

Emily gripped the photo. She didn't know how she held Armand's glare. She felt smaller and more insignificant than she had when the policewoman witnessed her breaking into a vault, taking the object, and returning it ten years ago.

"I didn't want to believe," he said. "All the pieces pointed to you, but I still can't believe it, and you're standing right in front of me. Why, Emily? Why?"

Emily put the photo in the box. "Why?" She put the newspaper in to avoid looking at him. "Because of my family. My biological family. When I was given up for adoption, I had a wooden figurine. The figurine fit perfectly into the first train car from Mrs. Halloran's store. The engraving on the side told a story. It told the story of my biological family." She took a peek. His gaze was fixed on her. She couldn't bear it and returned her attention to the box. "It could lead me to them." She closed the box. "As much as I knew it was wrong, and I shouldn't and didn't want to, I had to take the first train car and find the other two."

Armand stood up, heavily and slowly. "Did you steal the wooden horse?"

"No. I was returning it. That's when I found the first train car."

He switched on the light, closed his flashlight, and opened the door. "Will you tell me who took the wooden horse?"

"I can't." Tears filled her eyes, but she held them back. Her dreams and future were ruined. And all because of three wooden train cars with minimal financial worth but priceless to her. For a past and a family who gave her up and possibly still didn't want anything to do with her. "You can blame the theft of the wooden horse on me. I can't say who stole it."

He leaned against the front of the desk and placed his hands on the edges. "Someone in your family?"

She met his gaze, alarmed. "You've checked my family?"

"I'm a police officer, Emily. Yes, I checked them. Your parents' files are sealed. They had a criminal record. They are also the owners of Regal Master Locksmiths."

Emily picked up the box and put it back. She didn't want to see the disappointment and confusion in his eyes. "How did you put everything together? I know how not to leave clues or prints."

"The key to my handcuffs started it all. You said you used the key on my keychain to open them, but I didn't have the key on it. I found it later in my desk at the station. What did you use?"

"The hook of your pen."

He nodded, ashamed. She had humiliated him. It wasn't her intention and she kept her face averted.

"I was stumped and tried to push it aside, but I found two sets of shoe prints in the snow outside the Saunders' barn. A pair of women's runners and a pair of women's size seven Dr. Martens, which also happened to be the shoes our car thief wore—the one you met this morning and who hopefully will show up tonight to turn herself in. When you went into the bathroom earlier today, I took a snapshot of your runners and traced them on a sheet of paper. They were an exact match to the ones I found outside the Saunders' barn. They had the same spots and a pebble lodged in the tread."

Emily grinned. "The girl threw me off. You can't have any emotions when you're doing a job, but she pulled at my heart strings or there wouldn't be any shoe prints."

"You speak like a seasoned pro."

"I'm not. I was trained to be the best."

"Your parents?"

She couldn't implicate them or any of the other people who trained her. "I can't tell you."

"But you don't have a record."

"No, I don't."

"Protected by the law?"

"I can't say either."

"No, I suppose not. You'll need a lawyer to answer." He averted his gaze. "So what am I supposed to do now, Emily?"

"I guess you have to arrest me."

He laughed but shook his head in dismay. "And ruin you? Do you really think I can do that? Do you think I can take everything you're achieving away from you—your appraising and now your chance at doing art appraisals?"

"Can you live with yourself if you don't, Armand? You're an honorable police officer. You're an honest man."

Armand jumped up and moved to the window. He didn't want to look at her. She had sucker-punched him in the gut and twisted his heart. "I'm a conflicted police officer and a conflicted man. I'd be the scum of the earth if I turned you in but a worthless police officer if I didn't."

"I did it to find my biological family. It's the only defense I can offer and the truth. If you turn me in, I won't say anything about us."

"Do you think I'm thinking about me or what was between us now? I—I have to turn this over to my supervisor. I don't know what else to do. I've always done what was right. I have no idea what to do here. I have no idea what is right. All I know is everything is wrong."

Emily clasped the chair for support. Tears threatened to fall. She was ruined, and she did it with her eyes wide open. "Do what you have to do." Her voice was barely audible. "I won't hold it against you."

"I'll hold it against me!" He turned toward her, startling her. "Was anything between us real?"

Emily took a step forward. "Of course, it was real. I wasn't pretending. It's only been a few days, but I feel more for you than I can even believe myself."

"Yeah, well, you'll have to forgive me, but I'm sort of questioning how I think you feel about me and how I *know* or how I thought I felt about you. Do—"

"Uncle Armand? Emily?"

Emily swung around to find the girl who stole her cars standing at the door, holding a big garbage bag.

Armand was just as surprised as Emily. "Carli, what are you doing here?"

Emily turned on him. "This is your niece?"

"Yes. Nicole and Darryl's daughter."

Carli looked from her to Armand. "Is Emily the

woman you're in love with, Uncle Armand?"

Armand moved to the door. "I never said I was in love with the woman. I said I was interested in the woman."

"Whatever!" Carli shouted in frustration. "I heard everything you two said. Are you going to arrest Emily?"

Armand's gaze landed on Emily. "Could someone please tell me what's going on? How do you two know each other, and what the hell is in the garbage bag?"

Emily glared at him, her whole body going numb with fear, not for herself but for Carli. "Armand…" She didn't know how to tell him. "Armand, this—"

Armand's eyes widened, and his face went white. "Is this?" He stumbled for the words. "Is this the girl who stole your cars? The girl who is turning herself in tonight?"

Emily was just as wound up. She couldn't bring herself to say anything, let alone nod.

"I'll answer for myself," Carli shouted at Armand. "Yes, I *am* the girl who stole both her cars. She didn't rat on me. She gave me the chance to turn myself in and stopped me from running away and hurting my parents and—" She let the garbage bag fall. The Canada Goose coat, Ugg's boots, and Gucci sunglasses tumbled to his feet. "And I am turning myself in because of her. But if you arrest her, I will never tell you anything about the car thieves. I will never speak to you again." She ran off.

Armand's gaze went from the clothes to the door and to Emily. "Don't you dare run off on me, too. You have a lot of explaining to do. Carli!"

Chapter Twenty-Eight

Armand stormed after Carli. Trembling, Emily picked up the coat, boots, sunglasses, and garbage bag, closed the light, and locked the door. Armand yelled at Carli, but Emily couldn't hear her. She moved into the kitchen.

Armand pounded on the doors, leading into the restaurant. "Unlock the doors, now, Carli. You have to tell me what the hell is going on!"

"No! Go away!" came Carli's voice.

Emily put the coat on the back of a kitchen chair, the garbage bag and boots on the seat, and the sunglasses on the table as she settled her nerves. She had never seen Armand agitated. But screaming wouldn't get his niece to speak to him. He needed to calm down if he wanted her to talk. He had to remember he was a neutral police office at this moment and not her emotionally charged uncle. But he reacted as her uncle.

She moved to the restaurant doors. "Let me try, Armand," she said in a calm voice. She didn't know how she kept calm when inside she hurt like an open and bleeding wound.

"Really? She'll speak to you and not to me, her uncle?"

Emily ignored the sarcasm. She kept her gaze on him until he took a deep breath and swept his hand toward the door.

Emily advanced. "Carli, it's Emily. Can I come in, please?"

"I'm not going to tell him anything about the cars if he arrests you. I'll tell him I stole the trains, too."

Armand stomped to the doors. "She knows what you did? She's an accomplice to your handiwork, too?" His voice was close to shouting again. "Is there anything else she knows that I don't? Anything else I can't arrest either of you for?"

Emily knew he spoke out of anger, but she needed him to understand. "She left the bag of designer things in a garbage bin outside Colm Saunders' barn." She pulled him from the door. "And she put her dog in another bin," she whispered. "The people who forced her to steal my cars killed her dog."

Armand's eyes widened. "Bowwow? She said he was at the vet."

Emily glared at him. "What else could she say? She was frightened of the thieves and you."

Armand was at a loss for words. "Shit, shit, shit!"

"I heard!" Carli shouted. "I'm not coming out if you're swearing."

"Calm yourself," Emily whispered and moved to the doors. "Carli, what you said about taking the fall is the nicest thing anyone would want to do for me. But you don't have to worry. It's my problem, not yours."

"No. If he arrests you, I'll say it was me, and I'll never speak to him again."

Armand threw his hat at the door. "Unlock this door, Emily. Now. Pick it this instant. I'll even get you a pen."

Emily was appalled. "I am not going to pick this

lock. You are going to sit down and let me convince her to open the door and speak to us."

"To *me*," Armand yelled at the door. "She needs to speak to *me*. Now let me in, Carli."

"Are you arresting Emily?"

"I haven't a clue what to do with Emily. I haven't a clue what to do with you. So just let me in and tell me all you know about the car thefts."

Darryl and Nicole came in from the back door. "Mom and Dad are here," Nicole said. "They brought Carli. Is she here?" She held up a blue riding dress and flowered hat. "I have a costume for her." A tall man and woman somewhere in their early sixties came in after them. The man was dressed as a sheriff, too, while the woman wore an elegant traveling gown with a long flowing skirt.

"And there they are," Armand said, exasperated. "Hello, Mom and Dad."

They were confused. "We're here to be extras," his father said. "Don't know why you're so...tense." He took off his hat to show a full head of silver hair. "Well, hello, little lady," he said to Emily.

Armand's mother came closer and took Emily's hand. "Is this the Hepplewhite lady we've all been hearing about, Armand?"

"She's not the Hepplewhite lady, Mother. She has a name, and I chose not to tell you."

"Armand!" his mother rebuked.

Emily patted her hand. "It's Emily Atterberry, Mrs. Lecavalier. Armand is a little agitated right now."

"Agitated?" Armand shouted. "You think?"

Mr. Lecavalier came closer. "I'm this joker's sire." Emily shook his hand, too, keeping a smile on her face.

"But he doesn't seem to be in any joking mood right now."

"You're absolutely correct." Armand put his arms around them and led them to the back door. "Now you've met Emily you need to leave."

Both Mr. and Mrs. Lecavalier flinched. "Is something the matter?"

"Police business. Now go and do your extra actor bit."

"Lowan doesn't need us yet and it's cold out there," Mrs. Lecavalier said.

"What's going on, Armand?" Darryl asked. "Where's Carli?"

Armand indicated the doors. "Locked in the restaurant."

"In the restaurant?" It was Nicole. "Why?" She dropped the costume on the counter and moved to the door. "Carli, it's me. Is everything okay? Is the door stuck?"

"I want a lawyer," Carli shouted.

"A lawyer?" everyone asked.

Darryl moved to the door, too. "For what? What's going on, Armand?"

"Carli, let me in and we can talk about it," Emily said.

"Tell my uncle, parents, and grandparents to go away first."

Emily took Armand by the arm and led him to the table as Nicole and Darryl continued talking to Carli and Mr. and Mrs. Lecavalier joined them. "Let me talk to her, alone, please. She's not as emotionally tied to me as she is with you, her parents, and grandparents. I managed to convince her to turn herself in, remember?"

"To turn herself in?" Nicole stood beside them. "What's going on? What did she do?"

"She stole Emily's cars," Armand shouted.

Nicole, Darryl, and Mr. and Mrs. Lecavalier went still.

Emily shook her head in dismay. Armand was not handling the situation well. He was completely undone. "Armand, why don't you take Nicole and Darryl and your parents into the lobby for a few minutes and let me see if I can persuade Carli to come out?"

Armand's breathing was heavy. He stormed toward the door, leading to the lobby. He waved his hand like a crossing guard. "Everyone with me, right this minute. Move. Now."

None of them moved.

"Great, are we back to no one listening to Armand again?" he asked.

"Armand will explain everything while I talk to Carli," Emily said in a calm voice.

Hesitantly, they nodded and left. Once out of the restaurant, Emily knocked on the door. "It's just me, Carli. Your parents, grandparents, and uncle are in the lobby."

"There's no one else with you?"

"Nobody else."

The door clicked open and Emily slipped in. Carli locked the door, slid on the floor, and put her hands over her face.

Emily sat down beside her. "I'm glad you came, Carli. I knew you would."

"I didn't know you were involved with my uncle. He told me yesterday he met someone he liked."

"Your uncle is an excellent police officer and put

two and two together. He found out I stole the train cars."

"Asshole."

Emily couldn't resist a smile. "He did his job, and he did it well."

"I'm sorry. I guess he did."

Emily put her hand on Carli's knee. "You don't have to be. I'm sorry I deceived him, but you know why I did it. I wish I hadn't. I would have liked to get to know your uncle better."

She pulled a wry grin. "He's okay. And I guess he's okay looking, too. He made the King Court Calendar of hotshot men."

Emily laughed. "He's better than okay, Carli. That's the problem."

Carli brushed tears from her eyes.

"But enough of me and your uncle." She squeezed Carli's hand. "You came here tonight to tell your story. You now have to tell it. Armand may be your uncle, but he is also the police officer in charge of the thefts."

"I'll only speak to him with a lawyer. And if he promises not to arrest you. Otherwise, I'm not talking."

"Let's worry about what will happen to me later. Let's concentrate on you first. If a lawyer is what you want, then we'll get you one. Can we let Armand know you will only talk to him with a lawyer present?"

She nodded. Emily took her hand, and they moved into the kitchen. Darryl and Nicole sat at the table, their faces pale, while Armand paced circles around them. Mr. and Mrs. Lecavalier had left.

"Carli." Nicole jumped up as Carli ran into her mother's arms.

"I want a lawyer, Mom. Olivia. I saw her outside

with the film crew. I want Olivia. I want to speak to her with Emily first before I talk to," she glanced at Armand, "to the police."

"I'm really missing the love here, Carli." Armand raced outside.

"We're so sorry, Carli," Nicole said.

"Why? You're not the one who did anything wrong."

Darryl took Carli in his arms. "We won't let anything happen to you."

Carli moved out of his embrace. "I'm not a baby anymore, Dad. You can't protect me."

"You may not be a baby anymore, but you'll always be my daughter."

Carli's lips trembled, and her eyes filled with tears. Emily needed her to be calm. "Do you want something to drink, Carli?"

"I'll make you a hot chocolate." Nicole rushed behind the counter. "I'll make all of us a hot chocolate."

Armand stormed back into the kitchen followed by Olivia.

"You want to talk to me, Carli?" Oliva said.

Carli nodded. "As my lawyer, okay? Not as a saloon girl." She indicated the costumes. "It has to be private, too. I don't want to go to jail, and I don't want Emily to go to jail either. She didn't rat on me. She made me to do the right thing and turn myself in."

"Why don't I hear your story, and then I can discuss it with Armand, and we can take it from there?" Carli nodded. "Can we go somewhere private?"

"The restaurant is private," Emily offered.

"Do you want your parents with you?" Olivia asked.

"No." She looked at them. "Sorry." She grabbed Emily's hand. "Emily has to be with us."

Emily glanced at Armand who only nodded in frustration. They moved to the restaurant. The minute they sat down at a table, Carli broke down and told Olivia the complete story. She also told her that Emily knew who she was and gave a composite sketch to the police. When they met by accident, Emily convinced her to give herself up. She didn't want to go to jail and didn't want Emily to go to jail either. She wanted protection for both of them and for everything.

"Everything?" Olivia asked. "Should I know more."

"There is more," Emily said. "My story. But, later."

Olivia agreed. "Let me speak to Armand. He will need his supervisor's approval." She went to the kitchen.

"I'm afraid," Carli said.

Emily squeezed her hand. "You have every right, but everyone is supporting you."

"Even my uncle?"

"Believe it or not, even your uncle. Foremost your uncle."

"I've never seen him so upset. He's always so calm and collected. His hair moved out of place."

Emily held back a laugh. "He loves you."

"Just me?"

Emily's smile was wry. "Just you, Carli. He had his world rocked today. He has every right to be upset." And that was an understatement.

A few minutes later Olivia came back. "No one will go to jail. But you have to tell Armand the whole story. His supervisor will listen on her phone."

Carli nodded in agreement.

"You tell him who recruited you and where you brought the cars and you and the other girls will be spared any penalties," Olivia said. "You will have to testify against them though."

"Testify?"

"When we take them to court. I will approach the other girls and offer them immunity if they testify."

Emily squeezed her hand. "It's good, Carli."

They moved into the kitchen. Armand, Nicole, and Darryl sat at the table, cups of steaming hot chocolate in front of them. Emily, Carli, and Olivia sat opposite. Armand pushed his cup to Carli. His phone was on the table and he put it on speaker.

"Any time you're ready, Carli," Olivia said.

Carli nodded, put her hand around the cup, and with tears in her eyes spoke directly to Armand. "My driving instructor recruited me to steal cars. Her name is Josie Kemper. The driving school is Success Student Driving. She gave me the expensive coat, boots, and sunglasses and made me up to look beautiful. Then she insisted I steal a car for her, and if I didn't her associates would hurt my family. To prove it, they killed Bowwow. When I didn't bring Josie the first car, she said I had to get her another or she would hurt Mom this time. So I did. I was really afraid. I drove it where they're building the stadium to have outdoor concerts. Past the equestrian center. Josie waited with another woman. I think she may be one of the other driving instructors. I heard them mention a pond and driving over the bridge to Gatineau in Quebec. Josie then let me drive the student car back home. I don't know all the other kids who stole cars. But I'm sure one of them is Natasha Ivova, Sergei's daughter. She is the one who told me about the driving school. I know Diana Chang was forced, too, and they hurt her brother by almost running him down when she refused. They've been really upset. Like me."

"I know where the driving school office is," Armand said. "Anything else?"

Carli shook her head.

"Meet me at the station, Armand," came his supervisor's voice from his cell. "I'll call everyone in."

Armand disengaged and stood up.

Carli raced to the other side to hug him. "Be careful. I'm sorry. I'm really sorry."

"I'm not, Carli." He kissed the top of her head, strode out of the kitchen, and past the window.

"Do you think someone should tell him he's wearing the stupid sheriff costume?" Carli asked.

Nicole stood up. "Not me." She took Carli in her arms. "He'll figure it out sooner or later."

"Can I go see what they're filming outside?"

"Of course. I brought you a costume, too." She grabbed it from the counter.

"It's ugly."

Nicole grinned. "It was high fashion for the nineteenth century. You can change in the security office."

Darryl put his arm around her and moved toward the hallway.

Carli stopped, raced back to Emily, and hugged her. "Thank you."

"Thank *you*," Emily said. Carli hugged Olivia and left to change into her costume with her parents.

Emily turned to Olivia. "My turn now."

Chapter Twenty-Nine

It was close to midnight when Emily climbed into bed. She tossed and turned and finally got up. She put on a pair of jeans, a T-shirt, and hoodie and decided to wrap the paintings. After telling her story, Olivia could only guarantee her immunity from any involvement with Carli and the car thefts. Even though Carli insisted on carte blanche immunity, Olivia had to speak to Armand to see if he included dropping charges for the theft of the train cars, too. Whether Emily faced any court proceedings or not, the charges could still be made public. She was at risk of losing her job. With her job would go her future. Nothing was certain. The only sure thing was she and Armand were finished. She'd lost credibility. He didn't believe in her anymore.

She stepped out of her bedroom. The security office light was on. She knocked lightly and stuck her head in. "I wanted to—" Carli was fast asleep on an air mattress, curled up and looking younger than her sixteen years of age. "I wanted to see how Carli was doing," she whispered.

Both Nicole and Darryl came into the hallway. Nicole threw her arms around her. "She tried to run away?" she whispered. "And you convinced her to go home and turn herself in? You're her guardian angel, Emily. *Our* guardian angel."

Emily stepped away from her. "I'm far from

anyone's guardian angel. I listened to her. She didn't want to leave, otherwise no matter what I said she would have."

Darryl took her hands. "We don't know how to thank you."

"She protected me, too. If Armand—" she didn't know what to say.

"If Armand wasn't head over heels crazy about you and didn't trust you," Nicole said, "he wouldn't have given her the chance to turn herself in. Darryl and I are both ex police officers. What you did put a professional negotiator to shame."

Emily smiled. "I'll keep negotiator in mind in case this job doesn't work out. Carli's a good girl. Once the ordeal is over, she can be a good girl again. She told you what she did with her dog?"

"She did. We bought her Bowwow when Darryl and I got married and moved here to King Court. Bowwow helped her settle in. We told her we'd give him a real burial tomorrow."

"Have you heard from Armand?" Although he was a trained police officer, she worried about him.

"Not yet. We probably won't hear anything until the morning at the earliest," Darryl said.

"He can take care of himself," Nicole said.

"I know."

"But you worry. It's understandable. He is a police officer and puts himself in the frontlines of dangerous situations. We'll let you know anything the instant we do."

Emily's nod was brief.

"You look as worn out as we do but ready to start your day," Darryl said.

"Hard to sleep after everything we heard and saw."

"Tell me about it." Nicole rubbed her belly. "For me, it says a lot."

"If you need me or Carli needs me, just," Emily indicated her bedroom door. "Knock. If I'm not in there I'll probably be in the restaurant."

Darryl and Nicole went back into the security office as Emily moved into the lobby, put on latex gloves, and took down one of Marie-Anne Couture's paintings. She brought it to the restaurant, cleaned it, and wrapped it in a clear protective bag followed by a buffered envelope. When it slipped from her hands, she knew she was too drained. She needed to get some sleep. She returned to her bedroom and flopped on the bed, fully clothed.

All night, she thought of Armand. Where was he? Did he and the other police officers confront those driver instructors recruiting students to steal cars? Did he find the place where the cars were taken? Did he name the other thieves and arrest them? The thieves were dangerous. They not only killed Carli's dog but hurt one of the other girl's brothers. Was he okay?

She wanted to know if he was safe, but she couldn't call him. They were over. He was the best thing to happen to her, but she'd jeopardized the relationship to find something or someone about her past. She was a fool. She could have had a future with Armand. She could have loved Armand. He could have loved her, too. Instead, she thought only about her unknown past.

A tear rolled down her face. Could have loved. She ruined the chance to find out if she was falling in love with him. She ruined her chance to love him.

Through the turmoil of her thoughts and the tears seeping from her heart, one thing was clear. She knew what she had to do in the morning—if she could get a ride to Halloran's Antiques and Koffee & Tez.

Chapter Thirty

It was a long night for Armand. He and Bassam arrested Josie at her home on the outskirts of King Court. She cut a deal and told them everything. The cars were brought to an abandoned building on the outskirts of King Court, repainted, and shipped to buyers in South America. But there was more than one makeshift garage. There were a number across Ontario and Quebec, and she named them all.

With the assistance of the Ontario Provincial Police and the Quebec Provincial Police, Armand organized a coordinated raid on the makeshift garages. He raided the one outside of King Court with Bassam, Patricia, Sergei, and several other members of the King Court Police Force. But their station was small, and they couldn't hold the suspects. They brought them to an OPP detachment and held them there. Armand would question them later in the day.

Armand wanted to see Nicole and Darryl and especially Carli and give them an update, but he didn't get home until the early hours of the morning. When he did, he was so exhausted he fell asleep on the sofa with his coat and boots on. A couple hours later the incessant ringing of his cell woke him up.

It was Patricia. "Get over here, now." She hung up before Armand could open his mouth to reply.

It was 8:30. He had slept two hours at the most.

There were a number of texts and phone calls, mostly from Nicole, Darryl, his father, mother, Lowan, and one from Olivia. None from Emily. He was thankful. He didn't know what to do about her. He had a sworn duty to uphold the law and apprehend criminals. Emily broke the law. She was a criminal. But she was the criminal he loved—yes loved. What else could it be? The longing and need to see her and be with her. And now the pain that he couldn't, the deception that she had fooled him.

He'd agreed not to arrest Emily but how could he go about his job if he didn't report her?

How could he live with himself if he did?

He sprang up. He had to deal with the car thieves first. He took a quick shower, changed his clothes, and headed to the police station. But he needed a coffee first. The biggest Jessica had.

He parked his car in front of Koffee & Tez. Jessica was at the counter. "Jumbo dark roast, please."

Jessica poured him one. "Only one?"

Armand didn't understand what she meant and only nodded. He was too tired to ask.

"I heard what happened last night."

"The car thefts are big news for King Court."

"Not about the car thefts—even though I heard about them. Emily was here this morning. She returned the train car."

Armand flinched. "She what?"

"She told me and Mrs. Halloran the whole story."

The door of Koffee & Tez burst open and Mrs. Halloran rushed in. "Armand, Armand, Armand! I haven't thought about anything except Emily!"

His gaze jumped from one woman to the other.

"What did Emily say?"

"What didn't she." Mrs. Halloran grabbed his arm. "Can you imagine?"

"You have the train cars again?"

"Of course not."

Armand's grip slipped around the coffee Jessica handed him.

"They belong to Emily," Jessica said.

The cup was lead in his hand. Was he hearing things?

"I need to find the third train car," Mrs. Halloran said. "She needs to find her family."

"But…the breaking and entering," Armand said. "She…" he couldn't even bring himself to say it. "She took what wasn't hers."

"I would have done the same if I could crawl through my little window, tiptoe around the crates and boxes in my cluttered office and think straight enough to leave money and a note of apology," Mrs. Halloran said. "Arthritis and a scattered brain wouldn't work in my favor."

"I would have done the same thing, too, if I had the nerve and the skills," Jessica said. "Who could blame her for wanting to find her biological family? I can't."

Mrs. Halloran slammed her coffee mug on the counter. "I need another coffee, Jessica. I can only think about Emily and where the third train car could be."

"Extra-large cappuccino coming up."

"I've…" Armand didn't know what to say. "I've reported the thefts. I have to close the case and tell—"

Mrs. Halloran drew closer and stared at him like when he was in her grade ten and twelve history classes. "What thefts?"

Armand was bewildered. "You had a theft, Mrs. Halloran. Two actually. And so did you, Jessica, or rather your grandfather's barn was broken into and robbed."

"My grandfather's barn?" Jessica repeated. "I have no idea what you're talking about, Armand. I took a train and gave it to its rightful owner. My grandfather will applaud me. There was absolutely no theft." She handed him a ham croissant sandwich. "You are very much mistaken."

"I didn't order any sandwich."

"Didn't you?" She slammed it into his hand. "Well, I heard you order it, so it's yours. Happy Valentine's Day. I gave you the Valentine's brew, too."

"It's not Valentine's Day."

"Happy coffee and croissant sandwich day, then."

Armand took the sandwich but didn't know what to think or do.

"There were no thefts, Armand," Mrs. Halloran pronounced, looking at him as though telling him about his terrible dangling modifiers. "No thefts whatsoever in my store or in Colm's barn. I was mistaken and so was Jessica." She picked up a plastic spoon and tapped it against her hand.

"Very much mistaken, Armand. We're sorry if we took up your police time."

With his coffee in one hand and his croissant sandwich in the other, Armand backed his way toward the door. "I'll be in touch."

"No thefts." Jessica banged espresso grinds into the organic bin as Mrs. Halloran tapped the spoon against her palm. "No thefts whatsoever. They were gifts, understand?"

Armand rushed to his car and drove to the station. He could barely see the building. Media cars were parked everywhere while reporters crowded outside. He pushed himself through the throng of people. Inside wasn't any better. Reporters tried to get a statement from Patricia, who insisted it would come later in the day.

Olivia and a couple other lawyers rushed around, representing the young girls forced to steal the cars. The girls sat at every desk or bench in their high school uniforms. Their parents were with them, holding the designer clothes the thieves gave their daughters. The small police station never saw so much activity. The roof and walls would burst apart at any minute.

"We need to talk," Olivia told Armand as she rushed past him with a young girl and her parents. "In private. About Emily."

Armand stiffened. "Not now, Olivia." He couldn't talk about Emily. He didn't know what to say let alone do. He had to speak to Patricia first and tell her the deal Carli insisted on and she approved, exempting Emily from any knowledge of the car thefts but more importantly, the train car thefts. Telling Patricia meant exposing Emily. But he didn't have another choice. How could he live with himself if he didn't? As his supervisor, she had to know.

"I need to speak to you, Armand," Patricia said, leading some parents to her office. "When we have the chance."

But there was never a chance to speak to either Olivia or Patricia. The rest of the day was just as chaotic as the night before. He spoke to all the young girls forced to steal cars along with their parents and

Olivia or another lawyer present. By the time he left the station it was close to ten p.m. He didn't even have the chance to interview the suspects at the OPP station.

Nicole left more messages and he finally texted back. He would come soon. He went to her home, but no one was there. The Acadia Inn was the last place he wanted to go but, in all likelihood, they were there. He would have to face Emily. He had nothing to say to her even though he had everything to say. But he had to face Emily sooner or later. It may as well be sooner than he wanted.

Chapter Thirty-One

Armand parked the car at the Acadia Inn close to midnight. Only a handful of cars and film trailers were in the lot. Lowan had probably finished filming for the day and gone home.

He went to the back door leading to the family quarters and found it unlocked. He walked in, the hallway dimly lit, and his gaze went to Emily's bedroom door. A light filtered through. He wanted to knock but couldn't.

What would he say? He had no idea.

He knocked on the security office door and peered in. But no one was inside. He moved into the kitchen and found Darryl, Nicole, and Carli sitting at the table, sipping hot chocolate.

Carli zoomed up and threw her arms around him. "I left a hundred messages."

"I never saw any from you."

"Because I used Mom and Dad's cells." She dropped her arms and moved away, looking like he never saw before. Bashful. "I didn't know if you wanted to talk to me again, so I used their phones. Am I forgiven?"

He put his arm around her shoulders and led her to the table. "Well, Carlotta Abigail Stannard. You might have to shovel my drive this entire winter, mow my lawn in the spring, pull out weeds in the summer, and rake leaves in the fall."

She pushed him away and dropped into a chair. "I'll let you buy me a burger one day and we'll be even."

"Deal. Believe it or not you already did enough for me. You put me in the news and got me an invitation from the OPP to submit my resume. I may have a place in their theft department. Seems like us small-time police force in King Court, led by yours truly, cracked an Ontario- and Quebec-wide car theft ring." He sat down at the table and updated them on the case, including all the girls in Carli's school who were involved. They told him, they were relieved the car thefts were now over and none of them were hurt. "Everything's good here?"

Darryl put his arm around both Nicole and Carli. "Everything's good here. We buried Bowwow this morning."

Armand put his hands over Carli's. "I'm sorry about Bowwow."

"Yeah, it wasn't a wonderful way to go. But Mom and Dad are getting me a car now."

"I don't think so. Not so fast," came the replies from her parents. "How did you get from Bowwow to car in one breath?" Darryl asked.

"Thought I'd give it a try," Carli said. "They called my other mothers."

"Of course, we did,'" Nicole said. "They've been worried about you, too."

"Now they're flying out to see me. It's going to be a big Carli lovefest." She turned to her parents. "Mom, Dad, don't you have to go and check the monitors?"

"In other words, you want to speak to your uncle in

private," Nicole said.

"I've trained you well."

Carli waited until her parents left. She put her hands over Armand's. "I'm really sorry about everything."

"It's over, Carli."

"It's all okay with your boss and everyone? I won't go to jail?"

"No, you won't go to jail. None of the other girls will either. Oliva took care of everything. You and the other girls will, however, be called in to testify at the trial or trials. It's a big theft ring you helped me break."

"The OPP really invited you to join them?"

"They invited me to submit my resume, yes."

"It's what you want."

He unbuttoned his jacket. "It is."

"Then what's wrong? You don't look thrilled."

"Nothing's wrong. It's been two very long days and night. I'm exhausted, but I wanted to see you before I went home." He moved forward. "Will you answer me one question?"

"If you answer one in return."

He nodded. "Why? Why did you feel the need to take those cars? I know you. You would never do anything you know is wrong or don't want to do. You would have raced to me. Why not now?"

Carli pulled her hands away and moved against the chair. "I, well, I felt like an extra. I felt like I was being pushed out."

"Pushed out of what?"

"My family."

"I don't understand."

"Mom is having a baby. She and Dad tried forever

and all of a sudden one came around. I didn't belong anymore. I'm part of Dad's blood but not Mom's and my real Mom, my biological one, was too busy with her wife, and they're also thinking about having a baby. I didn't have any place with any of them."

"Did you tell your parents how you felt?"

"Which ones?"

"The ones who are under this roof?"

"I did."

"And?"

"Mom cried, as usual, and hugged me forever and Dad was ready to hand over his credit cards. Haven't told my bio Mom yet. Two credit cards are better than one."

"If you're not paying the statements." Armand moved forward. "You are this family, Carli. *My* family."

"I know. I make everyone better. Without me you'd be a big bore even with the nice suits."

"Yes, of course. I'd be lost without you, etc., etc., etc."

"I've trained you well."

His smile was wry. "Now what's your question?"

"Is Emily safe, too?"

Armand shifted in his chair. "It was part of your deal. Part of the "plea bargaining" so to speak. But I still have to report her."

"Why?"

"Because I wouldn't be much of a police officer if I didn't. I have to do what is right. It's what I swore to do. I can't pick and choose what to report and what not to. Thanks to you, she's guaranteed immunity, but I still have to put her in my report about the train car thefts."

"Even though you don't want to?"

Armand didn't want to answer. "What I want can't interfere with what I have to do and what is right."

"Reporting her is right? It's wrong. You know why she did it. You know what she did for me. You know her. She's good."

"I know, but what she did was still against the law."

"What about how you feel about her? Doesn't it make a difference?"

"Of course, it does. It hurts. How I feel about her only makes it more difficult. But what kind of police officer would I be if I chose what to report and what not to?"

Carli fell back in her chair. "You're going against the deal I made."

"No, I'm not. The deal is still on. She won't face any charges. Neither Mrs. Halloran nor Jessica Saunders are pressing charges. They've actually given her the train cars and the money."

"Then why report her if they aren't pressing charges? You can close your case, send your resume to the OPP, and continue seeing her. You can even follow Mrs. Halloran and Jessica's example and forgive her, too." She leaned over the table. "Like forgive her *now*, Uncle Armandillo. Right this instant and finally get to have a wonderful Valentine's Day celebration with a woman you like—or love…."

Armand's grin was bittersweet. "You're trying to put words in my mouth, Carlotta."

She shrugged. "It was worth a try. So…?"

Armand sighed. "Forgiveness is a little too…steep for me now. I can't do something I don't feel."

"Why? Because she hurt your feelings?"

Armand shook his head. "Because she broke my trust."

"Fix it."

"Doesn't fix fast."

"But isn't she why you're here now? You came to see Emily more than me."

"I came to see you."

"Right…"

He took his gloves out of his pocket, wondered why, and put them back in. "Is she here?"

"You're bad at pretending innocence. Of course, she's here. She's in her bedroom. I helped her pack the paintings by the servant girl from ages ago. Sort of like penance and community work put together. So many protective things." She stood up. "But she was quiet. Sad."

Armand didn't move.

Carli moved to his side, took a pack of Dubble Bubble, and offered him one. "I'm sure you'd prefer a scotch or gin or whatever you drink but this is the only thing I can give you until I turn nineteen."

Armand took one.

"I might not be able to double-date with you this Valentine's Day. Spiderman is busy saving the world," she pulled him up, "but you can still have a date. Just the two of you together. Doesn't it sound romantic or kinky or whatever you want it to be?"

Armand smirked but didn't move.

"You're kidding, right? You have cold feet?"

"Of course, I don't." He straightened up.

"Right, 'cause you're a he-man. I'm sure you know which bedroom she's in."

"And if I said no, I don't want to see her?"

"Like I said, you're a bad liar." She led him into the hallway and to Emily's bedroom door.

Armand put the bubble gum in his coat pocket and waited. What would he say?

"You are such a wuss." Carli knocked on the door and raced inside the security office. A few seconds later, Emily opened it, wearing jeans and a hoodie. He never saw her looking so casual. Without her business suit on, she appeared vulnerable. She was without spirit too. Her eyes didn't flash with excitement. No spitfire. Carli was right. She was sad.

But she was beautiful. Even though he knew what she did, he wanted to take her in his arms and comfort her. He was willing to forgive her and do what Carli said and close the case without reporting her. But being willing wasn't the same as being ready. She upset everything he believed in, and now he didn't know how to make it right.

Emily's eyes rounded in surprise. "Hey."

"Can I come in?"

"Sure." She moved aside and let him in. On the table was her laptop and a shoebox.

"I came to give you an update on the car thefts."

She indicated a chair, and he sat down while she sat opposite. He gave her a quick rundown. She nodded but didn't say anything until he finished.

"Sounds like you finally got your ticket to the big-time police force."

"Possibly. The investigation is still ongoing. I haven't had the chance to interrogate any of the suspects. Spoke with only the girls so far." He took a deep breath. It was now or never. "I went by Koffee &

Tez this morning. You told Mrs. Halloran and Jessica everything."

She fiddled with the shoebox. "I did. I returned the trains, but," she opened the lid to show him the two train cars, wrapped in pink and white dotted tissue paper. Inside the first train was the figurine she'd had since her adoption. "They gave them back to me. They said they were mine." She picked up the trains to show him an envelope, lying on the bottom. "They even gave me back the money I left." She pulled it out and showed him the money but put it back in the shoebox along with the train cars. "What happens to me now, Armand?"

"Nothing happens to you. You're part of Carli's plea bargaining. You're as protected as she and the other girls. My supervisor agreed, and she can't back out now, even if she doesn't know," he paused, "you took the train cars. Jessica and Mrs. Halloran aren't pressing charges, which null and voids the thefts."

"I didn't sway them, Armand. I don't want you to think I set out to make them feel sorry for me. I told them my story and why I took them."

"I believe you. You don't have to worry about it." He tapped the shoebox. "Can you tell me how this family business of breaking and entering and thieving came about?"

Her smile was wry. "If you're asking me as a police officer then I can't tell you. If you're asking me as a civilian, then I can but it has to remain between us."

"Civilian." He put his hand up. "Scouts honor."

"My parents were small time thieves but brilliant at cracking codes. The old rotary vaults, then any computerized system to come their way. They were arrested in their teens but avoided jail-time by helping the police and other agencies on a hush-hush basis. They were called to assist with delicate cases of cracking locks and vaults, taking things, and returning them without anyone knowing. They taught me and I taught my sister."

He sat up, appalled. "Did you do any jobs for the police?"

"I did a few. My parents' hands and senses weren't as steady as they used to be. They never wanted to involve me, but they were, well, sort of under contract with the police. I was headstrong and did the first assignment, so to speak, without them knowing. After that first time, well, there was no turning back. I took over the *family business,* and I was good. If we spoke about any of our break-ins, the police would deny them, my parents would be thrown in jail, and I would land in juvenile prison."

Armand shook his head. "Are you still in their employ?"

"No. The last job I did was ten years ago. A lovely policewoman decided to put an end to my extracurricular activities and whatever the police had over my parents. She wanted me to have a normal adolescence. Her compassion made a deep impression on me. My parents' court files were sealed, their crimes pardoned, and my association with the police was over and done with. No records, no files, nothing."

"Was your sister involved with the police, too?"

"No. Only me. But we used to *practice* together, so to speak. We would break into stores, take something, and return it. It was all for fun."

"Strange kind of fun."

"We didn't have an average upbringing."

"Then the wooden horse came your way. If you didn't steal it who did?"

"Still civilian and scouts' honor?" He nodded. "My sister. She saw the horse and thought my little figurine would fit onto it. I didn't know what she did until the next day. She wanted to see if she still had it in her and she did."

Armand shook his head in disbelief. "Mrs. Halloran is on a search for the middle train car."

"I know. I'm not."

He leaned forward. "Why not?"

"It's led to too many problems." She pushed the shoebox toward him. "I need you to do me a big favor. I need you to take it."

"Take it?" He was confused. "You mean take the train cars—and your figurine?"

"And the money."

He sat up. "But neither Mrs. Halloran nor Jessica want the train cars or the money back."

"Convince them. I don't want them either. I should have left things the way they were. I don't want to find the middle car."

"But what about the figurine? It's yours."

Emily shook her head. "I need to let go of it, Armand. It...keeps me back. Looking past ruined my future. I can't do that again. Give it to Mrs. Halloran with her train car. Quite honestly, do whatever you want but I don't want the train cars, the figurine, or the money." He didn't want to take them. Emily pushed it closer and stood up. "Please, Armand." Hesitantly, he got up and put his arm over the shoebox.

"I'm supposed to take the paintings to Toronto tomorrow. I need to know if I can go. If I can't, then—"

"You're not resigning, Emily. You can go. You not only have immunity, but no charges will be laid. I'll also make sure Jessica and Mrs. Halloran keep everything under wraps. I'm sure they will. They…admire you."

"Admire may be stretching it, Armand."

He squirmed. "I don't think so. They told me they would have done exactly what you did—if they could." It was just him who couldn't admire let alone respect what she did.

"What about you?" Her voice was above a whisper, but it shook with emotion. "What are you going to do? You still have to close the case on the train cars. You know what I did. You have to report me."

Would he report her as he knew he should? Was he going to tell Patricia everything as protocol and his own sense of morality dictated? What was he going to do? Nothing was as clear cut and straightforward as it was two days before when he discovered the woman he dreamed about, the woman he wanted to know inside out, committed crimes.

He ambled to the door. "You're free to…continue on with your work…and your life. No one will bother you about the train car thefts. I…won't bother you either."

Emily moved behind her chair. "For the record. There was no…deceit about me…about you. It was…honest."

Armand nodded but didn't say anything.

"Thank you, Armand, and I'm sorry."

Yes, he'd heard lots of "I'm sorry" in the last few

days.

He opened the door. "All the best, Emily." He rushed out of the room, down the hall, and outside. It was the first time everything he thought was right was a complete and utter blur.

Chapter Thirty-Two

Armand sat at the bar of the Coyote's Hole, staring into a full mug of beer. It was Saturday night and the bar overflowed with regulars as well as the crew and actors of *Intergalactic Wars*. The final scenes and episode had been shot, and it was time to celebrate.

"You're still on your first beer, Armand." Justin handed a lager to the man beside him, one of the series' camera people. "Not going down? I can get you another."

"It's fine. I'm just far away."

"The car theft ring you busted was big. It made the national news."

He traced the engraving on the glass. "Hard to believe so many young girls were recruited over the last several months and no one came forward."

"You're lucky Carli did."

"Yes, I am."

"Were any of the cars recovered?"

"Only a couple still being repainted. The others are long gone. We'll never see them again."

"When I see you are at the bottom of your mug, I'll get you one you haven't tasted yet. On the house. One of our newest brews. Haven't even named it." He moved down the bar to get some actors more beer.

Patricia sauntered in with her husband and two daughters. She moved toward him while her family went upstairs to the restaurant section. Armand didn't want to talk to her. He didn't want to talk to anyone, but she flashed her badge to the camera person beside him and got his stool.

"Isn't that against the law?" Armand asked.

"I could have played the old lady card, but this works faster."

"Glass of Merlot, Patricia?" Justin asked.

"Yes, please. "She took off her coat and put it on her lap. "I never thought I'd say it, but you look like crap."

Armand twirled the glass. "I'm not working."

"Even when you're not working, you're impeccably dressed. You put all of us to shame."

"First time for everything."

Justin brought her the glass of Merlot. She raised it to Armand. "To a job well done."

Armand tapped his glass to hers.

"And to Emily and the train cars," she said.

Armand choked on his beer. "Emily? How do you know about Emily? I haven't written my report on the train car thefts yet."

"Yes, I noticed you opening the report and closing it again. Taking a stab at it and moving on to something else. Now, tell me the truth. Were you going to name Emily as the thief in your report?"

Armand held the glass between both hands. After a long moment he shook his head. "I'm sorry. I know I should, but I can't. It's why you haven't seen it on your desk."

Patricia patted him on the back. "Don't look so glum. It doesn't make you less of a police officer if you can't report someone or something. It's the beginning of a well-rounded one. A *seasoned* one."

"Seasoned?"

"We make judgment calls all the time while doing our sworn duty to uphold justice. Sometimes they don't agree with what is written in law books."

Armand put his glass down. "You don't think less of me?"

"I respect you for it. You made a moral call. I'd say you're ready for the OPP or whatever big-time police force can get their hands on you."

Armand took a sip of his beer. A weight had lifted from his shoulders, but his heart was still heavy. "How do you know about Emily and the train cars? Did Olivia update you?"

"She did, but…" She moved her stool closer to him. "Do you know everything about Emily?"

"What do you mean do I know everything about her? What do you *know* about Emily?"

Patricia sipped at her wine, a smirk curling her lips. "Well, before I answer, I need to know how much you know. Did she tell you everything? About her family history?"

Armand sat up. "She did. But it's supposed to be hush hush. I'm not supposed to know. Does this mean you know everything? You know her family history?"

"We're dancing around each other and not very well. Yes, Armand. I know her history and story very well. I only knew her by her first name. I thought of her immediately after I heard about the return of the wooden horse but refused to consider it." She leaned closer. "I'm the one who took her out of her history ten years ago."

Armand's eyes widened. "You left the Toronto

Police Force and moved here because of Emily?"

Patricia nodded and took another sip of her wine.

He couldn't pull his gaze from her. "Holy shit."

Patricia laughed. "What the brass at the police force asked her and her family to do was not only unfair but unethical. Her parents paid for their small crimes many times over during their years in police employment. They were good. Emily, however, was better. But it had to stop. I couldn't stand by and see a young girl taken advantage of. She was the same age as my oldest daughter. She needed to be an average teenager, not some top-secret police weapon, who couldn't live her life as she wanted."

Armand shook his head. "Small world."

"It certainly is." Her husband waved, and she nodded. "You can still write me your report—however you want to write it. Whether you name Emily or not, I won't hold anything against you. Only you can make the call." She pinched his shirt. "But from the less than impeccable condition of your shirt, the stubble around your jaw, and the out-of-place hair, I think you've already made the decision and don't know it yet." She slid off the stool. "Will I have the opportunity to meet Emily again?"

"She's coming back soon. She hasn't finished her work at the Acadia Inn."

"Yes, I heard she's done very well for herself. I'm happy for her. She even met a nice man, an impeccable dresser with solid credentials, and a high moral code. Maybe I'll drop in on her. Give her another surprise she isn't expecting." She put her hand on his back. "Don't take it too hard. You're not the first police officer who can't do what he thought he had to do. Not everything is black or white. Welcome to the world of policing."

Don't take it too hard? He turned away as Patricia left. Of course, he took it hard. He was ready to arrest the woman he cared deeply about, before he pushed her out of his life and walked out on her. And all for the sake of what he believed in. In what he was told was right.

Lowan landed in the stool, startling him. "Hey, buddy. So many beautiful women are in this bar ready to cozy up to Mr. February and our sheriff's stuntman stand-in, but if I'm not missing the mark, the beautiful woman you want isn't in this room, is she?"

Armand turned away. "It's over."

"Is this why you're moping?"

"I'm tired. Been an exhausting week."

"I've known you since junior kindergarten. You don't mope." He rubbed Armand's cheek with the outside of his fingers. "Is this scruff?"

"Why is everyone concerned about how I look? I can't have scruff?"

"You'd shave twice a day if you could." His gaze dropped to his shirt. "Do I spy a wrinkle on your shirt?"

"I can't have a wrinkle on my shirt?"

"You iron your T-shirts. I bet you iron your boxers."

"Go away."

Lowan laughed. "You're coming undone, bro. Why don't you call Emily?"

"And say what? I'm sorry I almost threw you in jail?"

Lowan's eyes rounded. "You almost threw her in jail?"

"You didn't hear me say anything."

Lowan swirled Armand's stool toward him. "Holy smokes. Why?"

"I never said anything." He faced the bar and took a sip of his beer.

"Fine." Lowan drank some beer. "She's coming back tomorrow."

Armand swirled toward him. "She is?"

"I thought it'd get your interest."

"How do you know?"

"Katrina told me. The paintings are in Toronto, and she still has a lot of appraising to do at the inn."

"How nice." Armand took a sip but didn't taste much.

"Really? That's all. How nice?"

"What do you want me to say?"

"Look, whatever was between you two, it's obviously not over for you and possibly for her either."

"Go away and let me drink in peace."

"You're drinking it like a liqueur. You're mocking beer etiquette."

He downed his beer, his gaze fixing on a little ledge above the bar. "Better now?" He did a double take and followed the ledge running over the mirrors, highlighting the bar and around the entire place. "Justin!" He knocked Lowan's beer out of his hand as he fell over the counter. "Justin!"

Justin rushed over. "You ready for my new brew?"

"What happened to the train going around here?"

Justin looked up at the ledge. "Which one?"

"You have more than one?"

"We have the Christmas one we removed last month and the regular one we haven't put up yet."

"Both of them."

"They're in the basement along with—"

"Show me. Now!" Armand jumped over the counter, knocking over Lowan's beer, and landing beside Justin.

Justin straightened the bottle. "Now? Why?"

"What is with you?" Lowan wiped beer from his shirt.

Armand ignored Lowan. "It's part of a case. An important case."

Justin called his father at the end of the bar. "Armand needs to see something, Dad. I'll be right back."

His dad nodded and moved toward the center of the bar.

"This I have to see." Lowan slid over the bar and landed between Armand and Justin.

Justin led them past the bar to the kitchen and down a flight of stairs to the storage room in the basement. There were a number of boxes on shelves. He found several marked trains and put them on a table. "Here you go. I'll be upstairs if you need me."

Lowan moved to the table. "You're really looking for a train?"

"One very specific train car." Armand tore the duct tape off the first box. "It's made of basswood."

"Of what?"

"Basswood—like some of those other pieces in the curio of the Acadia Restaurant. The one I'm looking for will have an intricate design on the side. Evergreen trees and possibly a house."

Lowan didn't move. He stared at Armand as though he were crazy.

"Are you going to help me or not?"

"I don't understand you these days." Lowan opened the box and started pulling out train cars. "Just so you know, I could be partying with beautiful women who fall at my feet. Instead, I'm helping you find a train car."

"I'll name my first son or daughter after you."

"He or she might not be too happy."

"Are you looking or not?"

"Does this have to do with Emily?"

"Keep looking."

Lowan stopped. "Armand, my good buddy. I do believe you have fallen in love."

Armand stopped taking pieces out of the box. He opened his mouth to make some retort and closed it again. There was nothing to retort. He *was* in love with Emily. There was no other explanation as to why he was so torn about her or why he couldn't write the report about the train car thefts and implicate her. It was why he couldn't rest, and why he didn't care if he shaved or ironed his shirts again.

"Maybe."

"Maybe? And so, one of us falls," Lowan sang.

"Stop being so dramatic."

"I'm an actor, bro. It's in my blood. You're in love, my dear friend."

"Yeah, yeah, yeah. Still too much drama." His gaze landed on the train car Lowan held. "Stop." He grabbed it. The front was painted white and red with Santa Claus, snow, and his sleigh but he could feel the engraving of a scene underneath it. The back was untouched. It was basswood. "This is it. This is the one." He scratched at the paint, but it wouldn't come off. "Shit. I have to get it cleaned up. It has to be cleaned up."

Lowan flinched, the amusement in his eyes disappearing. "Okay, but what is it?"

"Your dad."

"My dad?"

"Your dad can clean it up, can't he? Is he at home or the Acadia Inn?"

"Acadia Inn."

"I have to go."

"Now? The party just started."

"Now. Tell him I'm coming now. He can't go to sleep. I need him."

Lowan took out his cell. "So much for beautiful women tonight. You fall in love, and I hold you up."

****

Armand and Lowan sat at the kitchen table of the Acadia Inn, watching as Jerome removed the paint on the train car with cotton swabs dipped in a gentle varnish. Wilhelm sat beside him, handing him more cotton swabs or soft brushes. The other two train cars with the figurine sat on the table. The shoebox holding the money neither Jessica, Mrs. Halloran, nor Emily wanted was on a chair.

Wilhelm moved to the stove. "Anyone want tea?"

"I'll have a chamomile," Armand said, keeping his focus on Jerome cleaning.

"Chamomile?" Lowan said. "When did you drink chamomile?"

Armand ignored him.

"You really have fallen. I'll have a chamomile, too, Wilhelm."

"Chamomile for everyone," Wilhelm said, filling the kettle with water.

Several hours and refills later, Jerome put his brush down. "All done."

"Can I take a look?" Wilhelm asked. Jerome handed it to him. Wilhelm examined it for a long while and gave it to Armand. "It's a beautiful piece of art. Excuse me for a minute." He disappeared into his office.

His hands shaking, Armand placed it between the other two train cars, hooking them together via little clasps. The division between them was noticeable but the engraving was clear and exact and flowed with ease from one train car to another. It was of a house, surrounded by evergreens. On the house were engravings of a cuddly bear with a big bow tie, a moose with a bowler, a rabbit with a floppy tie, and on the side a tall tricycle with a mouse. In front was a sign with a heart and a feather."

"It is a set," Lowan said.

"It's a beautifully-crafted set," Jerome said. "Weren't those the train cars taken—"

"They weren't taken. They belong to Emily," Armand said. "Emily was adopted when she was one year old. She had the figurine. Mrs. Halloran had the first train car, Colm Saunders had the last one, and Justin McQuaide had the third one you just cleaned."

"You mean someone from her biological family made them?" Jerome asked, incredibility in his voice. "And left the figurine with her?"

Armand nodded.

"I want to cry," Lowan said.

"The artist could be her father or mother," Jerome said.

"Possibly."

"This could lead to her family."

Armand moved the trains. "Unfortunately, I don't know where this house is—or even if it is a real house."

Wilhelm walked into the kitchen, holding a folder, and waving a photo. "The home is real, and I know exactly who made the train set and where the house is."

Chapter Thirty-Three

Emily took her overnight bag out of the car she'd rented at the Ottawa airport and headed toward the Acadia Inn. The grounds and the inn looked strange without the hustle and bustle of actors, film crew, equipment, cars, and trailers. It was surprisingly peaceful. Just as a country inn should be.

She had taken the red-eye flight out of Toronto, and it was only eight o'clock. She hoped the front doors were open or she'd have to wait out in the cold. She smirked. She could pick the lock, but she wanted none of that ever again.

In Toronto, she met Isla and had what her sister called a monster cry. Emily told her everything about Armand and how they ended as well as her near brush with jail time. She never wanted to hear of breaking and entering and stealing anymore. She even left her lock picking tool kit with Isla. It was another way to say that part of her life was over—just as giving Armand the train cars and figurine. She could have been happy with Armand. Instead she put the relationship on the line. She returned to the Acadia Inn to finish her job and get the hell out of Dodge as quickly as possible. She hoped she didn't run into Armand while she was here.

The front doors stood open and the warmth of the lobby was welcoming. Marilyn flew back to Toronto but Lubna and Tatyana were staying on for another week. A number of other appraisers would join them soon. She hoped her stay wouldn't extend past a week.

She moved into the kitchen, expecting to find someone but there was no one. Coffee wasn't brewing but a number of dirty mugs and plates sat on the counter, telling her people were awake. But it was Sunday. Where were they?

Pink and white dotted tissue paper like she had used to wrap the train cars was flung on a chair. She moved toward it. It wasn't alike. It *was* the paper she had used. It could be a coincidence, but the dots bore the name of the National Gallery in London where she bought mugs with Van Gogh's sunflowers on them.

"Hello?" She waited. "Is anyone here?" The inn was big but Darryl or Nicole or whoever monitored the security cameras should have seen her walk in and greeted her.

She moved into the hallway. Her bedroom door was ajar. The room was hers until she left. She still had clothes in the closet. No one should be inside.

She peered in and blinked several times. On the table were the two train cars she'd found and, she couldn't believe it, but the middle one, too. She pushed opened the door and stopped short. Armand was sound asleep on her bed, sprawled on his back. He must have been dead tired—or had had one too many beers. He was fully clothed and even had his shoes on.

She closed the door, moved to the table, put her bag down, and sat in a chair. The middle car showed a house decorated with toy animals wearing a piece of clothing. A tall tricycle with a mouse was next to the house while a heart and feather were in front. She didn't realize it until a drop stung her lips that tears flowed down her face.

She brushed them away.

It was complete. The train set was complete and so was the scene. The figurine of the girl looked so happy in the first train. The figurine couldn't look happy. It was her. She projected her happiness on the figurine of the girl and her sense of completeness.

Armand found the last train car and set it up for her. It could only be him. She gave him the train cars and figurine.

She took off her coat and moved to the bed. Tears still rolled down her face. She didn't know if she cried about the discovery of the middle train car and a major clue to her biological family's whereabouts or Armand. He never wanted to see her again. But without Armand, she would have nothing. It was him. Only him.

She touched several days of beard growth. He groaned, and his eyes flickered. She caressed his cheek again.

His eyes slit open and closed again "Hey, Em." He rolled toward her and closed his hand over hers.

"Looks like someone is sleeping in my bed, said the little bear to the mama bear. And I think he's still there."

Armand's eyes flew open and he zoomed up. "Hey." He swung his feet over the side. "Sorry. I didn't realize—" He saw her tears. "What's wrong?"

She took his hand and kissed it. "I love you."

Armand's eyes narrowed. "It's a problem?"

"It was. Or so I thought."

Armand placed his hands around her face and kissed her eyes, cheeks, and lips with a gentleness, an urgency, and a longing all rolled together, until she swooned. "So did I. But not anymore. Not at all. I love you, Emily. "'I love you to the moon and back,' said the parent to the child."

Emily laughed. "Getting ready for bedtime stories?"

"Well, I think we can wait on it. I want you with me, Em. I'm sorry I trapped you and couldn't let go of what I thought was right. Being with you is right. Everything else isn't. I'm sorry I didn't believe you. I've been the most miserable man since I wished you well. I love you. I hope you can forgive me."

Emily threw her arms around him.

"I hope this means yes you can forgive me, and you're happy."

Emily nodded. "I'm very happy."

"Good, 'cause you're soaking me, babe."

Emily laughed and pulled away, drying her eyes with the back of her hand. "How?" she indicated the train. "When? Where?"

"The Coyote's Hole."

"The bar?"

He nodded. "The McQuaides always have a train set above the bar. It's usually stationary but the Christmas train set moves around. I noticed there wasn't one when I was there last night."

"Last night? You found it last night?"

"I did. Justin—you met him I think—big, strong red-head?"

"You mean Mr. March?"

Armand's eyes widened. "Have you been looking at other men, Ms. Atterberry?"

Emily kissed him. "Isla has. She told me."

"Good. Justin let me look through boxes of train

sets and I found it. It was covered in paint and had a Santa Claus scene. Jerome cleaned it up for me. Happy Valentine's Day, Emily."

Emily kissed him and with her cheek rubbed his stubble.

"I look terrible, I know. I haven't shaved in a couple days."

"You look ultra-sexy. Ready for Valentine's Day."

"Really?"

"With scruff and without." She ran her hand through his hair. "With your hair all messed up or perfectly in place. With your wonderful clothes on and most definitely without. You're always perfect to be my Valentine."

His eyebrows rounded. "Well, it's something I've never heard before."

"Everything's good about you, Armand."

"Even when I was ready to arrest you?"

"Even then. You're righteous and honorable, and I love you for who you are."

"I couldn't write the report."

"You'll have to."

"No, I won't. Both Jessica and Mrs. Halloran insist they gave you the train cars. No one is pressing charges. Technically, there never were any thefts."

"I'm grateful to them, Armand." She kissed him again, moved to the train set, and picked up the middle car. "Jerome did a wonderful job. The etchings and details are so clear." She turned it over, checking all sides. "But there's no signature. The house could be real or fictitious."

Armand sat in a chair and pulled her into another. He kept his hands on hers. "It's real. Wilhelm knows the artist and the home. I can take you there."

Emily went cold. He could take her? Could she do this? Could she go? Was she ready to meet someone who could be or could lead to her biological family? Tears overflowed again. "I don't think I can. What if— if they didn't want me? What if they don't want to see me? I don't want the past to conflict with my future again. I want to look only ahead. Only to you."

Armand removed the figurine from the engineer's seat. "They left this with you. You are the conductor, Emily. You can go anywhere you want. To the past and bring it forward. Make it part of your future, too, with me. You can go to them. They want you to go to them. They want to see you."

Chapter Thirty-Four

Emily clasped the figurine as she sat in the passenger seat of Armand's Jeep. She wasn't sure where he was taking her on the long winding road. All she saw were trees covered in snow or ice. The sun was bright, which meant it was colder than it appeared.

It was warm inside the car, but she was cold. She called her parents while Armand went home to clean up. All they said was if she found someone from her biological family, they would fly out and be with her. They wanted her to go. She had to go.

Armand put his hand over hers, startling her out of her thoughts. "You're squeezing the poor figurine like you're going to lose it."

"I want to turn back."

"Do you really?"

"Yes and no."

"Everything will be fine." He removed his hand. Emily wished it was still over hers. It gave her comfort.

They passed the First Nations Reserve of Algonquins of Pikwakanagan but continued until they arrived at a lake. Ice glimmered like a sheet of silver. Armand followed it until they came to several stores and a church. People gathered around the front doors of the small Catholic church, talking to each other or the priest, or waving goodbye and getting into cars.

Armand drove past, following the road into a

wooded area. Emily could see sparkles of the frozen lake peeking through the trees. Stuck in between them were wooden houses.

Her heart beat faster. Evergreen trees, just like the etching.

"It can't be much farther." Armand said.

She saw a fence and her breathing quickened. Armand stopped in front of a house. Emily froze.

It was the house. It was a wooden, one-story house surrounded by evergreen trees. On it was the cuddly bear with the big bow tie, the moose with the bowler hat, the rabbit with the floppy tie, and on the side the tall tricycle with the mouse riding it. In front of the house, just outside a wooden fence was a heart-shaped sign with a feather. *Art by Baptiste*

Emily wanted to throw up. She had seen this place before. Not on the side of the train cars but in person. She was here. An awfully long time ago. But it was vague, like a long-forgotten dream.

This was it. Inside the house could be her family. But the family that put her up for adoption.

"I can't go in, Armand."

"I'll be with you."

"I know what you said, but, really, what if they don't want to see me? It's been twenty-five years since they let me go."

"If you want to go back and wait for another time, maybe come back with your parents and sister this time, we can. Just say the word, and I'll turn the car around and return to King Court."

Emily closed her eyes. She wanted to cry but stemmed her tears and fears. "No. We came all this way. It has to be now. It either stops or begins again here."

Armand stepped out of the car and helped Emily out. She stood in front of the walkway unable to move forward.

"It looks like a gingerbread house," Armand said.

"It is picturesque. I just hope there's no evil witch inside."

Armand squeezed her by the shoulders. "There isn't. They didn't let you go until you were one year old." He led her up the walkway to the front door. "Ready?"

She nodded.

Armand knocked as Emily leaned against him, then turned into him for support. But no one came to the door. He knocked again. Still no one. He checked the driveway. "There's a carport but it's empty."

"That decides it. Let's go back. I'm not ready for this." She raced to the car and jumped in, closing the door firmly.

Armand opened his door. "Are you sure?"

She nodded. "I'm sure. We can come back another day, or I'll send them a letter. An old-fashion snail mail type of letter. If they answer it and invite me, then I'll come back."

Armand turned into the driveway and backed up, going the way they came. They went as far as the second house when a red minivan passed them.

"Stop," Emily cried, looking behind.

Armand stopped the car as the minivan turned into the driveway of the gingerbread house. A man in his late sixties or early seventies moved to the side of the van and opened the door. He extended planks of metal from the van to the driveway. A few moments later a woman of about the man's age came out in a wheelchair.

Emily put her hand over Armand's. The man and woman became blurry. Tears confused her vision. She wiped them away with her other hand.

"Go back?" he asked.

She nodded.

Armand turned the car around and headed to the house. The man drove the car forward into the carpark as the woman waited at the side door.

Emily stepped out and stood at the end of the driveway. Armand stood beside her, his arm around her shoulder.

The man got of the car, holding down a checkered Fedora and keeping his dark coat from flapping in the wind. The woman removed her gloves and took out keys from her small purse. Emily couldn't resist a smile. They wore their Sunday best, just like her mother's parents. They were coming back from church.

The man saw Emily and stopped in is tracks.

"Arthur? What's wrong?" The woman in the wheelchair turned to see what made him go cold. The keys fell to the ground.

Emily wasn't sure how, but she walked toward them. The man approached the woman, and there were tears in their eyes, just like in hers.

Emily opened her mouth to say something, but nothing came out. They were as speechless as she was.

She held out her hand and showed them the figurine.

The woman gasped. "Emily?"

She nodded.

"I knew you'd find your way home one day." She

opened her arms and Emily moved into them. The woman sobbed, her chest moving against Emily's. Someone tugged at her coat. Emily shrugged out of the woman's embrace and into the man's arms.

The man pulled her away but held onto her. "You're so beautiful. Your father will be very happy to hear about you." He smiled. "You have his eyes."

"My father?"

"Yes, your mother, my youngest child, is not with us anymore. We hope she is with God, but your father never gave up hope you would come back here."

"And my mother?"

"It's a long story, Emily. She was troubled and disappeared right after she and your father gave you up for adoption. We've searched for her over the years but nothing. She just disappeared."

Emily brushed tears away from her eyes so she could focus and think. "And my father?"

"Your father moves around a lot. He's in the military. Has another family now. Two boys—your half-brothers—with the same beautiful silver eyes as you. Your father is in Ukraine on a training mission. His family lives in Quebec City."

"Is my father Ukrainian?"

"Oh, no, my dear. His family is from Hungary, but he speaks a number of languages. I can call him, and you can speak to him, if you'd like. I know he'd be beside himself to hear you…to know you found us."

The woman took Emily's hand. "If you're wondering who we are, we're your grandparents. I'm Margarite Baptiste and this is Arthur. You're First Nations on your grandfather's side and a mix of French, German, and Swiss on mine. That's why you're so beautiful. It comes all from my side. Your father's side of the family is Hungarian."

They laughed, including Emily. "Well, it definitely explains my looks."

Arthur took the figurine from her. "I made this figurine for you and put it in your hands when your parents put you up for adoption. They didn't want to, but they were only fifteen. Soon after, your father went into the military and your mother disappeared. Your father was too young, his family moved too often, and we were too old, your grandmother confined to a wheelchair, too."

Margarite's hands squeezed hers. "Or we would have kept you, Emily. God knows we wanted to keep you, but we couldn't offer you anything. You've turned out beautifully." Her gaze went to Armand. "Now, who is this handsome young man who has been quietly observing us? We haven't extended him any civilities."

Armand came forward as Emily took his hand. "This is Armand Lecavalier."

Armand shook hands with both.

"You look military," Arthur said. "Very clean shaven, straight and strong."

"Close but no, I'm a detective with the King Court Police Force."

"King Court? You must know my old friend Wilhelm Sherrer."

"He told us where to find you."

"I found your train set," Emily said.

"The one your figurine sits in?" Arthur said.

"Yes, it really was quite the find."

"I'm glad you did." He threw his arms around her again. "It brought you back to us."

"Why don't we get inside," Margarite—her grandmother—said. "You must stay for lunch. We have so much to talk about." Armand handed her the keys she had dropped. "Thank you."

Arthur wheeled her inside.

Emily took Armand's hand and kissed it. "Thank you. This is the best Valentine's Day I could ever have."

"You found them."

"I found you."

He brought her hand to his lips and kissed it, too. "I'm thinking of it as an investment. I want you with me every Valentine's Day from now on."

She moved against him. "Investment made—the best I'll ever make."

"Look what I found." He pulled the top portion of the red furry handcuffs from his coat pocket.

Emily gasped and pushed it back inside. "Not here."

"Of course, not here. Later tonight. When it's just you and me and Valentine's night."

The wheelchair stuck on the carpet. Armand stepped inside. "Let me help, Arthur."

Emily watched as Armand helped her newfound grandfather maneuver her grandmother inside.

All in one day, all in one most beautiful day, she found her past *and* her future and because of a beautiful man she wanted to spend the rest of her life with.

It was indeed the best Valentine Day she would ever have. And, to think. There were so many more to come.

A word about the author…

Kirsten Paul is the pseudonym for Franca Pelaccia, author of the romantic comedy series the Calendar Men of King Court. The first book, *The Hockey Player and the Angel*, came out in July 2019. *The Detective and the Burglar* is the second book.

Writing under her real name, Franca is the author of *Moses & Mac*, a women's action/adventure (or what some call "chick-lit") and the first book of the Vatican Archaeological Service series. The second book, *Mac & the Magi*, is in progress.

Writing as Francesca Pelaccia, Franca self-published *The Witch's Salvation*, a historical paranormal novel, which won the Beck Valley Reviewers' Choice Award for 2013.

An avid reader, Franca reviews novels for the Historical Novel Society.

Visit her at:

http://francapelaccia.com

Thank you for purchasing
this publication of The Wild Rose Press, Inc.

For questions or more information
contact us at
info@thewildrosepress.com.

The Wild Rose Press, Inc.
www.thewildrosepress.com